NEAR NEIGHBOURS

Molly Clavering herself wrote, 'My life has been uneventful, apart from six years in the W.R.N.S. during the war.' Uneventful maybe, but very full. Born in 1900 in Glasgow and educated in Bristol, she lived in the country from an early age. Her first novel, *Georgina and the Stairs* was published in 1927, followed by two more, *The Leech of Life* and *Wantonwalls* and four under the pseudonym 'B. Mollett' before her war service in the W.R.N.S. In 1947 she moved to Moffat in the Scottish Borders, where she lived alone with a series of large black poodles, the first of which was a gift from her friend and neighbour, D.E. Stevenson. She participated fully in the life of the small town, becoming its first and only woman magistrate, served on the Town Council for nearly a decade, was involved with the Girl Guides and Rangers and became president of the local Scottish Country Dancing Association. The rest of her time she filled with her writing: seven more novels under her own name, and twenty-four additional works serialised in *People's Friend* between 1954 and 1976. All but one of these were later issued as *People's Friend Pocket Novels,* most in the 1980s, and one as recently as 2007. She is also believed to have written for *The Scots Magazine.* All these ephemeral works are now nearly impossible to find, as are many of her novels in book form. Molly Clavering died in 1995.

NEAR
NEIGHBOURS

MOLLY CLAVERING

Greyladies

Published by
Greyladies
an imprint of The Old Children's Bookshelf

© Molly Clavering 1956

This edition first published 2015
Design and layout © Shirley Neilson 2015

Greyladies would like to thank Scott Thompson, who blogs as
Furrowed Middlebrow, for biographical information.

ISBN   978-1-907503-45-0

Set in Sylfaen / Perpetua
Printed and bound by CPI Group (UK) Ltd, Croydon CR0 4YY

NEAR NEIGHBOURS

CHAPTER 1

THE ELEGANT OVAL of Kirkaldy Crescent was placed on the downward slope from Queensferry Street with such consummate art that it looked as though it had arrived there by happy chance.

When first built it had really been a crescent, a half-moon of tall Regency houses with pillars on either side of each front door, which was further embellished by a semi-circular fanlight above it with wrought-iron balconies in front of the first-floor windows, and looking out over a green garden set with fine trees running right to the edge of a stream.

The stream was still there, confined between stout railings above walls, but it would not have been visible to the Crescent, for the gardens had dwindled to a meagre lawn where the last of the trees still lifted sooty heads towards the sun, and the leafy distance was occupied by the other side of Kirkaldy Crescent.

This other side was broken in two places by the entrances to side-streets, and it lacked the harmonious symmetry which made the older part of the Crescent such a pleasure to look at, but the houses were good, for all that, and it was they which had turned the half-moon into the beautiful oval spreading down the hill.

As the nineteenth century progressed, town planning degenerated to a race to build enough houses for the ever-increasing population. Behind Kirkaldy Crescent, especially on the north or original side, there sprang up street after street of high ugly dwellings, which backed on to their high-walled strips of garden. Now the "other side", saved by the stream from sharing this fate, could speak pityingly of "those dreadful slums" opposite, so close to their superior

1

neighbours. Fortunately for them, none could look into the future. In their worst nightmares they never dreamed of the days to come, when almost every house on both sides of the Crescent would be converted into flats, and their roomy, beetle-haunted basements, once occupied by kitchen premises, became the abode of separate tenants, taxi-drivers who parked their cabs beside the garden railings in the centre of the oval, or bus conductors, and their noisy families.

The changes wrought by two world wars brought this to pass, and of the whole stately Crescent only two houses remained unaltered. These were Number Six and its next-door neighbour Number Four, at the lower end of what the owners of Number Four still called "the good side of the Crescent". Number Six hardly counted, for it had been bought cheap by a Mrs. Lenox, a widow with several children to bring up, who found the good schools in Edinburgh sufficient recompense for the dull neighbourhood.

But Number Four was different. The Balfours had lived and died there for upwards of a hundred years; and now the last remaining member of the family was sitting crouched on the window-seat of the top-floor back room, staring down at the rectangular greens and gardens far below her.

Miss Dorothea Balfour was nearer seventy than sixty, but there was something childlike about her, partly her undignified attitude, curled up as she was, partly her slight figure and the mouse-coloured hair which hardly showed any grey, taken back from a high wondering forehead to a small bun at the nape of her thin neck.

She felt rather like a child, a lost, bewildered child, and she was doing what Belle had always objected to so strongly: staring out of the window at "those rather odd persons next-door, as if their washing could have any possible interest for you!"

Almost she expected to hear the door open briskly behind her, and her elder sister's sharp voice saying these words, and ending with the plaint, "Really, Dottie, I sometimes think you have no sense of what is fitting. If you must gaze out of the window in that imbecile fashion, at least you might look at the gardens in the Crescent."

But she would never hear Belle's voice again. She would never see Belle looking down her handsome aquiline nose in disdain at her, for Belle was dead. The whole house still felt so full of Belle's overpowering presence that Dorothea could not really believe it, though she had followed the motor hearse in a car with Mr. Ferrier, the lawyer, and old Doctor Kinnaird at a decorous pace through the sunny streets to the Crematorium only a few hours earlier. At the thought of the Crematorium Dorothea shivered.

"I will not be cremated!" she said aloud, and after glancing guiltily and automatically over her shoulder, realized that there was no one left to decree how her bones should be disposed of: no one but herself. She could make a will and put in it that she wanted to lie in the little country kirkyard at Kersland, and the lawyers would have to see that this was done. How extraordinary, how unbelievable, to know that she could do as she wanted, without reference to Belle or Papa!

For as long as she could remember, Dorothea had lived in a continual state of giving-in: to Papa at first, and after he died, to Belle. It had not been so bad while Mamma was alive to share this bondage, but during the last ten years, alone with Belle in the big gloomy house except for Edna far below in the basement, life had become almost unbearable. Belle's temper, always domineering like Papa's, had grown really shocking, and Dorothea had borne the brunt of it, for to have raged too openly at Edna might have driven that handmaid, long-suffering though she was, to give notice. So Belle called her a lazy slut (to Dorothea) and found fault with her up to a certain point, but beyond that she did not

3

go. There was no need, however, for her to restrain herself where Dorothea was concerned.

"She'll be the death o' you, Miss Dottie!" Edna exclaimed sometimes, after a more than ordinarily ferocious outburst, and Dorothea had thought this quite probable.

But she had not. Instead, she had died herself. She had finished one of the enormous midday meals which she ate with such relish, fallen off her chair at table with her face all drawn sideways, and died in three days of a stroke.

"I don't want to think about it. I won't think about it!" said Dorothea, and turned again to the window which had been her solace ever since the room it lighted had been her nursery.

The outlook had changed for the worse, with the streets of mean houses rising at the farther end of the long walled strips of garden belonging to the Crescent. Other rows of tall tenements ran at right angles to the end house, Number Two, away to the noisy main street where the electric tram-cars bucketed clanging to and fro.

When the sun caught the slate roofs after rain, they were touched momentarily to the sheeny purples and greens of a pigeon's feathers, but there was only one thing of real and lasting beauty to be seen from Dorothea's window, an ash-tree growing high and slender in the corner of the Balfours' garden.

It was interesting to watch the starlings and sparrows which chattered among its branches, but far more interesting were the glimpses of the teeming life in the grim-looking houses to the side of it. Sometimes, when the lights were switched on, as they had to be quite early in the afternoon, for these houses were dark, Dorothea could see right into the rooms.

She would watch, absorbed, while the children rushed in from school, were given huge "pieces" of bread and jam, cut on a newspaper on the cluttered table, and rushed out again for their evening's play in the streets. Later, when the men came home from work, she could see them hastily sluicing face and arms at the sink, eating the meal dumped before them on the same newspaper, and then settling with the sports edition, or following the children out, perhaps to the local pub, perhaps to go to "the dogs" by the bus that passed the end of the street. The girls, too, would drink tea and then mince off in their shoddy best: the older women seemed never to go out. They stayed behind in the hot bright rooms ironing, or washing, or occasionally doing nothing but sit, while the wireless blared and bleated unnoticed.

Dorothea saw quarrels and reconciliations, children being cuffed or petted, girls washing their hair. Once she watched with fascinated horror a free fight, when a drunken man tried madly to get at a jeering woman: they threw plates at each other and overturned the poor bits of furniture, until suddenly a policeman walked in and took the man away, while the woman yelled with laughter.

It never occurred to the lonely watcher, who would have been genuinely shocked at the idea of listening to other people's private conversation, that she was looking into these people's private lives. To her it was like something seen on a stage, and though vivid, quite unreal.

Belle, who never looked out of the back windows at all if she could help it, spoke of the inhabitants of Linden Terrace as "squalid" and "disgusting". Dorothea found the squalor, where it existed, pitiful, and was much more impressed by the cheerful thrift and hard work which she was sure predominated. She accepted the fact that their standards were different from her own, but she was far from condemning them wholesale on that account. When there was nothing else to see, she could look at the washing hung like dingy banners from iron poles outside the windows. They were

5

banners, she felt, flying in the cause of respectability and cleanliness, but the washing in itself was not a very attractive sight, and when she had noticed that the big sturdy woman three houses down Linden Terrace had scrubbed her two younger boys' corduroy shorts again, Dorothea was apt to turn her gaze downward to the garden of the house next door to hers on the left: the garden of Number Six Kirkaldy Crescent.

It really *was* a garden, with a neat rectangle of lawn down the middle, and flower beds running the whole length under the high enclosing walls on either side. Only the far end was used as a drying-green, and it was hidden from the house by a trellis on which rambler roses had been trained. From her eyrie, of course, Dorothea could see it quite as easily as the rest of the garden. There was only a small corner hidden from her view up aloft, the corner by the back door.

She was a little shy of watching the garden of Number Six. The Lenoxes were their nearest neighbours and though Belle had refused to call on them and would not even recognize them if she met them in the Crescent, Dorothea could not resist giving Mrs. Lenox or her pretty daughters a timid half-smile when she saw them. It was always returned, often with a comment on the weather, so Dorothea felt that in an unofficial way she did know them.

To be caught staring down into their garden, watching them have tea on the lawn beside the ramblers on a fine afternoon, or picking flowers from their borders, would be dreadful. To her mind it was entirely different from looking at the people of Linden Terrace. She could not have explained why, but Dorothea had not a logical mind.

In spite of her fear of being caught, she never could resist having "just a peep" at their drying-green. Such pretty things hung on the line between two stout wooden posts;

even the dish-cloths were gay multi-coloured checks; and if one of the girls did happen to come out to take in garments ready for ironing—well, that was just a lucky chance. Even to herself Dorothea never admitted that it was the Lenoxes she waited to see, not merely their washing. The family had a fascination for her, they represented youth and gaiety and colour, all the things she was starved of in her own life.

It was most astonishing, she thought, as she gazed downward into the garden of Number Six on this never-ending summer afternoon, herself discreetly hidden by the curtain, how much she could tell about her neighbours from their washing.

There was Murray, the only son. He must be a great deal more interested in his appearance than Miss Balfour had always understood young men to be. His pyjamas were silk, blue silk that flapped richly and heavily in the wind, and he seemed to wear four or five shirts every week, his socks and handkerchiefs and collars were too many to count and, except for the collars, as brilliant as the flowers below them. As usual, a passing glance sufficed for Murray's belongings. Dorothea's real interest was in the feminine undergarments which blew airily on the line. She knew to whom they belonged. Mrs. Lenox's were all white, exquisitely fine, but very plain. The schoolgirl Holly's were plain too, but more solid, made to resist a considerable amount of wear and tear. But the three older girls had wisps of pale-coloured nylon, filmy lace, delicate *ninon* . . . "how they don't catch *cold*—!" thought Miss Balfour, even while she admired, and wondered what it would be like to go clad in such things.

To-day, as she peered out, she saw that Willow's special nightgown was out. Willow was the eldest, married to a young man in the Merchant Navy, and the appearance of this diaphanous affair of palest pink always meant that he was home from sea. In a moment of madness, Dorothea had once remarked on this to her sister, and Belle, after one swift glance of shuddering distaste, had pronounced her verdict that "the young woman" was shameless, and her husband probably greatly to be pitied.

Dorothea had not agreed, but knew better than to say so. And yet—Belle was the married woman, not the old maid. It seemed odd that she should be so easily shocked, even though her marriage had been so strange and unsatisfactory, and of course, so very short . . . for six months after she had married Montagu Milner, Belle had returned to Number Four Kirkaldy Crescent alone, and had lived there ever since as if she had never left it as a bride. . . . No explanation had been given to Dorothea, nor had she expected it. Belle's official title was Mrs. Milner, but in herself she was the older Miss Balfour, increasingly ill-tempered and finding something shocking in what, to her younger sister, was often only natural.

But then, Belle would have said, Dorothea ought to have been shocked too, and would have been, if she had not "common" leanings, inherited through Mamma from those unfortunately plebeian grandparents whose part in the Balfour family history had always been resolutely ignored by Belle and Papa. The inference was that Mamma—and Dorothea, who took after her—were of coarser grain than Papa and his elder daughter.

Dorothea had never minded this, perhaps because she had grown up accustomed to being slightly despised, and she infinitely preferred to resemble Mamma in nature as well as looks. Only—Mamma had had this one great advantage: she was necessary, really necessary, to Papa. No matter how cavalierly he might treat his wife, he could not do without her. Whether he had lost a collar-stud or the bottom had fallen out of his pet shares, he shouted for her as if she were a dog, and like a dog she would come running to him, to find what he had lost, pick up what he had dropped, comfort and help him in any way he needed.

The rather tousled hair, the eager anxious brown eyes, the little pointed face, all heightened Mamma's resemblance to a shepherd's collie, and Dorothea was exactly like her, except that after Mamma died, Dorothea began to look like a collie that is lost. There seemed to be no place for her in life. Papa had never needed her, and Belle needed her, if anything, less than Papa had. . . .

And now they were all gone and she was quite alone in the world. It was a strange feeling, free yet rather frighteningly lonely, to know that she could do as she wished without criticism. She could look out at her neighbours as much as she liked, and a really daring idea came to her so suddenly that she gasped aloud. She could call on Mrs. Lenox. She could even invite her to tea. . . .

"Goodness!" thought Dorothea. "What *would* Belle say?"

Then, in a rush, the realization that Belle would never say anything to her again swept over her in full force, and she was crouched, trembling on the window-seat of the old nursery, a little elderly spinster, alone in the world— and desolate.

A girl's voice floated out from a window on the floor below in the next house, a charming voice, soft, yet clear.

"Rowan! Oh, Rowan! Be an angel and bring in my nightie! I'm sure it's dry enough to iron!"

The back door of Number Six fell to with its muffled bang, and as light footsteps crossed the small courtyard, Dorothea's bowed head came up in time to see Rowan's face, vivid with laughing protest, raised to call back to her elder sister above.

"You lazy thing, Willow! Why can't you bring in your own washing?"

Willow's fair head, pale gold as the pollen-sprinkled catkins of her name-tree, was thrust far out.

"Don't be so mean, Rowan. You're down there and I'm up here—"

"You'll lose the use of your elegant legs soon, my girl," answered Rowan, but the threat only made Willow laugh.

"Go on, bring it in, like a dear," she said. "I want to iron it before we go out, and Archie's champing at the bit already—"

"Well, will you lend me your white petticoat if I do? The frilly one—"

Willow moaned. "You'll tear the frill!"

"Of course I won't tear it. You needn't speak as if I were Holly!" cried Rowan hotly.

"All right, all right! And as you were speaking of legs a minute ago, I never knew anyone whose leg was easier to pull! You can have it this once—but for goodness sake bring in my *nightie!*"

From her post at the high window next door Dorothea Balfour listened entranced to the girls' voices, her own forlorn loneliness forgotten for the moment. This, she thought, was how sisters should be, at ease with one another, arguing, teasing, quarrelling if need be, on equal terms.

She leaned further forward than usual to watch Rowan Lenox stripping the line, gathering the fragile half-dry wisps under one arm, tossing the pegs into a basket on the grass, all her movements instinctive with the careless grace of youth and good health. Finally, with a dazzling pirouette and a swoop like a diving swallow's, Rowan caught up the basket of pegs and turned to go into the house. As she did so, straightening her lithe body, she saw the sad little face with its pointed nose and lost eyes at the top window of Number Four; and though Dorothea shrank back instantly, she knew that she had been seen. A painful flush rose to her thin cheeks. She felt dreadfully ashamed of herself, caught like this peering at her neighbours, and only a few hours after Belle's funeral. Somehow that seemed to make it worse. She crept away from the window and began to go slowly downstairs through the silent house.

CHAPTER 2

ROWAN, letting the back door thud behind her, stood in the empty stone-floored passage which ran towards the area in front, with the big kitchen and various dark cupboards and small dismal basement rooms opening off it.

"Poor old thing!" she thought. "How ghastly it must be for her, left all alone like that—"

There was a quick patter of high-heeled shoes on the stone stair down from the hall, and Willow burst into the passage.

"For Heaven's *sake*, Rowan!" she cried in angry expostulation. "What have you been doing all this time? I won't be able to do my ironing now! It's a bit too much, when I promised you my petticoat too! I've a dashed good mind to say you can't have it!"

Rowan's only reply was: "Do you know, Willow, I'd completely forgotten about poor old Miss Balfour. What selfish beasts we are!"

"I don't see why." Forgetting her haste and indignation, Willow looked more closely at her younger sister as she stood in the shaft of dusty sunlight pouring in through the glass panel above the area door, and saw on her face that expression known to the family as Rowan's Crusading Look.

"I really don't see why," she repeated rather uneasily. "Mrs. Milner and Miss Balfour have always made it perfectly plain that they didn't want to know us. Mrs. Milner used to avoid us as if we were a particularly dirty puddle she was afraid of stepping in, and—"

"She's dead now, and Miss Balfour is all alone," said Rowan. "Think how awful it must be for her, Willow."

"Personally, I should think it couldn't be anything but a blessed relief. You *know* Mrs. Milner was a bitch, Rowan. There was no other name for her!"

12

"Here. Take these." Rowan thrust the bundle of washing into Willow's arms. "I'm going next door to see her."

"No, Rowan! Rowan, you simply can't! You mustn't! I'm sure Mummy wouldn't like it!" cried Willow despairingly.

"I'm going. Now," said Rowan.

She slipped past her sister and ran up the stairs. In a moment the front door banged. Willow, still clasping the damp armful of undergarments, followed quickly enough to see, from the dining-room window on the ground floor, that Rowan was standing at the door of Number Four with her hand on the bell.

"They won't let her in, of course, and she'll come back a bit chastened, I expect," Willow thought. "Poor old Rowan!"

The same thought had occurred to Rowan herself, as she stood, hatless and in her gay red and white cotton frock, listening to the bell jangling far away inside the big almost empty house.

As the seconds passed she began to hope that no one would come in answer to her ring: what could she say if she did see Miss Balfour? She had salved her conscience by coming so far—and at that the door opened slowly, just enough to allow a face like a white rabbit's, with a quivering pink nose, to be seen against the strip of dark hall behind it.

Her red-rimmed eyes, timid yet disapproving, looked quickly at Rowan and then away.

This is awful, thought Rowan. She summoned all her resolution, and said, more loudly than she intended: "I—I suppose I couldn't see Miss Balfour for a minute?"

The white rabbit shrank away appalled, murmuring in a thread of a voice, "Oh, *no*, miss, I don't think so!"

"Oh—well." With a sudden inward rush of relief, Rowan was turning to go, when Miss Balfour herself spoke from inside the hall.

"What is it, Edna? Who is at the door?"

Rowan stopped, and the white rabbit said: "It's one of the young ladies from Number Six, Miss Dottie."

"If she has a message for me, you had better ask her to come in, Edna, and not keep her standing on the doorstep."

It is probable that Dorothea Balfour had never spoken so decisively in her life; certainly the effect on Edna was astonishing.

With her rabbit's eyes bulging, she opened the door wider, whispering feebly, "If you'll please come in, miss."

And Rowan, squaring her shoulders, walked into the dim hall, still without the slightest idea of what she was going to say to its owner.

Years before, when the young Lenoxes were still children, they had often beguiled wet afternoons in planning how to capture the stronghold next door, by strategy or direct assault. Number Four was the giant's castle, the witch's cave, the dragon's lair, and Mrs. Milner, Miss Balfour's sister, was in each case the giant, the witch, or the dragon, Miss Balfour herself the victim to be rescued from her wicked clutches.

Rowan was the only one who still played this game. To her it had become a secret romance. And now here she was inside the stronghold, but the dragon was dead and buried and Miss Balfour set free by no human aid from her years of bondage.

Edna had scuttled out of sight down the basement stairs, leaving her to go on alone, but after a few steps Rowan halted uncertainly, once more wondering why she had been such a fool as to come.

The hall seemed very long, perhaps because it was so much darker than their own hall next door. Midway of its length it was divided across by a half-glass door with tall narrow panels of glass set in dark wood on either side of it. The only light there was filtered in through the fanlight above the front door, and fell palely down from the glass cupola in the roof. Rowan, blinking after the sunlight out-side, saw a small figure all in black standing on the bottom step of the stairs, gazing at her.

"I'm sorry. I—I couldn't see very well, coming in from the light," she heard herself say apologetically, and came forward to stand, once more tongue-tied, in front of Miss Balfour. Holly could not have behaved more awkwardly, she thought, furious at having uttered this inane remark instead of saying simply that she had come—but then, why had she come? To say she was sorry? It would sound so absolutely feeble, and she could not think of a single other thing.

It was Miss Balfour who broke the silence. In her gentle, rather hesitating voice, she said: "Yes, the hall is very dark. But I suppose yours is the same?"

Rowan could answer this. She seized on the topic eagerly. "No, it isn't," she said, shaking her head. "That bit in the middle where the glass door is—we haven't got that. Our hall is all in one."

Miss Balfour appeared to be interested. "Really? I am sure that must make it a good deal lighter," she said, and went on: "What sort of wall-paper have you in your hall?"

"It's a creamy-yellow one, quite plain. Of course, it shows the dirt, and lots of people said it was silly in town," Rowan explained, suddenly quite at ease. "But Mummy wanted to open the door and walk into a bright hall, and not a dark cave, she said, and so she had it. But yours is a very good paper, much better than ours—"

Miss Balfour looked at the sombre walls, papered from floor to ceiling and all up the stairs in a rich chocolate brown embossed with large flowers and leaves all of the same colour.

"I daresay," she answered. "My father chose it when he did the house up on his marriage, and it has lasted ever since. Seventy-three years."

15

"Goodness!" exclaimed Rowan, and added, "But haven't you got—rather tired of it? I mean, I know it's *good*, but—"

"Yes, I have been tired of it for a long time," said Miss Balfour with a faint ghost of a smile. "I think, do you know, that I shall have to have it re-papered." And went on:

"Won't you come upstairs to the drawing-room and sit down?"

Rowan, about to refuse, suddenly realized not only that Miss Balfour wanted her to stay, but that she had made a great effort in asking her.

So instead of mumbling that she would have to go home, she answered clearly, "Thank you very much," and followed her hostess up the gloomy stair, carpeted in the same brown as the walls, from which dark old engravings glared down on her head as she passed them.

The drawing-room was at the top of the stairs to the left, on the first floor, exactly as in Number Six and all the other houses on this side of the Crescent, but apart from its shape—an L with the upright very long and the other leg very short—and the three high windows facing the oval of the Crescent garden, it was quite different. It was impossible to imagine two rooms more different than the Lenoxes' drawing-room and this into which Miss Balfour now ushered Rowan.

Everything seemed to be mud-coloured or a peculiarly ugly dingy green. It was like being at the bottom of a dirty pond, Rowan thought as she sat down on a mud-coloured velvet chair. There was not a single bright or pretty thing in the whole room.

Dorothea Balfour, from her seat on the sofa between two windows, where she could look across at Rowan, was perfectly certain that there was, at least for the moment, one bright and pretty thing in the drawing-room. Though the sunlight always had a struggle to get in between the *écru*

16

net covering the lower panes, the blinds drawn halfway down, the heavy velvet curtains looped back with cords, the deep pelmet, it was not possible to keep it out altogether on a June afternoon, and now the golden shaft lay full on the girlish figure, touching the lights in her dark, brown hair, showing up the red and white of her dress, the red of her lips, the brightness of her brown eyes. All the light in the room seemed to be concentrated on her; it was almost as if she shone back at the sun with a radiance of her own.

"You are Miss Rowan Lenox, aren't you?" asked Dorothea, though she knew this quite well already.

Rowan smiled and nodded. "Yes, I'm Rowan, the third girl."

"You are very like your name," said Miss Balfour.

"Am I? I never thought of that. We think it was rather awful of the parents to call us after trees, and we envy Murray—my brother, because he escaped it by being a boy."

"I think it is a charming and original idea," Miss Balfour said with most unusual firmness. "Especially as you are all like the trees you are named for."

Rowan laughed. "Isn't that rather hard on my younger sister? Her name is Holly—"

"The holly is a very beautiful tree," answered Miss Balfour.

"But very prickly."

"Not the top branches, where they are out of reach, and then, the leaves are such a deep glossy green, and the berries are so gay, and the little white flowers so pure and fresh." Miss Balfour was speaking in quite an animated way, as if the subject really interested her.

"I think it's clever of you to know which of us is which," said Rowan.

Miss Balfour's thin cheeks were suddenly flushed. "I'm afraid," she said, painfully embarrassed, "that—that I have fallen into the bad habit of—of looking at you from that top

17

window. You—you are all so gay and lively, it gives me a great deal of pleasure to see you."

Rowan's instinctive sympathy made her answer at once quite composedly. "Oh, do you look at us? Because, you know, we've often looked at you!"

Miss Balfour forgot her embarrassment in surprise. "I should never have thought that we were at all interesting to watch," she exclaimed.

"Oh, but you are! Awfully interesting! You see, we made up all sorts of stories about—" Rowan broke off just in time. "About you and your horrible sister," she had been about to say.

A small gilt clock striking six in a fussy tinkling chime saved her as she sat stricken to silence, her cheeks scarlet with shame.

"Oh! I must fly!" she said thankfully, springing up from her chair. "We have high tea at six—"

"High tea?" Miss Balfour echoed the words. "Do you always have high tea? Aren't you very hungry later?"

"Well, we don't always have it. Sometimes we have cold supper. But we like to have the evenings free in summer when it's light so long," Rowan explained. "If we feel hungry at bedtime we have milk and cake or biscuits or—oh, anything. You see, Murray and Hazel play tennis, and they don't get any time except in the evening. And Holly is always so fearfully hungry when she comes home from school. Really high tea is the best arrangement for us."

"And do you play tennis, too? Are you going to play this evening?"

"Sometimes I play. I'm not very good, though. *This* evening I'm going to dance," said Rowan.

She was standing quite still as she spoke, but Miss Balfour was aware, most vividly, of an impression of swift graceful movement, airy as a bird's flight.

18

Almost uneasily she looked at the tall, slim young creature who had brought a momentary warmth and brilliance to the big dreary room. Surely she was different from other girls? Not that Dorothea knew any other girls, but she felt sure that they could not all be like Rowan Lenox, so glowing, so vital, and so sympathetic. . . . Aloud she said, though more as if she were talking to herself: "So that is what the frilly petticoat is for!"

Rowan stared at her. "Goodness, did you hear all that too? Oh—!" Her voice rose in dismay. "Miss Balfour, I must fly! I'll have to iron it, and there are yards and yards of frill—"

"Of course, my dear," said Dorothea, and led the way from the room, down the dark staircase to the gloomy well of the hall.

Here, as she opened the door, letting a long stream of sunshine in, she said: "It was kind of you to come. Thank you."

"Oh!" Rowan paused on the step. "I—I never said any of the things I came to say, Miss Balfour! I'm so sorry—"

"You didn't need to say them. I knew what you meant quite as well without," said Miss Balfour. "I hope you will come again, and soon."

"I will!" cried Rowan. "I really will, very soon!"

And with a smile and a wave, she was gone, darting down the steps of Number Four and up the next door ones almost in one bound. Dorothea Balfour turned back into the hall. She felt cheered and in some way younger. As she passed the top of the stair winding down to the basement she paused and sniffed. There was a pleasant smell of cooking wafting up from the kitchen regions, a most unusual smell, that of something frying.

After a second's hesitation she went into the dining-room, where she saw that the table was already set for her supper, and rang the bell. It was never any good calling over the stair to Edna, for the echo only came back up the dark

19

well, and one's voice was not heard in the kitchen. Besides, Belle always insisted that Edna should be summoned "properly", by ringing the bell. Having rung it, however, Dorothea went back to the hall, and as soon as Edna's pale scared face appeared below, she called down to her.

"Edna! What is that smell?"

"Oh, Miss Dottie! It was just—I thought you should take your supper early this evening. I'm sure you've hardly had a proper bite all day," said Edna. "And—I was frying the fish, 'um, in egg and breadcrumb, an' doing it up with a nice little bit of parsley an' lemon. Seemed ter me it would be more tempting-like than steamed. But I've only just begun it, Miss Dottie. I can still steam yours if you'd rather."

She did not look up, but Dorothea knew quite well what she was thinking. Belle had never allowed them to have their fish fried. It was always steamed by her orders.

"I am sure it will be very nice fried, Edna," said Miss Balfour. "And how thoughtful of you to put supper forward. I will take it whenever you are ready."

"Yes'um, Miss Dottie. I'll only be a few more minutes," said Edna, and dived back to the basement like a rabbit to its burrow.

"What a good soul she is!" thought Dorothea Balfour. "But how I wish she wouldn't call me Miss Dottie! I've always hated being called Dot and Dottie. . . . I wonder if I could persuade her to say 'Miss Dorothea' instead? It is really a nice-sounding name, Dorothea. Dignified. . . ."

CHAPTER 3

IF ROWAN had not realized already that she was late, the tinkle of cutlery on china, the buzz of voices from the dining-room would have told her.

The dining-room door was half open, and the aperture was filled by the back view of the youngest Miss Lenox's sturdy form as she argued hotly with persons inside the room.

"Well, I'm *going* to get it! But all the same I think it's a beastly shame to send me when it was Rowan's turn to set the table."

"Horrors!" thought Rowan. "It was my turn to set the table, and I forgot all about it!"

And as Holly, with an indignant flounce of the tartan kilted skirt which she insisted on wearing, regardless of her figure's rather pronounced curves, erupted backwards into the hall, Rowan said mildly:

"I'll get whatever it is, Holly. I'm sorry."

"Ho!" snorted Holly, her cheeks very red, her dark eyes flashing. "So you should be!"

"Well, what have you come for? Tell me and I'll fetch it." When Holly was on the war-path she was very prickly indeed, and it was useless to try to appease her.

"Jam," replied Holly curtly. "Though why anyone should want jam after wolfing stuffed eggs and salad and lemon meringue pie and iced coffee, I just don't know!"

"Iced coffee? Good for Mummy . . . who does want jam, Holly?" said Rowan.

"Darling Murray, of course, so don't get anything dull like last year's plum. It's a scandal the way Mummy spoils that boy," she said darkly. "Favouritism! Rank favouritism!"

As always, her own eloquence had restored her to good humour, and now she grinned quite amiably.

21

"I'll come and help you to find the jam," she said, tucking her hand through Rowan's arm and leaning heavily on her. "And I might as well see if there are any biscuits at the same time."

"After wolfing stuffed eggs and all the rest?" murmured Rowan, making for the pantry.

Holly squeezed her arm. "Now, don't be a pig!" she begged. "I need nourishment, because of the amount of brain-work I have to do for those horrible Highers."

"Dear me," said Rowan, as she reached for a pot of raspberry jam, and scooped its contents into a glass dish. "Do they work you harder than Murray has to for his C.A. finals? I've always been told they were very stiff."

"I bet they aren't any worse than Highers," retorted Holly. "Oh, joy! There are squashed fly biscuits as well as digestive! I'll take some of each, I think—don't scrape any more off that spoon, Rowan, I want to lick it!"

"Put it in the sink when you've finished, then," said Rowan. She handed over the spoon, still with a generous blob of jam on it, and made her way to the dining-room.

"Oh, there you are, Rowan! You're terribly late," said Mrs. Lenox. "Have you seen Holly? She is supposed to be fetching some jam, but from the time she is taking she might be making it and picking the fruit into the bargain!"

"I've brought the jam. Holly is just coming. And I'm sorry to be so late," said Rowan, sitting down at her place between Murray and Hazel.

"Who set the table?" she added. "Was it Holly, by any chance?"

"Holly? Of course it wasn't. She didn't get in until six. Hazel set it. And I must say, Rowan," said Mrs. Lenox, "that though you are usually very good about remembering your turn, you chose a very awkward day to forget it, when you are all going out."

"I'll wash up for you, Hazel," said Rowan.

"You'll be late for dancing if you do."

"No, I won't. It doesn't start until half-past eight, and I can do it in ten minutes by bus, if I'm lucky. But—oh! I forgot, Willow said I could have her petticoat—the white one with the frills—and I haven't ironed it. Blast!" cried Rowan despairingly.

"It's all right. I've done it," said Hazel.

"Angel! I suppose you did Willow's nightie as well?"

Hazel nodded, smiling. "I got home early, for once, and I had something of my own to iron, and the whole lot only took twenty minutes. But where *were* you, Rowan?"

"I'll tell you later," began Rowan in a cautious undertone, glancing at the other members of the family. Then, realizing that the uproar created by Holly trying to convince Mrs. Lenox of her urgent need for extra nourishment in the shape of biscuits would drown any other conversation, she turned to Hazel and said quickly and softly:

"I went next door to see Miss Balfour. I wonder Willow didn't tell you."

"She only said that you had gone off on one of your madder crusades," answered Hazel. "But what made you do it, Rowan?"

"She looked so lonely, so lost, somehow. I saw her peering down from that top window, you know how she does?"

"Didn't she mind? Didn't she think it was a queer thing for you to do? What on earth did you say to her?"

"No, she didn't mind, I think she was glad to have somebody to talk to," Rowan said slowly. "She would like to be friends with us, Hazel. I don't believe she knows anyone. I think her sister never allowed her to make friends."

"Poor old soul!" said kind-hearted Hazel. "I'm sure Mummy will be nice to her if she is given a chance—"

"You tell Mummy, Hazel. I feel rather a fool about it," said Rowan. "All the same, I'm not sorry I went."

23

"Now, girls, if you've finished, you ought to be clearing away and washing up. It's after seven." Mrs. Lenox, speaking briskly, put an end to their talk, and all three girls jumped up and began their various jobs with the speed of practice.

While Hazel and Rowan piled the used dishes and silver on a tray, Holly, heaving care-worn sighs and muttering that she had an essay to write, put away the salt and pepper and folded the table-cloth.

"What's your essay about, Holly?" asked Hazel.

"The Poet, the Mystic and the Lover are all God-intoxicated Men," said Holly, with gloomy pride.

"Good Lord! What do you know about mystics and lovers, my girl?" demanded Murray, who was standing near the window idly twirling the tassel of the blind-cord. "Let alone poets! Anyhow, you've got it all wrong. It should be—

'The lunatic, the lover, and the poet,
Are of imagination all compact'."

"That sounds better than the one the Beetle gave us," said Holly critically. "Is it Shakespeare?"

"It is, my ignorant pet. *Midsummer Night's Dream.*"

"Well, I'll put it in my essay. It ought to please the Beetle. She's always complaining that we don't read the classics," Holly said, shutting the sideboard drawer with a hearty bang.

"I don't like to hear you speak of Miss Beadnell by that stupid nickname," said Mrs. Lenox.

"Oh goodness, Mummy, everyone calls her the Beetle," said Holly indulgently. "I'd feel a fool if I started calling her Miss Beadnell."

"Well, run along now and write your essay," said Mrs. Lenox, giving it up as useless. "You can do it in the study, as Murray is going out."

"Don't meddle with my papers, then, or touch my pens and pencils!" shouted Murray, as Holly left the room, crashing the door to behind her.

Shortly after eight o'clock silence descended on Number Six Kirkaldy Crescent.

Mrs. Lenox looked in at Holly, struggling inkily and with many groans over her Poet, Mystic and Lover ("absurd subjects they give these children to write about!" she thought privately) and having frequent recourse to the paper bag of fruit drops at her elbow, presumably for inspiration.

"Don't make yourself sick on those sweets," said Mrs. Lenox automatically.

As automatically Holly replied that it was impossible to be sick on quarter of a pound of wholesome boiled sweets, and her pocket-money did not permit her to buy more.

"I am glad to hear it. They are shockingly bad for your teeth," said her mother and left her before she could think of a really crushing retort.

It was too fine an evening to spend indoors, Mrs. Lenox thought, so she made her way down to the basement, collected her gardening gloves and a small fork from the huge scullery which was now used almost entirely to house bicycles and tools, and went out to weed the end border.

At fifty-two, Edith Lenox was still a very pretty woman. Her dark hair was so lightly sprinkled with silver that it looked as if it had been touched by hoar frost. Her eyes were bright, her skin soft and smooth, her figure slim and upright. It was difficult to believe that she had a married daughter and that the youngest of her five children was sixteen.

"Of course, Edith will marry again," her sister and her friends had said confidently, after John Lenox had been killed somewhere on the bitter road to Dunkirk in 1940. "She is much too pretty not to. Besides, she needs a man to look after her."

25

But the years had gone on, and Mrs. Lenox remained a widow. She removed to Edinburgh partly because it had been her husband's home as a boy, partly on account of the good educational facilities it afforded. It was safer, too, for the children during the War. She had bought the house in Kirkaldy Crescent at a low price—it was too large for most people—and settled down to bring up her family with competent composure.

If she ever felt lost or frightened without her husband no one was allowed to know it. She went on her way quietly, cooking, mending, sewing, and later, as the children grew up and were able to help, turning the bleak rectangle behind the house into a garden.

To her own surprise Mrs. Lenox discovered that the digging and planting and weeding which she had begun as a duty because the garden had been an eyesore, soon became a pleasure. She liked the feel of earth in her hands, the warmth of sun on her bent back, and there seemed to be time to think while she wrestled with obstinate weeds, no matter how hot it made her. This evening she was having one of her periodical mental reviews of her family, lining them up and inspecting them with what she fondly imagined to be a dispassionate eye. There was nothing wrong with their appearance: between them she and John had produced five exceedingly nice-looking children. Not one of them was outstandingly handsome, but not one was plain enough to be overshadowed by the others.

As Mrs. Lenox always insisted that they had inherited their good points from their father, she felt free to admire them without any false modesty. Thinking of Willow's slender silvery fairness, Hazel's nut-brown hair and green-flecked eyes, Rowan's grace of movement and brilliant colouring, Holly's dark curls (of course, Holly could hardly be judged fairly at her present rather, lumpish stage)—Mrs.

Lenox never failed to congratulate herself on having given her daughters the names which suited them so well, though they were apt to grumble over them at times.

Apart from their looks, they were good girls; not perfect, naturally, but as far as she could judge, a great deal more agreeable than most of their contemporaries. At least they did not treat her as if she were feeble-minded. Holly was a little inclined lately to attempt to be crushing, but the others promptly sat on her if she showed any symptoms of over-stepping the line which they drew so rigidly. And then, poor pet, one had to remember that it must be very difficult to keep one's end up with four older ones!

Holly made heavy weather of her school work, moaning over her "prep" every evening, but she was certain to do well in Highers, or so her head-mistress at St. Gregory's said. When that was over, there was trouble ahead, for if Holly imagined that she was going to hang about at home until she was old enough to be taken on as a nurse at the Princess Elizabeth Hospital, she was mistaken. No, thought her mother, vigorously loosening the soil round the roses, she would take a course of advanced classes in French and lit-erature, and acquire a little of the polish she needed. . . .

It was a pity that Rowan had never shown any leanings towards a profession. She had done well while at St. Gregory's, carrying off more prizes than the other three put together, dancing at school concerts, playing Rosalind in the school's inevitable production of *As You Like It*. After she left Greg's she appeared to have no further ambition and now she was looking after three obstreperous children and perfectly happy, doing country dancing in the evenings, quite uncon-cerned about the lack of prospects in her present post. She was not even well paid, her mother thought resignedly; if she had had a little of Hazel's doggedness and Hazel some of Rowan's brains, both might do better.

Not that Hazel was not doing well, bless her. By sheer determination and hard work she had made up for being less clever than the others, and now on the secretarial staff of the Empress Hospital she held a responsible position without rousing envy. Everyone liked Hazel, and wished her well. In many ways she seemed more like the eldest of the family than Willow.

Mrs. Lenox frowned at a weed which she had just pulled up. She was beginning to be afraid that Willow would never realize the responsibilities of marriage as long as she (and Archie, when he was not at sea) continued to live at Number Six. Willow ought to be making her own mistakes and learning from them instead of helping a mother whose housekeeping had been brought to a fine art. Besides, the house was not large enough for them all. It looked enormous, but there were not very many rooms, unless you counted those areas in the basement, which were really only fit for growing mushrooms, in Mrs. Lenox's opinion. There was Holly, still sharing Rowan's room, and Murray sleeping on a divan in the study. And though Holly could and should, as soon as her mother could get it papered and painted and the odd bits of old furniture cleared out of it, be moved into that little place on the top floor between Hazel and Rowan, there was still Murray to be considered.

Actually, thought Mrs. Lenox, it would be fairer to put Murray in the little place, since the study was more or less sacred to him, give Rowan the room now occupied by Willow and Archie, because it was bigger and better than her own, and leave Holly in sole possession of the room she slept in now. But, of course, none of this could be accomplished while Willow and Archie were there. If only Archie, dear fellow, would assert himself more. Willow responded to firm handling, but Archie either could not or would not see that. Because Willow preferred to live with her family, he had given up trying to find a place of their own, and made feeble excuses which would not have deceived a six-months-old infant for doing so.

"Really, Archie is as spineless as a jelly-fish!" Mrs. Lenox exclaimed angrily to her son. "I cannot imagine how he ever manages to give an order on board that boat of his!"

"Be fair, my pet. After all, he doesn't have to give orders to *Willow* on board," Murray said. "It's only with her that he is entirely invertebrate. And Willow—well, she can reduce any man, except a mere brother, to pulp with one of those big-eyed looks of hers."

Murray was quite right. Her whole family had watched with weary resignation the devastating effect of Willow's impact on men young, old and middle-aged. Nor could one blame Willow for being Willow. She meant no harm, and then, she was so very pretty.

As usual, Mrs. Lenox's musings had brought her back in a circle to their starting-point; as usual she had reviewed her four daughters and hardly glanced at her only son. When it came to Murray, however, Mrs Lenox was quite unable to consider him with the same cool, unbiased attention. Being an honest woman, she admitted this to herself. Murray was too much like his father for her ever to see him clearly as she saw the girls.

He was not faultless, of course. For one thing his temper was quicker, his tongue more biting, than his sisters', but he looked at her out of John's grey eyes, he spoke with John's voice, he was a constant living reminder to Edith Lenox of the husband she had adored. And so, where Murray was concerned, she was the same as any other mother of a beloved only son.

"Anyhow," said Mrs. Lenox to herself, rather defiantly, as she gathered up her basket and fork and turned to go into the house. "Anyhow, he is a good son and a good brother, too! And he is working so hard to pass his finals—and he is so good-looking. No one could deny *that*!"

Then, for she had spoken aloud, she looked round her guiltily in case she could have been overheard. There was no one within hearing, but at one of the top windows of Number Four she saw a slight movement as if somebody had been looking out and drawn back hurriedly.

"Dear me!" thought Mrs. Lenox. "That must be Miss Balfour, poor soul!"

Across her mind flashed the remembrance of a remark flung at her by Willow as she left the house with Archie several hours earlier. Something about Rowan's having gone next door to see Miss Balfour. . . .

"Really, Rowan is much too impulsive!" thought her mother. "I do hope she didn't horrify the poor old thing—"

But she had her own impulsive moments, and before she had given herself time to think, she had waved towards that top window.

There was a shadowy response from above, as if Miss Balfour were half afraid of what she was doing.

"I must find out from Rowan about this call of hers, and then I think I shall call myself," thought Mrs. Lenox. "After all, we *are* her nearest neighbours, and I've always had a feeling that she would like to be friends. Perhaps now that her sister is dead, she will be able to know us at last."

And she went in, to drag Holly away from her lessons and send her to bed.

CHAPTER 4

WHILE their mother gardened and thought about them, and Holly reluctantly dealt with her home-work, the rest of the Lenox family enjoyed their evening in different ways.

Murray's was quite simple and always the same. He walked straight up the hill to the courts belonging to his tennis club, and played until it was too dark to see the ball.

He usually played with Hazel as partner or opponent, for she played a good game and had a really strong forehand drive. But this evening he walked up the street alone, for Hazel had some mysterious date about which she would say nothing except that she was going to the movies. The movies, thought Murray disgustedly. After being indoors all day, to go and frowst in a picture-house all evening! It was just like a girl, but no doubt some boy-friend had asked her, and they would sit holding hands in the warm darkness. . . .

"If ever I take a girl out," thought Murray, pushing open the creaking door in the high wall and finding himself in his favourite surroundings, "we'll go for a long walk over the Pentlands, or play tennis or do something sensible."

He waved his racquet cheerfully in answer to a shout of welcome from the pavilion verandah, where a group of white-clad figures were seated, waiting for their turn to play. Murray walked along the path outside the high wire mesh, keenly noticing the games in progress on all four courts.

Good Lord! There was a girl who should never be allowed to play except on a moss-grown grass lawn at a country tea-party! If she succeeded in hitting the ball she spooned it up as if she were putting sugar in coffee, and with just about as much strength. It would be funny except that the possibility of having to play with her made it enraging.

"I'll go home early," he thought. "I'll just have one or two sets and then I'll leave."

He joined the others on the pavilion steps, and sat down beside his friend John Drummond.

"Any chance of a game?" he asked. "Or are you all fixed up?"

"Well, not exactly," said John. "But I think it would be asking a bit much to expect you to join in our four." He leaned towards Murray and lowered his voice. "Did you happen to notice a girl on Number Three court as you passed? A stranger, I mean—"

"Not the little one who can't play for toffee?" said Murray, staring at his friend in horror. "But why do *you* have to—"

"Because she's a school friend of Pam's, and she's staying with us. She's a nice kid, really. It's only her tennis that's so ghastly. Her name's Susan Rattray."

"Will she want to play again as soon as she comes off?" Murray sounded hopeful, but John shook his head.

"She may not want to, but she'll play, all right," he said gloomily.

"The thing is," he went on, "her mother was first-class, or very nearly. Played at Wimbledon and did pretty well there. Ruby Vincent—"

"Good Lord! And that rabbit is her daughter? What rotten luck!" exclaimed Murray.

"Yes, it's rotten luck," agreed John, rather drily. "On Susan. You mean on her mother, I suppose. But nobody can help it if they aren't any good at games, can they? And Mrs. Rattray has made Susan's life absolute hell ever since the girl was thirteen. Extra tennis at school, coaching all through the holidays, and when the coaches threw in their hands and said it was a waste of time and money to go on, Mrs. Rattray did the coaching herself. The result is Susan's got such an inferiority complex that she's almost afraid to speak. I think her mother must be a proper bitch."

It was unusual for John to talk at such length and so hotly, and Murray was surprised. Could John be keen on this girl, he wondered. That also was not like John, who had never shown any interest in girls except as partners on the tennis court. It was obviously his cue to say he would make up their four, he thought, and he said, "It's queer how one-idea'd women get on anything they're good at, isn't it? I daresay Ruby Vincent —I mean Mrs. Rattray—is a pretty difficult parent. I'll make one of your four, John, of course."

"Thanks, Murray. That's decent of you. It'll mean that you'll have to play with Susan," John said anxiously. "You are much stronger than I am, so Pam and I—"

"Yes, that's all right by me," said Murray, now feeling an agreeable glow of magnanimity.

It still warmed him while he was being introduced to the small dark girl, and tinged his voice with a hint of patronage which made Susan Rattray think resignedly: "This is another of them! Playing with me to please John and Pam. Oh, well —it won't last so very long!"

As she walked on to the court the resigned feeling, to which she was only too well accustomed, suddenly yielded to rebellious rage. She could not have said why the pitying look in the tall fair young man's grey eyes had seemed the last straw, but it was so; and something deep down inside her was boiling up into a resolution never to hold a tennis racquet again, no matter how angry her mother might be.

Murray, noting with careless approval that she was perfectly turned out, and thinking that it was something in her favour, was startled to find her slamming the balls back at their opponents like a fury.

"Look here," said Murray, when they were leaving the court after beating the Drummonds six-two. "You're a fraud, Susan Rattray. I saw you playing pat-ball like a rabbit

33

when I came in, yet just now you were a tigress. What's the meaning of it?"

Susan looked up at him with a confidence she had never felt before in her dealing with young men. "The meaning of it is that I was in a rage," she replied.

"Then you must always play in a rage!" Murray said, laughing.

Susan shook her head. "I've made up my mind never to play again—and you've no idea what a relief it is!"

"What do you like to do, then?" he asked.

"Oh, so many things!" Susan's pale face grew delicately pink, her eyes shone. "Sailing and riding, and walking—"

To his own intense astonishment Murray Lenox heard himself say: "I can't do anything about sailing or riding, but we might go for a good tramp one evening, if you liked?"

"But then you would miss your tennis."

"I don't think it would do me any harm to miss it now and then," said Murray.

*   *   *

As Murray had supposed, Hazel was sitting quietly in the dim warmth of the picture-house on Adam Ferrier's left, but he was not holding her hand. She was acutely conscious of his nearness. If she moved at all her sleeve brushed against his, so she sat absolutely still. He was so close to her in body, so far away in mind. Adam liked her because she was sensible. He had said so; and that was why he had asked her out with him this evening. It was terrible to be liked because you were sensible, but better that than not to be liked—by Adam.

All the younger members of the clerical staff at the Hospital, and some of the nurses too, were interested in Adam Ferrier. They showed it in different ways: some by pretending to ignore him, some by saying they couldn't stand him because he was so pleased with himself, some by dog-like devotion. Hazel had tried to behave to him as she did to the other doctors, with cool impersonal politeness.

And Adam went on his way absorbed in his work, and never noticed any of the feminine attitudes struck for his benefit. Nobody knew anything about his private life.

"It's my belief," said Christine Rennie solemnly to Hazel, "that he just doesn't exist outside the Hospital. He materializes as he walks in at the gates, and dissolves into thin air when he goes out."

Christine, a green-eyed red-head with a milky skin, whose hair flamed like a torch under the lights of the Out-Patients' Department and attracted every male glance, had so many young men that she could go out with a different one every night for weeks on end. Therefore, if she insisted that her interest in Adam Ferrier was purely a naturalist's in some strange new specimen, she must be supposed to be speaking the truth.

She had a shrewd common sense oddly at variance with her romantic appearance, and this remark of hers about Adam's having no existence beyond the Hospital had a grain of truth in it which Hazel, though she had laughed at Christine, had thought over and found bitter.

They all knew how the other young doctors and surgeons liked to spend their free time: Doctor Lister played Rugby football, "Ginger" Smith played the flute, Montford played the fool and was popularly expected to be booted out in the near future if he didn't lay off whisky and women; Pincher Martin was crazy about amateur dramatics . . . but Adam Ferrier never gave anyone the slightest hint as to his tastes and activities.

She knew that he thought her sensible because Ginger Smith had told her so.

"The Mystery Man approves of you, Hazel," he had said, grinning until his sandy moustache quivered. "He said just now, 'for God's sake get that Lenox girl to do those notes. She's the only sensible one of the whole bunch!' I hope you feel honoured!"

Hazel had only smiled and edged past Ginger, whom she did not like very much.

"Well, he knows you, and he knows your name, which is more than can be said about the rest of us!" This was Christine's comment. She had been standing near enough to hear what Ginger Smith said.

It was no use trying to edge past Christine with a smile.

Hazel said: "If it's true and not just one of Ginger's fairytales, it's only because Doctor Ferrier is so particular about his case-notes. You know he gets into a frenzy if they aren't perfect."

And the day after that, Adam Ferrier asked her to go to the pictures with him. . . .

Even now it was almost incredible to Hazel that she should be sitting beside him, that she should be with him at all, and in surroundings so utterly unlike the Hospital.

"Why can't I just enjoy the outing and the picture?" she thought miserably. "Why do I have to bother so much about *him*? I wish I were more like Rowan—"

For a moment her mind flew to the sister with whom she was most in sympathy. Rowan, called after a fairy tree, born in the fairy's month of October, who sometimes seemed not altogether mortal in her happy detachment from the sentimental troubles that afflicted her sisters periodically. Lucky Rowan!

*   *   *

Rowan, her slender feet in ballet flats moving through the intricacies of a strathspey, was calling herself lucky too.

36

The big hall, in spite of open windows, was stiflingly hot, and the dancers were wilting, but not one of them would have changed places with their friends enjoying the summer evening outside.

All their hours of practising had reached the culminating point when, out of their number, a team was to be picked to perform in one of the Festival productions. All of them who were left, eight girls and eight young men, were good. It would be difficult to choose among them. Rowan was glad that she was dancing and not selecting. She wondered if she would be picked; she was a little on the tall side—(why were the good men dancers almost all so very short?)—but since she had been taken away from her usual partner in the practices and told to dance with this taller man, she was beginning to think that she would be one of the reserves.

Her new partner was looking sulky. Perhaps he resented having to dance with her? Certainly his former young woman, now dancing at the bottom of the second set, a hideous girl, Rowan thought, with a great big ugly mouth, but beautiful feet, was resenting it—and Rowan—bitterly.

"You can have him, and welcome!" said Rowan to herself, gliding into the *allemande*. "I don't want him—once the dance is over."

But it was a delight to have a partner as tall as this, and he did dance beautifully. When they had made their bows and curtsys to one another and were standing about trying to get cool, Rowan was surprised to find him still at her side. And still looking sulky.

"Well," he said abruptly. "It's going to be you and me, is it?"

"But—they haven't picked us yet, have they?"

"If you're dancing with me, you're in the team," he said impatiently.

Rowan was amused. "You seem very sure of it."

"Sure? Of course I'm sure. I know I'm in the team, so if they've put you to dance with me, you're in too."

"What a conceited creature he is!" thought Rowan. "How Murray would hate him! I wonder if he's right, though, about me being in the team? Do I want to be, if I've got to dance with him?" And then: "Yes, of course I want to be in the team—and he does dance most beautifully. . . ."

Aloud she said nothing, but stood quietly, her hands clasped in front of her waist.

The selection committee, two women and a man, now stopped their consultation. The man adjusted his spectacles, cleared his throat, and said:

"Er—ladies and gentlemen! The team is as follows:" Here he fumbled with a slip of paper, and Rowan clasped her hands so tightly that they hurt. Would he *never* start to read it out?

"Er—first couple. Miss Lenox and Mr. Angus Todd."

Rowan heard no more. First couple, she thought. Then the conceited creature had been right. . . . She caught his glance, the little superior smile which seemed to say "What did I tell you!" Suddenly, brilliantly, she smiled back at him, and Angus Todd, taken by surprise, could only blink.

*　　*　　*

"Oh, let's go home, Archie! This is terribly *drab*, don't you think?"

Willow had seemed perfectly content throughout the excellent—and expensive—dinner at which she had only nibbled while Archie ate everything with appetite. Now, as he still sat peacefully sipping his brandy, she pushed her empty coffee cup away from her, and spoke petulantly.

"Half a minute, darling!" he protested. "Don't make me gulp my brandy!"

"Well, leave the horrible stuff, then! I'm bored with this."

"I thought you wanted to see that picture—?"

"I've changed my mind, and it's too late to get decent seats now," said Willow. "Do hurry up, Archie—"

"All right, I'm coming," he said. "Must pay the bill, though—"

It was extraordinary how restless Willow was, he thought ruefully, laying notes on the discreetly folded bill brought by the waiter. Everything seemed to bore her after a few minutes. . . .

When they were walking slowly back towards Kirkaldy Crescent, Willow's mood changed again. Crossing the Dean Bridge she tucked her hand into his arm, and said, "Much nicer to be out, by ourselves, than sitting in that stuffy restaurant, isn't it?"

"You know I don't care a damn where we are as long as we're together," said Archie, rather shakily.

Willow could still make his heart thump and race as it had done at their first meeting.

"Darling Archie!" she cooed now. "I feel just the same—"

CHAPTER 5

FOR THE SECOND TIME in her life Rowan stood on the newly scrubbed top step of Number Four. Her hand was on the knob of the shining brass bell, but instead of pulling it she waited, repeating to herself in varying forms the message which she was to deliver from her mother.

"Oh, bother!" thought Rowan, and gave the bell a tug which set the echoes jangling through the house. "I'll have to leave it until I see her."

Edna opened the door in her reluctant fashion, but when she saw Rowan, a wavering smile flitted over her face.

Yes, Miss Balfour was in, and would be pleased to see Miss Lenox, she said, and led Rowan upstairs to the drawing-room, where she announced:

"It's the young lady from next-door again, Miss Dottie."

"*Miss Dottie*! How perfectly ghastly to be called that!" thought Rowan, so shaken by the name that she was able to greet Miss Balfour and add quite naturally, "I've brought a message from Mummy. She would like to come and see you, if she may."

"I should be very pleased," said Miss Balfour, prim with shyness, but smiling and turning faintly pink.

"Miss Balfour," Rowan burst out. "Why do you let her call you 'Miss Dottie'? It's so ugly—"

"I know," answered Miss Balfour. "But you see, I have always been called Dottie. My sister—"

"Oh, I'm sorry! I shouldn't have asked! It was frightful me!" cried Rowan in distress. "Of course, if your sister called you that, and you like it."

"But I don't like it at all. I never have, and I am intending Edna to call me 'Miss Dorothea' or 'Miss Balfour', when I find a suitable opportunity."

Rowan, at once full of sympathetic interest, said, "I daresay it won't be easy for her at first, but I'm sure she would come round to 'Miss Dorothea' fairly quickly. Besides, it is such a pretty name, and dignified, too. It suits you."

"Do you really think so?" Miss Balfour, unused to having anyone to take an interest in her affairs, was pleased. "I am glad. But it does seem a pity that now I am able to use it there should be no one left to call me by it except Edna."

She sounded so wistful that Rowan said: "I would love to call you 'Miss Dorothea' if you didn't think it cheek."

This was such rapid progress towards intimacy that Miss Balfour was startled. Then, reminding herself that everything moved more quickly nowadays, and feeling delightfully daring and up-to-date, she replied: "Do, my dear, I shall like it very much."

Mrs. Lenox, in spite of being much more used to the manners and customs of the young than Miss Balfour, raised her eyebrows when Rowan announced: "Miss Dorothea would be very pleased if you'd go and see her, Mummy."

"You seem to have got to know Miss Balfour very well in a very short time, Rowan," she said mildly. "Perhaps you should come with me when I call."

"She's seen me twice now," Rowan said. "I expect it would be more fun for her if one of the others went."

A dissentient muttering rose from all round the table. The evening meal was in progress, so the whole family was present.

"This is Rowan's pidgin. The old lady is her protégée," said Murray. "Not that I imagine even Rowan thinks that I should be the one to go with Mummy."

"I don't see why not. Old ladies usually fall for you," Willow chipped in.

"I propose to go on Saturday afternoon," said Mrs. Lenox, raising her voice slightly. "So you will all be free. You had better make up your minds between now and then which of you is going."

"I'll come with you, if you like. I don't mind," Holly said, in a negligent tone which did not conceal her passionate curiosity to see the inside of Number Four.

"No, Holly dear. *Not* you," said Mrs. Lenox firmly. "I'm sorry, but you are altogether too overwhelming. You must wait until Miss Balfour has had time to get accustomed to the family."

"Breaking the poor old thing in gently?" murmured Hazel. "It really had better be Rowan."

And in the end it was Rowan who accompanied her mother.

"Well, how did you get on? What's the house like? What's *she* like? Was it very heavy going?" This chorus greeted the two deafeningly when they returned from their call.

"Children! Children!" cried Mrs. Lenox, putting her hands over her ears and knocking her neat little straw hat sideways. "What a dreadful noise! Is tea ready? Because I'm not going to tell you *anything* until I have had some."

On Saturdays and Sundays the Lenoxes had what Holly called "low tea" at half-past four, with supper later, so they hurried their mother into the dining-room, where Hazel had just set the big blue tea-pot on its stand at one end of the table.

Murray pushed Mrs. Lenox into a chair, Willow poured her out a cup of tea, Holly offered her scones.

"Now tell us all about it!" said Willow. Mrs. Lenox drank some tea and obligingly embarked on a detailed account of Miss Balfour and the house next door.

Mrs. Lenox said at last: "That's all. I've told you every single thing I can remember. Why don't you ask Rowan?"

"It's no use asking Rowan," Murray said. "She's a very nice girl, but her habit of turning all sorts of fowl—

not even geese, very often—into swans makes her an inaccurate reporter."

"Miss Balfour was the one whose geese were all swans this afternoon," Rowan said. "You should have heard her about Mrs. Lenox's beautiful, talented, charming children!"

"Didn't it make you squirm?"

"No, because the poor pet obviously doesn't know the first thing about people of our age. What *did* make me blush," said Rowan candidly, "was Mummy being all maternal!"

"*Never!*"

"Gospel truth. I expected to hear her talk about her chicks at any minute."

Mrs. Lenox's other daughters moaned loudly, but Murray said, "just wait until you find yourself the mother of a bouncing grown-up daughter when you still feel quite young and lively, and see how you like it!"

"Dear Murray. Always so understanding," murmured Hazel, with a mocking lift of her eyebrows.

Mrs. Lenox looked bewildered. "I don't know what you are all talking about," she said, "but Murray is perfectly right—"

("He always is," said Holly, in a stage aside.)

"And as I have asked Miss Balfour to come to tea to-morrow," Mrs. Lenox continued, with a quelling glance at Holly, "you—and she—will be able to judge at first hand for yourselves."

And having dropped this bomb, she got up, smiled at her family, and went away to take off her best hat.

Like so many other things that are looked forward to with dread, the tea-party for Miss Balfour was a great success. The young Lenoxes assured their mother that she had made them so self-conscious beforehand that they were certain to be at their worst, either completely tongue-tied or far too talkative. But as soon as they realized that Miss Balfour was much more nervous than they were, they threw themselves whole-heartedly into the business of putting her at ease.

Dorothea Balfour sat between Mrs. Lenox and Hazel, rather silent, rather dazed by the noise made by so many cheerful voices, but enjoying the friendly warmth of the atmosphere. She smiled and nodded, and thought how much better everything tasted when it was accompanied by laughter and talk. But she realized, with a guilty pang, that she found her recent meals, eaten in solitude with a book propped against the water-jug, infinitely preferable to those partaken of when Belle had sat munching at the head of the table, and nothing had broken the silence except the sound of chewing, or an occasional diatribe from Belle on Edna's general unsatisfactoriness. It was dreadfully sad to remember one's sister only as a fault-finder, and it made Dorothea feel wicked, yet all her memories of Belle were like that.

Belle had never changed; the last words she spoke, just before she had her stroke, had been characteristic: "Don't be a fool, Dottie."

These same words, uttered in a clear voice, brought Dorothea back, blinking, to her place at Mrs. Lenox's table.

"Oh, don't be a fool, Hazel!"

It was Willow, leaning across from her place opposite, who spoke, and Hazel only laughed.

"They aren't my best ones," she said.

"I should think not!" said Willow. "But if you lend *any* nylons to Holly, you *will* be a fool, Hazel! She'll bring them back in ribbons!"

"Children!" cried Mrs. Lenox. "Will you stop calling one another fools, please? What do you suppose Miss Balfour can be thinking of you?"

"Oh—but —" said Dorothea in her gentle, deprecating manner. "They don't really mean it, do they? And that is what matters, I think."

"There, you see, Mummy. It's all right, Miss Balfour *understands*," said Holly, giving Dorothea a look of such ardent approval that Dorothea blushed.

"It is lucky that she does," retorted Mrs. Lenox. "Miss Balfour, if you really won't have another cup of tea, shall we go upstairs and sit in the drawing-room, or would you rather go out to the garden?"

"The garden, please," said Dorothea, and Holly, as they all went down to the basement, took her arm confidingly.

"You *do* understand," she said, into Miss Balfour's ear. "Nobody with any sense would want to sit inside on a lovely day like this, now would they?"

Dorothea, gratified, but finding progress on the dark stair difficult because of Holly's bear-like clasp, murmured, "No, no!" rather breathlessly.

"Of course, the garden's very small, but it's quite decent—for a town garden," Holly went on. "Do you know, when the people in Linden Terrace don't have their wireless on too loud, and we're lying on the grass beside the rose-trellis, Miss Balfour, you can almost believe you're at Kersland."

"Kersland!" In her amazement Dorothea tripped on the door-step and was only saved from falling by Holly, but she hardly noticed it. "Did you say Kersland?"

"Yes. Do you know it, too? It's the dearest little Border village and we go there in the summer. Before the War, when the others were quite young, we used to have a house there—of course, I wasn't born then," Holly explained, guiding her dazed captive towards the far end of the garden. "But even since the War we used to stay at Kersland all summer. Now we can't go for more than a fortnight because

45

of the older ones having jobs. I'd like to stay there all the time. Did you say you knew Kersland, Miss Balfour?"

"Long, long ago, when I was very young," said Dorothea.

She sounded regretful, and Holly, interpreting her tone as sorrow for her lost youth, gave her arm a comforting but very painful squeeze.

"Never mind, you aren't really so *terribly* old!" she said consolingly. Then a thought suddenly struck her. "Oooh! Do you remember Queen Victoria?" she asked.

Dorothea said, "Well, I was fifteen when she died, you know, and I can remember quite well how upset everyone was. People all wore black . . . and I remember the Diamond Jubilee, and being allowed to sit up late to see the bonfires across the Forth, on the Lomonds in Fife. And the volunteers singing 'Good-bye, Dolly, I must leave you', on their way to fight in Africa. Dear me, how long ago it is—"

"Fifty years in history is *nothing*," began Holly, in a lecturing tone all too familiar to her family. "When you begin to think in centuries, you—"

"That will do, Holly," said Mrs. Lenox. "It's all very interesting. I'm sure, but we have heard it before."

Holly looked sulky. "Miss Balfour hasn't," she said.

"Perhaps you would come and see me one day by yourself," Miss Balfour suggested. "And then you could tell me all about it."

"You don't know what you've let yourself in for, Miss Balfour," said Murray, from the grass where he was sprawling in careless ease, a daisy held between his teeth by its stem. He spoke with feeling though rather indistinctly. "Holly on History is apt to be pretty long drawn-out."

Holly turned her back on him with a haughty flounce of her skirt. "Mummy," she said, "Miss Balfour knows Kersland, too! Isn't it super?"

"Really? That's interesting—and strange, too, when one remembers what a small place Kersland is," said Mrs. Lenox, adding, as she glanced at their visitor's face, suddenly very pinched and small: "We must have a talk about it, Miss Balfour, but not now. My noisy family has tired you, I think—"

"No, no indeed!" Dorothea said hastily. "It has been delightful, and it was so good of you to ask me. But I think perhaps I should be going home now."

Directly she was outside on the pavement, with the words of their farewell still in her ears, Dorothea was annoyed with herself for being, as she put it, "so silly about Kersland". Why could she not have said that she loved the little place, and that her mother's grandfather had been the blacksmith there, and had once shod Sir Walter Scott's cob when it cast a shoe? She was not ashamed of her great-grandparent, as Belle had been. He had been a very good smith, and various wrought-iron gates in the neighbourhood proved him to have been a craftsman besides. If they had asked her whether she was related to old Dod Armstrong and his descendants, she would have acknowledged it immediately and without embarrassment. But Kersland meant so much to her, and she had had to keep this love secret in her own heart for so many years, that to hear it mentioned suddenly was almost impossible to comment on with reasonable composure.

Kersland: Dorothea had been sent there to stay with her mother's relatives while she was recovering from a bad attack of measles. She had been four years old, and she had never forgotten the smallest detail of that visit. The people, as well as the place, remained diamond-bright in her memory.

The village straggled down a gentle slope along a ridge, with a tiny school at its upper end, and the smithy at its lower. The cottages faced each other across a dusty road and grandfather's was just beyond the smithy. It was the last house in the village, a little apart from the others, and had a bigger garden. There was no longer a church in Kersland. All that remained of it was a crumbling gable-end smothered in ivy, standing among the grave-stones of the old church-yard. Of course, people still went to church, but they had to walk down the side of the ridge by a grassy track between high thorn hedges until they came, down in the hollow, to a bigger village with a large parish church. Dorothea had been too small to walk so far, and she had always stayed with grandfather in the sunny garden, while Aunt Elsie, wearing a black costume and hat, had gone to the morning service. The sound of the bell used to come floating up the hill when the wind blew from the north, telling people it was time for church. . . .

How it all came back to her on this Sunday evening in summer, while other bells, those of the many Edinburgh churches, rang for evening service! Dorothea, looking about, half-expecting to see the blooming cottage gardens, the dusty hedges, the red-tiled roofs, found that she had walked up to the far end of Kirkaldy Crescent without noticing it.

She stood for a moment beside the scarlet pillar-box. Suddenly the thought came to her: "I could go to Kersland. There's nothing to stop me now." Perhaps it would be foolish to go back after so long; perhaps Kersland had changed, as so many things had changed. But Holly Lenox had spoken of the place as if they all loved it, and Dorothea was inclined to believe that if the Lenoxes found it enchanting, it must still be so.

CHAPTER 6

MRS. LENOX, packing neatly and swiftly, thought what a blessing it was to have Miss Balfour next door to keep an eye on the house and its occupants while she and Holly were at Kersland for the summer holidays. Miss Balfour would never interfere unnecessarily, and her advice would be so gently offered that Willow would accept it without realizing that she had.

At this point in her preparations Mrs. Lenox paused, stood erect with two pairs of Holly's stockings in her hand, and said aloud:

"How extraordinary!"

Yes, how extraordinary it was to think of Miss Balfour, who until a few weeks ago had been the less disagreeable of the two old ladies at Number Four, as a blessing!

It had come about so naturally, so simply, so imperceptibly, starting from that afternoon when she had put on her new hat and gone next door to see Miss Balfour. Or rather, it had begun before that. Rowan had begun it by paying her impulsive visit only a few hours after Miss Balfour's sister's funeral. The new friendship was really due to Rowan and her unorthodox behaviour. Of course, she must not be encouraged to do such odd things, thought her mother, frowning a little.

Rowan was different from the rest of her children, there was something unaccountable in her which made her more vivid, and gave her the capacity for feeling more intensely. She rode so high on the crest of her wave of happiness that Mrs. Lenox sometimes felt afraid of the depths to which sorrow might plunge her.

So far and fast do thoughts range that Mrs. Lenox, though she spoke severely to herself for day-dreaming and wasting time, had only stood clutching Holly's stockings for a minute, before she bent and stuffed them into a convenient corner of the suitcase.

It was impossible to save Rowan, or any of them, from the sorrows that life might bring. Her good sense told her so, but it was not very comforting, she thought, as she went on packing. What did bring her comfort, and it was not sensible at all, was the recollection of the odd old Highland cook who had been with them temporarily just before the War, when Rowan had been three or four years old!

She had always said that Rowan belonged to the Little People, and that they would guard her from sorrow and strife. . . .

"Ridiculous!" muttered Mrs. Lenox, annoyed that the old woman's words could still console her. "Quite ridiculous— an ignorant old creature—and she wasn't a very good cook, either! Terribly extravagant . . ." but she was fond of the children, especially Rowan, and Nannie was away at the time, and even Holly, the baby, loved her.

At the thought of Holly, Mrs. Lenox's mind sprang back at one bound to the present. Where *was* Holly? She should be home by now, she should be helping to pack. . . .

Of course, St. Gregory's had broken up for the summer holidays, and the child was enjoying her freedom, but at the same time, she ought to remember that there was a lot to do at home.

Holly was much nearer home than her mother supposed. With two companions of her own age she was proceeding very slowly down Kirkaldy Crescent, on the far side, stopping at intervals of a few yards for no apparent reason, and then strolling on again.

All three walked with a slight but noticeable waggle reminiscent of ducks on the move, which caused the full skirts of their cotton dresses to flounce about them, and all were giggling.

Miss Dorothea Balfour, standing at one of her drawing-room windows, watched their antics with puzzled wonder. They had reached the lower end of the Crescent, and so were directly opposite her, and they halted there as if undecided whether to turn back or walk on. As they hesitated, swinging their skirts and chattering, two tall boys on bicycles came down the hill, wearing the badge of a well-known Edinburgh day-school on their caps. They passed the girls without a sign of recognition, and pedalled on out of sight. The girls tossed their heads, turned and walked up the Crescent again.

In a few minutes the boys reappeared, rode up the near side of the Crescent, passed the girls near the top, and continuing their circular tour, passed them once more.

"Dear me!" said Miss Dorothea, as the meaning of these apparently senseless manoeuvres broke on her. "Dear me! They seem very young to be starting this sort of thing. I wonder if their mothers know?"

She remained at the window, watching for Rowan, whom she was expecting to tea, and saw the bus reach its stop at the upper end of the Crescent.

Rowan jumped lightly off, and a minute or two later joined Miss Dorothea in her drawing-room.

"Did you ever see such young ostriches as Holly and her friends?" she remarked indulgently, observing her hostess at the long window. "As if it doesn't stand out a mile that they are hanging about waiting for some pimply boy to notice them!"

"Surely they would not want to be noticed by a boy with pimples, my dear?" said Miss Balfour.

"I think the point is to be noticed, whether the boy has pimples or not, at that age," said Rowan. "I never bothered much about them myself—I mean the boys, not the pimples—but I remember Willow used to keep a little book and put down all the boys who looked twice at her. If she didn't know their names she put 'fair hair', or something. And Willow was much prettier than Holly, so I expect Holly isn't terribly particular."

"I can't help feeling that your mother would not be pleased if she knew."

"No. She wouldn't be pleased. She'd be furious," was Rowan's candid reply. "But what's the use, Miss Dorothea? It's just something that happens when you get to about seventeen."

Very few people are so strong-minded as to be proof against the flattery of being treated as contemporaries by those young enough to be their grandchildren.

Miss Balfour was not so strong-minded. She was perfectly willing to believe that Rowan was right. Her own common-sense told her that if the game Holly was playing was foolish, it was quite harmless, but she said rather diffidently:

"I am sorry if it annoys your mother, my dear. Do you think that perhaps if Holly knew—"

Rowan shook her glossy head.

"No good. You can't stop a—a force of nature. Holly would go underground, that's all. I don't see why she shouldn't amuse herself like this. Mummy's a darling, Miss Dorothea, but she doesn't seem able to understand how girls feel at that age. It's funny, isn't it?"

Miss Balfour, who felt in some obscure way that it would be disloyal to Mrs. Lenox if she agreed, heard Edna clanking the tea-tray outside the drawing-room door with a sigh of relief and said: "Here is our tea, my dear."

"Lovely! I'm starving!" announced Rowan, and as Edna staggered in with the enormous silver tray and its gleaming burden of tea-pot, cream-jug, hot-water jug, sugar basin, cups and saucers and a covered dish from which rose a delicious smell of hot scones, sprang to help her.

"That's far too heavy for you, Edna," she said.

"You know," observed Miss Balfour mildly, picking up the heavy silver tea-pot and pouring out tea for them both, "I have suggested that we should put all this paraphernalia away in the silver-chest and use a wooden tray and a china tea service, but Edna won't hear of it. She seems to enjoy being a martyr over polishing and carrying it."

Rowan blushed. "Miss Dorothea!" she cried. "I never meant—it was only that Edna looked so overloaded!"

"I know, and I didn't mean to sound as if I were scolding you," said Miss Balfour.

Rowan sprang up, circumnavigated the table, and dropped a kiss on the little black velvet bow which Miss Balfour liked to wear on top of her hair.

"You are a pet!" she said. "And I'd hug you if you hadn't a cup of hot tea in your hand!"

Miss Balfour blinked to rid herself of two tears of pure pleasure. It was so comforting to be told she was a pet by this delightful young creature; and so far had her spirit progressed towards emancipation during the weeks she had known the Lenox family that the thought of Belle's disapproval did not even cross her mind.

"Dear child," she said, steadying her voice with difficulty. "I am going to miss you when you are at Kersland with your mother and Holly."

Rowan, who had gone back to her chair, looked at her old friend and blushed again. "But I'm not going to Kersland, Miss Dorothea," she said.

"Not? Are your employers not going away after all then? I understood from Mrs. Lenox that they were spending the next two months at North Berwick," exclaimed Miss Balfour.

"Oh, they are! They are there already and the children have been parked with an aunt who keeps a maid to look after them," said Rowan. "But I can't leave Edinburgh just now. I'll have to stay to practise with the rest of the team."

"The country dancing team, of course. I had forgotten," said Miss Balfour.

How strange, she thought. Rowan doesn't seem to mind missing Kersland and staying in town all through her summer holidays.

"Is it really worth giving up a summer in the country for?" she asked wonderingly.

"To dance? Oh, *yes*!" Rowan answered. For a moment she struggled to try to express what dancing meant: the lovely stirring tunes, grave or gay, the ordered beauty of the pattern traced by the changing formations, the exquisite precision of footwork which yet must not give the faintest hint of stiffness, the harmony of music and movement, the known touch of her partner's hand as he led her—no, it was quite impossible to convey any of it even to a person as sweet as Miss Dorothea.

So she only repeated: "Oh, *yes*!" and took a bite of the gingerbread which Miss Balfour had cut for her.

She thought about her partner, Angus Todd, and realized with astonishment how differently she saw him now that she had been dancing with him regularly for the past five weeks. He was still the same, yet though she winced when some particularly blatant expression of self-esteem set her teeth on edge, she made excuses for it and for him.

Poor Angus! He had had rather a miserable life. Adopted by a sedate, narrow-minded elderly couple who meant well enough but knew nothing about children, he had been brought up strictly, and never allowed to forget his good fortune in having been rescued from an orphanage and given a home and a name. Rowan had been told this by his former dancing partner, the girl with the ugly mouth.

"So you needn't think you're getting anything very great in the way of a partner, after all!" she had finished with a sneer.

"What does all that matter? He dances far better than any of the rest of us—*that's* what counts!" Rowan had said.

"D'you mind? I must dash, I'm late—" and she had slipped past the other girl and fled across the empty echoing floor towards the door and the sunlit street beyond it.

The effect on her of this unhappy story was the exact opposite of what the teller had intended. Rowan, with her vivid sympathy, could imagine just how the boy had been soured by the constant calls on him to be grateful, the reminders that he had no real name of his own. His defence had been to armour himself in self-satisfaction, to use as weapons a barbed tongue and a rough, gibing manner. Pity was the last thing he needed or desired, it seemed, and Rowan, though desperately sorry for him, was careful not to show it.

There was never any opportunity to show or hide much during the dancing practices, of course, but Angus had taken to seeing her home afterwards. And then, as they went by short cuts through the quiet grey terraces and crescents where the heavy-leaved trees in the gardens brought twilight early, they talked. Or Angus talked, bragging, jeering, at odds with the whole world, and Rowan listened, wishing she could help him to see everything with a less jaundiced eye.

Miss Balfour wondered why she suddenly looked so grave, but being accustomed to watching other people without interrupting, she said nothing, and in a moment Rowan came out of her reverie with a start.

"I'm so sorry," she said confusedly. "Did you ask me something?"

"No, my dear. You were talking about your country dancing," was Miss Balfour's placid reply.

"The old pet! She hasn't noticed anything," thought Rowan, much relieved.

Aloud she said: "You must come and see us dance, Miss Dorothea. Do say you will. I'll get you a ticket—"

"That would be delightful. Thank you," said Miss Balfour, inwardly deciding that it would also be interesting to see Rowan's partner; for, of course, the child had been thinking about him. Anyone with eyes in her head could see that.

Rowan was standing now, thanking Miss Balfour for her nice tea, and saying that she must go home.

"Mummy gets in a bit of a flap when she's going away," she said. "So I'd better be there in case she wants me to do anything."

Mrs. Lenox, when she came round later in the evening to say good-bye, showed no sign of flurry, apart from a slight and very becoming flush in her cheeks.

"Holly asked me to say good-bye for her," she said, as she sat down near Miss Balfour in the big drawing-room. "She wanted to come with me, but really she *had* to tidy her room—or rather her half of the room she and Rowan share. It looks as if she has been turning everything over with a pitch-fork."

"Dear Holly, she is probably at an untidy age," murmured Miss Balfour.

"I'm sure *I* was never—" began Mrs. Lenox.

Then she broke off, frowned, and smiled rather unwillingly.

"Oh, well! Perhaps the children are right when they say I fuss," she admitted. "But it's difficult not to. I think it's a kind of mothers' disease. Some show it, some don't."

"I am sure you show it very seldom," said Miss Balfour.

Mrs. Lenox sighed. "It's just going off and leaving them to their own devices for so long," she said. "I can't help worrying a little. For the last two years we only went away for a fortnight, and they all managed to get their holidays at the same time, so we just shut up the house. And before that, of course, with Murray doing his National Service and Rowan still at school and Hazel at the University, everything was quite easy. If only Willow looks after them properly and remembers to feed them."

"Oh, surely—" Miss Balfour could not help showing her surprise.

"No. You don't know Willow. She's very sweet and very pretty," said Willow's mother dispassionately. "But she's lazy and selfish. I ought to have insisted that she and Archie should find somewhere to live on their own, but it seemed so—so brutal to turn one's own daughter out of her home!"

Miss Balfour nodded. It could not be easy to tell a daughter who apparently preferred living at home to go, and it would be more difficult now than if Mrs. Lenox had hardened her heart when Willow was newly married.

"If I can help," she began, a little diffidently.

"Dear Miss Dorothea, it is such a comfort to me just to know that you are next door," said Mrs. Lenox. "And if you really wouldn't mind just keeping an eye on them, and giving Willow the help of your good advice, I should be so very grateful. But you are not to let them—especially Willow—be a trouble to you."

"She will be no trouble to me," Miss Balfour assured Mrs. Lenox.

And then, though years of repression had made her almost inarticulate, she added shyly, "It—it is the *greatest* pleasure to me to have you all for my friends. You could never believe how much it means."

They parted with feelings of mutual respect and affection, and on the following day Mrs. Lenox and Holly left for Kersland.

CHAPTER 7

FOR THE FIRST WEEK the household at Number Six appeared to be running as smoothly as if it had been oiled.

Hazel, Rowan and Murray, who all came in to see Miss Balfour more than once, were loud in their praises of Willow's efforts.

Murray added that he hoped they would last, but this ingratitude was received with such adverse comment from his sisters that he withdrew the remark.

"Under duress," he added darkly, and muttered something about the everlasting triumph of hope over experience, which Hazel and Rowan prudently pretended they did not hear.

Of Willow herself, Miss Balfour only had fleeting glimpses, flying across the garden to hang dish-towels on the line or to pick a handful of parsley and mint and chives for a salad. Once or twice they met in the busy street at the far end of Linden Terrace, where the trams clanged to and fro, and the pavements were always thronged with people shopping. Willow, her prettiness enhanced for some reason by the large basket she carried, smiled and waved and cried, "Good morning!" as they passed, but quite obviously had no intention of stopping to talk.

Possibly she resented being told by her mother to turn to her elderly neighbour for advice, and was afraid that Miss Balfour, given the smallest opportunity, would try to interfere. Miss Balfour was sorry, but her good sense (inherited from Mamma, though Belle would never have credited either with possessing it), told her that the best thing she could do was to leave Willow alone.

What mattered was that she seemed to be keeping house quite successfully, and as for Murray's scepticism, Miss

Balfour had often heard that brothers were apt to judge their sisters rather severely.

So she and Willow continued to smile and say "Good morning" with complete amiability, and the last days of July passed, one very much like another.

Miss Balfour had discovered, not long after she took the reins of Number Four into her hands, that Edna adored doing the household shopping, and as it gave her such delight, her employer saw no reason why she should not do it quite often.

The procedure followed was always the same, and soon became regular routine. Miss Balfour, having dusted the drawing-room and her bedroom, came downstairs to the dining-room, and there awaited Edna's return.

Every single purchase was then laid before her on the table by Edna, who displayed a mixture of the hunter's pride in his bag and the zeal of a well-trained retriever in fetching it home.

On a morning almost a fortnight after Mrs. Lenox had gone on holiday, Edna, having accounted for the money she had spent and bundled her shopping back into the basket, took up her position near the door to regale her mistress with a commentary on her passages with the shop assistants who had served her and whom she invariably suspected of intent to defraud.

Miss Balfour was not really interested in this recital, but she felt it was unkind to deprive Edna of this innocent enjoyment, so as usual she listened, or appeared to listen, which did just as well.

Suddenly her wandering attention was brought sharply back by the mention of a name.

"What was that, Edna?" she asked. "I'm afraid I didn't quite catch what you were saying."

"I was saying," Edna repeated in an unnecessarily loud

voice. "That young Mrs. Harper from next door is fairly going it. I came into MacSween's Creamery while she was there, and you should have heard her! Cream and a chicken and eggs! And telling Mrs. MacSween she wouldn't be able to pay the book this week— I don't know what Mrs. Lenox would say to that, I'm sure! She paid all her books like clockwork."

"Oh, well, Edna, perhaps there is some special reason," said Miss Balfour. "Just take the things down to the kitchen. You have done very well."

She spoke so firmly and cheerfully that Edna was forced, though with reluctance, to remove herself and her basket from the room. But when she was alone, Miss Balfour's face reflected thoughts that were troubled.

She had never been told in so many words that Mrs. Lenox's income was only just enough for her family's needs and left nothing over for expensive luxuries, but that sort of thing could be guessed without anything said.

Miss Balfour felt extremely worried, and all the more so because she was uncertain what she ought to do.

Just then a dapper little elderly gentleman who had been hovering on the doorstep of Number Four for some minutes seemed to come to a decision. Stretching out a hand in a spotless wash-leather glove, he rang the bell.

"Willow, do come and look! There's such a funny little man at Miss Dorothea's door!"

Rowan, reaching the window during a rather sketchy dusting of the Lenoxes' dining-room, had taken the opportunity to look out, and now called her eldest sister to come and look too.

"Only selling vacuum cleaners," said Willow languidly.

"No. I'm sure he isn't selling anything, he's far too well-dressed. Natty is the word . . . now he's ringing the bell—"

"Well, if you're so anxious to find out all about him, why don't you go and ask your precious Miss Dorothea?" said

Willow, still languidly, but with a waspish sting to her voice. "You're always rushing next door to see her—"

"I don't know why you should be so beastly about Miss Dorothea," said Rowan, flaring up at once. "You're in a foul temper this morning—"

"My God, if I *were*—though I'm not, as it happens—" cried Willow, pushing herself erect and shaking her bell of fair hair the better to glare at Rowan across the table. "It wouldn't be surprising! I'm bored to *tears* with cooking and shopping and housework! I'm *sick* of it!"

"Considering that the shopping's rather fun and Mrs. Baird and I do most of the house-work and Hazel washes up nearly every evening—" began Rowan, when she suddenly realized how absurd they must both look, glaring at one another like two angry cats, and she burst out laughing.

Willow promptly started to cry, and after one or two vain attempts to comfort her, Rowan went away, knowing that Willow would stop when she wanted to and not a minute sooner.

"Perhaps she misses Archie," thought the younger sister. "Poor old Willow!"

Then her thoughts returned to the little man in his neat grey flannel suit whom she had seen on Miss Dorothea's doorstep, and she washed up the breakfast dishes—there was no Mrs. Baird to do them on Saturdays—still wondering who he was, because he seemed so very unlike the sort of person who could be an acquaintance of dear Miss Dorothea's.

In the dining-room next door Miss Balfour stood gazing in frozen astonishment at her visitor. She had not moved since Edna, with a scared face and bulging eyes, had announced hardly above a whisper: "Mr. Milner to see you, Miss Dorothea," and shown Belle's long-vanished and almost completely forgotten husband into the room.

Looking for the first time at the neat little man—so utterly different from the bullying oaf of her imagination, who had driven Belle to leave him after six months—as he tripped round the end of the big dining-table towards her, Dorothea Balfour felt that the scene had the distorted reality of a bad dream.

It was in keeping with this that he should appear perfectly composed and cheerful; and to her alarmed embarrassment was added a sudden wave of angry sympathy with her dead sister.

She stiffened her backbone, held her head high, and said without a quaver, in a remarkably good imitation of Belle's chilliest tones:

"To what do I owe the honour of this—this most unexpected call?"

Much to her relief, it had the effect of halting him in his approach. His outstretched hands dropped to his sides, but as he stood in front of her, too close for comfort, he continued to smile, at the same time shaking his head in a gently admonishing fashion which she found acutely irritating.

"Yes," he said, after a pause which seemed endless to her. "Yes, there *is* a resemblance, after all. Not in looks, but in manner. I didn't notice it until you spoke. What a pity!"

Miss Balfour, now wondering if perhaps he was mentally unsound, said: "I don't understand you. What are you talking about?"

And instantly regretted it, because this time she did not sound like Belle in the least, but like her own gentle fluttered self.

The little man was beaming at her so infectiously that to her horror she almost smiled back.

"Ah!" he exclaimed with great satisfaction. "That's better! That was the real Dorothea speaking. The other was only a copy of Belle—and not a very life-like one, I am glad to say!

My dear Dorothea, how delighted I am to make your acquaintance after all these years!"

Advancing upon her he kissed her lightly but firmly on both cheeks.

No man had ever kissed Miss Balfour before, except Papa, who, she realized vaguely, hardly counted as a man in this connection; and she was so shattered by the novel experience that she could only say weakly:

"I don't think you ought to speak about Belle like that."

She was surprised and mollified when he became serious at once, and replied: "No, I ought not. You and I are alive, and she is dead, poor soul."

After this a silence fell again, which might have lasted for ever as far as Miss Balfour was concerned, because she could not think of anything to say. Her brother-in-law, not afflicted by shyness or undue delicacy of feeling, remained quiet for just the proper length of time to suggest respect for the dead, and then spoke.

"Do you not think we might talk more comfortably if we sat down?" he said gently.

An appeal to Miss Balfour's hospitality never failed. On realizing that they were still standing face to face in the dining-room she was so shocked that, forgetting how very recent was her intention not to talk to him at all, she said they would be more comfortable in the drawing-room, and led the way upstairs.

She supposed that he wanted to talk about what she called "business" without really knowing what she meant; or perhaps he was going to express contrition for having treated Belle unkindly.

But once seated in a corner of the big sofa between two of the long windows, Mr. Milner leaned back against the cushions and proceeded to chat amiably on a variety of impersonal topics.

When the door opened and Edna looked in, her mistress was amazed to find how fast the time had passed.

"Will the gentleman be staying to lunch'm?" asked Edna.

"Oh—" Miss Balfour hardly knew what to say. Her conscience was pricking her, for in the interest of exchanging views with Belle's husband, she had quite forgotten his misdeeds.

Not understanding why she hesitated, Edna said: "There's plenty, Miss Dorothea," and Mr. Milner was accepting the invitation which had not been given with cheerful alacrity.

Edna lingered at the door. "There's that bottle of sherry in the hall cupboard, Miss Dorothea," she said meaningly.

Miss Balfour gave in. There seemed to be nothing else to do.

"Please uncork it carefully, Edna, and bring it up," she said.

After a surprisingly short interval—so short that if Miss Balfour had been capable of thinking about it she would have realized that Edna must have already drawn the cork—the sherry made its appearance on the best silver salver, with two of the cut-glass wine-glasses beside it, and a plate of biscuits.

Setting it down with such hearty good will that everything rattled, the faithful handmaid announced:

"I've put clean towels and a fresh cake of soap in the top bathroom'm," and once more withdrew.

"That's a very good maid you have, the real old-fashioned kind," Mr. Milner said approvingly. "I can see that she knows how to look after you."

"Yes—oh, yes," replied Miss Dorothea distractedly. "Won't you pour yourself out a glass of sherry?"

He was beside the tray in a flash, he was pouring out the wine, exclaiming reverently, "Pre-war Amontillado! My dear Dorothea, this is indeed a treat!" He was bringing her a brimming glass, he was drinking to their better acquaintance. . . . It really was like a dream, though not such a nightmare as she had thought at first!

Yet throughout the meal that followed, while her guest ate heartily and prattled on like Tennyson's brook, Miss Balfour, emboldened by sherry, was making up her mind that she really must ask him why he had called on her, and show him quite clearly that Belle's wrongs were still remembered.

She waited until they had gone back to the drawing-room for coffee. Then she cut across his praises of Edinburgh as seen by morning light from the train.

"I think it is time that I should know why you have come to see me, Mr. Milner," she said.

" 'Mr. Milner!' " he answered reproachfully. "Surely, surely, my dear Dorothea, that is a very cold, stiff way of addressing a brother? Montagu, please, or even better, Monty, as all my friends call me—"

"This is the first time I've ever seen you, and I really cannot call you anything but Mr. Milner," said Miss Balfour.

("And I wish," she added to herself with unwonted irritation, "that you wouldn't talk in that stupid affected way, like an out-of-date play!")

He sighed. "I am sorry. I always think of you as Dorothea. My sister Dorothea."

"Why have you come to see me?" asked Miss Balfour firmly.

"I felt that two people, alone in the world save for one another, might find mutual comfort in companionship," he said with dignity.

Miss Balfour felt this to be quite ridiculous.

"Considering the nature of the relationship between you and my poor sister," she said coldly, "I cannot think that you and I would ever become good companions."

To her horror she could hear herself speaking in the same stilted manner as her brother-in-law.

" 'Let the dead past bury its dead', Dorothea," he replied. "I do not complain. Why should you?"

"*You* have nothing to complain about," Miss Balfour said.

"But I have. When I think that you treated Belle so badly that she was forced to leave you, it—it makes my blood *boil!*"

Mr. Milner stared at her.

"I know one should not speak ill of the dead," he said. "And I have eaten your salt, Dorothea, and so must not quarrel with you, but—"

"That is such a silly saying, I always think," said Miss Balfour, "as if salt were the only thing one's guests ate! And," she continued, in case he might think she had been side-tracked, "whether we quarrel or not, you can't deny that if *Belle* had to leave you, things must have been pretty bad."

"Look here!" he said, jumping up and walking about the room. "I agree that if Belle had left me, you might be right. But, you see, she didn't. *I* left *her.*"

Miss Balfour could only stare at him speechlessly. For some reason, perhaps because he had dropped his old-fashioned actor's rolling phrases, she believed him. Her honesty told her that this version of the old story was much more credible than the one she had always believed. The little man trotting up and down the floor in such agitation was not capable of ill-treating anyone, certainly not Belle, who could have picked him up and carried him under her arm!

He had come to a standstill and was staring down at her unhappily.

"It was a rotten thing to do. I was a coward," he said. "But I really got to the stage when I simply couldn't stand it—so I bolted. I don't suppose I need to tell you what it was like."

Miss Balfour shook her head.

"No," she answered almost inaudibly.

"I was a fool, of course," he went on. "If I'd been willing to wait a little, I might have seen what she was really like, and escaped. But—well—she was a big handsome creature in those days, and I was in love with her. And she—she liked me, you know, and didn't mind my knowing it. And she seemed to be well-to-do, and I was on the rocks. It served me right, I daresay."

"I don't suppose it was all your fault," said Miss Balfour.

"If she had been more like you—oh, well, it's all over now," he said. "By the way, where *were* you, when we got married? You never appeared."

"I was at Kersland," Miss Balfour said, looking back more than a quarter of a century at herself, painfully young and shy though over thirty, at Belle, six years older but in the full bloom of her good looks, handsome, dashing and over-bearing. "Mamma and I went there because her father was dying, and after he was dead Papa sent for Mamma to come home, but I stayed on with my aunt. She is dead now, too, of course. . . ."

"So you and I are the only ones left, and you live all alone in this great house?"

The tone of his voice did not escape Miss Balfour.

"Yes," she said. "And you—where do you live?"

"Oh, here and there, you know, here and there!" he replied, with a return to his affected manner. "Wherever my roving fancy takes me. I am a rolling stone, my dear."

She nodded. "And I suppose you haven't gathered any moss?" she asked.

"I flatter myself that you will not find any moss growing on me," he said, with an airy laugh.

"That was not what I meant," said Miss Balfour quietly.

He sat down, carefully hitching up the knees of his trousers.

"How did you guess?" he said. "You are quite right, of course. I've never had a bean, and at the moment I am utterly and completely broke to the wide."

"I don't know," said Miss Balfour. "I just guessed. Is that why you didn't come to see me sooner? I mean, Belle died several weeks ago."

"Yes. I saw it in an English paper that some tourists left on a table outside a cafe," he told her. "It was in Italy. You can live wonderfully cheaply in Italy if you know the ropes. It took me a long time to scrape the fare together to get here."

"I think," said Miss Balfour. "That you had better fetch your luggage from wherever you left it, and come here— for a visit, at least."

There was nothing impulsive about this invitation. Ever since she had learned that Belle had driven him to leave her, Miss Balfour had been feeling more and more strongly that some recompense must be made to him. He had been a coward, as he had admitted himself, but remembering what life with Belle could be, Miss Balfour did not blame him very much.

But the effect on him of her suggestion astonished her, for looking across at him she saw that his eyes were full of tears, and in great embarrassment she hurriedly looked away again.

Monty Milner had not bargained for this. He had hoped to talk his sister-in-law into helping him, it is true. He had intended, if need be, to base his appeal on the grounds that Belle had once loved him, or failing this, to hint that a husband had rights to his wife's property by law.

Something about Miss Balfour had prevented him from doing this, had made him tell her the truth, and now, as he blinked the easy tears away—he had always been emotional—he heard himself saying:

"That's uncommonly good of you, Dorothea, but I think you should consult your lawyer first. He might not approve."

To himself he said with surprised congratulation: "You're not such a bad little b—— after all, Monty!"

"My lawyer? But what can it possibly have to do with Mr. Ferrier?" asked Miss Balfour, bewildered once more.

"I wouldn't feel comfortable about it if you didn't tell him," he replied doggedly. "Ring him up and make an appointment to see him—I'll come with you, if he wants me to," he added, thinking ruefully that the lawyer would probably recommend Miss Balfour to have nothing to do with him, and he would have done himself out of a good home for—what? For the sake of the transparent honesty and kindness that had looked at him out of his sister-in-law's faded, but still pretty brown eyes.

CHAPTER 8

IN HIS DETERMINATION to be noble and protect Dorothea from himself, Mr. Milner had lost sight of the fact that it was Saturday afternoon.

He was rather dashed when his sister-in-law pointed out that it was no use trying to telephone to Mr. Ferrier or any other lawyer before Monday, and Montagu had much better be sensible and spend the week-end here at Number Four.

(She called him "Montagu" firmly, though with a blush, because she had decided it was silly not to, and his pleasure in being accepted as a brother-in-law, as this seemed to show, made it worth while.)

Accordingly, still protesting, he fetched what he grandly called his baggage, which turned out to be a small cardboard suitcase and a dilapidated basket of Italian raffia-work, and was installed in the bigger of the two enormous spare bedrooms on the top floor.

He settled in at once, as if he had lived there all his life, and Miss Balfour had to confess to herself that it was pleasant to have his cheerful company. Edna was even more delighted, and said so openly. "It makes a bit o' life about the house having a gentleman to do for," she told her mistress.

When the people whom it really concerned were all content, it was a pity that young Mr. Ferrier should have been so extremely disagreeable about it. Miss Balfour had rung him up on the Monday and asked if he could see her at his office. Mr. Ferrier, making an appointment for Tuesday morning, and hearing the reason for it, had wanted to know her brother-in-law's address in Edinburgh.

Miss Balfour said he was staying with her at Number Four Kirkaldy Crescent. Whereupon Mr. Ferrier, with complete if temporary loss of his legal suavity, had said quite

70

sharply that he considered it very ill-advised of her to have invited Mr. Milner to be her guest under the circumstances.

It was bad enough to be barked at down the telephone by Mr. Ferrier, who had been so kind and helpful when Belle died, and explained everything to her so carefully that she had not had the heart to tell him she was none the wiser for his trouble. Yes, that was quite bad enough, but the thought of the interview to come had made Miss Balfour feel quite sick.

"And it was even worse than I expected," she thought. "I almost lost my temper with Mr. Ferrier, he was so *rude* to poor Montagu!"

It was Tuesday afternoon, and Miss Balfour was so shaken by her morning at the lawyer's office that she had retired to the drawing-room as soon as lunch was over, to spend an hour or two on the sofa with her feet up.

She was alone in the house. Her brother-in-law had gone on some errand of his own, about which she neither showed nor felt curiosity; Edna, who always went out during the afternoon, ostensibly to get some fresh air, was quite certainly chewing caramels (so bad for her teeth) in the nearest cinema.

The sofa was comfortable, and Miss Balfour, with a thin old Paisley shawl over her slippered feet, ought to have felt peaceful and drowsy too.

But though her body was at ease, her mind continued to turn over the outcome of her interview with Mr. Ferrier. She must really try to make herself understand about the money, which had made Mr. Ferrier so terribly angry. . . . "An iniquitous arrangement," he had called it. . . . "My uncle should never have allowed Mr. Balfour to make such a will, leaving all his property to his elder daughter with the proviso that you were to be looked after by her, Miss Balfour! See what has come of it!" he had said—as if anyone, least of all herself, could have made Papa do anything he didn't want to—"On Mrs. Milner's death, instead of your being owner of half the estate, you find yourself dependent on your brother-in-law!"

Miss Balfour sighed. Of course, Papa had always treated her as if she were half-witted. She had often appeared almost so with him.

She had said so to Mr. Ferrier, but he had only glowered at her.

If that had been all, Miss Balfour would not have minded so much, in spite of the shock of discovering that almost all her possessions seemed to belong to Montagu; but then Mr. Ferrier had turned and rent her brother-in-law, which had been most unjust.

"I understood you were dead," he had said, in a tone clearly showing his indignation that this was not so. "I have always believed that Mrs. Milner was a widow."

"I assure you I am very much alive, my dear fellow," Montagu answered, at his most jaunty and annoying.

"You will have to prove your identity to my satisfaction," Mr. Ferrier had said. "And let me tell you that though your legal rights to this estate may be adequate, in my opinion your moral rights are nil. Mrs. Milner could have divorced you for desertion any time during the past twenty years."

"Yes, but, you see, she didn't," Montagu had said. "There's no need to get into such a temper, though it does you credit. I have no intention of depriving my sister-in-law of her property."

"Then it is a very great pity that you came here at all," Mr Ferrier had retorted. "And I must say, in spite of your protestations, it looks as if you had come for just one thing—"

"So I have. To make the acquaintance of my charming sister-in-law."

"No. For money," Mr. Ferrier had said brutally.

But at this stage in the proceedings Miss Balfour had interrupted.

"Oh, please!" she had said faintly. "This is horrible! Of course, my brother-in-law must have what is due to him, Mr. Ferrier. And—and if you don't mind, I think I must go home now. This has been very upsetting—"

Both men had turned to her at once. Mr. Ferrier, suddenly seeming very young, had muttered an apology for causing her distress, and immediately added: "You will hear from me, Mr. Milner," in a threatening voice.

Montagu, all solicitude, had led her away and insisted on taking her home in a taxi.

As they were bowling westwards over the Dean Bridge, with a glimpse of trees, green lawns and the shrunken Water of Leith far below, Miss Balfour had pulled herself together and said, "I am so sorry. I have never heard Mr. Ferrier being unpleasant in that way before. He is usually such a very polite, considerate young man. I do apologize."

Her brother-in-law, however, had shaken his head. "That is a very decent young fellow, Dorothea," he had said soberly. "A bit hot-headed for a lawyer, perhaps, but he really is thinking of your interests, and I liked him for it."

Having muddled over the affair to its conclusion, and decided that until she knew her financial position in simple terms of pounds, shillings and pence it was no good worrying, Miss Balfour closed her eyes. She drifted into a light uneasy doze remembering Montagu's tribute to Mr. Ferrier, and thinking, as women so often have and so often will, that men were strange creatures.

The gentle opening of the door roused her, and she started up, blinking, to see Edna beside the sofa.

"It's tea-time, Miss Dorothea," she said. "And one of the young ladies from next door says can she speak to you a minute?"

"Yes, of course. Ask her to have some tea, Edna, please," said Miss Balfour, patting her hair into place and kicking the shawl off her feet.

"Will Mr. Milner be in to tea'm?" asked Edna.

"I don't know. He didn't say," replied Miss Balfour. "Put three cups on the tray and then you needn't bother about it."

"I think the young lady wants to see you *alone*'m!" said Edna.

Her voice was so heavy with mysterious meaning that Miss Balfour guessed that the afternoon's film had been a thriller, and with great kindness did not show any impatience, nor ask which of the Lenox girls it was.

"Very well, Edna. Ask her to come up, and don't bring tea for half an hour," she said.

"Or you could ring'm," suggested Edna, who, for some reason of her own, adored answering bells.

"Very well," said Miss Balfour again, and while Edna went away, she sat wondering if it were Hazel or Rowan who had come to see her.

When the door opened, it was their elder sister Willow who came in, looking nervous and defiant, though enchantingly pretty in spite of it.

Miss Balfour did not know Willow as well as the other Lenoxes, but she smiled at her warmly.

"Come in, my dear," she said. "What a very pretty frock, and how becoming it is to you."

Willow's face brightened, and she gave a swift glance at the long narrow mirror on the wall, where her slender figure in the grey glazed cotton, patterned with green and black, was reflected dimly as if under water, and her pale gold hair shone like spring sunshine.

"It is very nice of you to come and see me," Miss Balfour went on, doing her best to encourage her visitor. "Because

I was feeling rather cross and worried, and not liking my own company."

"Oh!" cried Willow. "*Oh!*"

She flew across the room and fell on her knees beside Miss Balfour's chair.

"Oh, Miss Dorothea, that's just how *I* feel—cross and worried!" she babbled. "And it isn't a bit nice of me to come and see you. I should have come days and days ago, only when Mummy told me to ask you if there was anything I needed help about, I made up my mind I could manage perfectly well by myself!"

"Why shouldn't you?" said Miss Balfour, as Willow paused for breath.

"Only you see," Willow said dolefully, "I couldn't. I've got into the most awful mess, and there's no money left. I don't know where it's all gone, and Mrs. Baird said this morning she wouldn't come back till Mummy's home again if she couldn't get her money regularly, and—"

Miss Balfour listened while Willow poured out her tale of woe and mismanagement. She could not always make sense of money and business as talked about by Mr. Ferrier, but weekly or monthly tradesmen's books and household economy were simple to her.

"Didn't you keep an account of what you were spending?" she asked, when it became plain, from Willow's muddled statements, that she had succeeded in spending the money left by Mrs. Lenox for the first month in just under a fortnight.

"Well, I did, at first, but it was such a bore," said Willow. "I hate adding and subtracting, and anyway, the money I had left never came out right with what I'd written down."

"It has a nasty habit of not squaring," Miss Balfour agreed, remembering how anxiously she used to work over her household accounts before submitting them to Belle's sharp eyes and acid comments.

She looked at Willow, kneeling among the crumpled folds of her pretty frock, and thought hard.

"Have you any ideas about what you are going to do, my dear?" she asked, in a brisk, business-like way.

Willow's beautiful grey eyes widened. "I—I thought perhaps *you* would help me," she murmured trustingly.

"So I will, if I can. But we must think what would be the best way."

"If only Archie weren't on that horrid long run I could ask him for the money," said Willow. "But he won't be home for weeks."

"That wouldn't be very fair to Archie," was Miss Balfour's comment, and she spoke rather drily. "He gives you an allowance, I suppose?"

"Oh, yes, of course! But I seem to have spent nearly all of it already—"

Miss Balfour sighed. She was beginning to see why Mrs. Lenox worried about her eldest daughter's lack of responsibility. "I think," she said, "that we should see just what you have. Is there any of the housekeeping money left?"

Brought down to hard facts, Willow became much less helpless, produced the remnants of the housekeeping money, and after some shrewd questioning from Miss Balfour, remembered that she had a Post Office Savings book with quite a respectable sum in it.

"Then you must use that," said Miss Balfour. "The only alternative that I can see is to ask your brother and sisters to help you out."

But Willow not unnaturally was against this. "They'll be horrible about it, and never let me hear the end of it," she said, and she sighed. "I'll just have to use my Post Office savings. I meant them for a new fur coat."

"Perhaps your husband will give you a fur coat some day," said Miss Balfour. "Would you mind ringing the bell?

I think we would both be the better for a cup of tea."

Willow, feeling a little aggrieved and looking a little sulky, because she felt that the sacrifice of her fur coat had been treated altogether too lightly, went over to the fireplace and pushed down the handle of the old-fashioned bell, with its garland of small bright flowers painted on a white china surface. She had hoped, without putting it into words even to herself, that Miss Balfour would have offered to lend her enough to carry on. Archie would have paid it back as soon as he came home. ... It seemed unfair that she should have to use her own savings, when, after all, she had spent the housekeeping money on Murray and Hazel and Rowan far more than herself . . . well, of course, she *had* borrowed enough to buy the grey glazed cotton. . . . Everything was a muddle, and so boring that she could scream.

Turning impatiently from the bell, Willow saw Miss Balfour standing by the window with the hard light of an August afternoon full on her face. She looked old and frail and tired. Compunction smote Willow so hard that she bundled the fur coat and her boredom to the back of her mind, and crossed the room to stand beside Miss Balfour.

"I'm afraid I've made you tired," she said. "I'm sorry, truly I am. I am very selfish and thoughtless, and you've helped me out of my muddle, and I've never thanked you."

"My dear child!" Miss Balfour smiled, and now the tired look had gone, to Willow's relief. "You haven't tired me at all. I was thinking how much pleasanter it would have been if I could just have given you the money you need. But I know your mother wouldn't like it, and—"

Willow broke in impetuously, quite forgetting that she had been thinking exactly the same only a minute earlier.

"Of course, Mummy would have had a thousand fits!" she cried. "Of course, you couldn't give me the money. It's my own fault for being so careless and extravagant and—and my old fur coat will do another winter perfectly well!"

"You mustn't feed your household so nobly," suggested Miss Balfour, laughing openly.

"At least, we won't be down to porridge and kippers and bread," Willow said.

Then, rather hesitantly, she bent and kissed Miss Balfour's faded cheek. "You're a darling, Miss Dorothea!" she said. "The others always say so, but I've never quite believed it until now."

"It is very sweet of them, but perhaps they have rather rammed me down your throat," said Miss Balfour. "And one is usually apt to dislike the unfortunate person whose praises one hears sung too often."

"Yes, like the books people say you *must* read because you'll be certain to love them," agreed Willow.

And then Edna came in with the tea, and shortly afterwards Willow went home full of good resolutions and feeling a somewhat unmerited glow of virtue because she was giving up her new fur coat.

"Well," thought Miss Balfour, when she went to change her dress for dinner—since Montagu Milner had come to stay the evening meal had blossomed into dinner—"Well, I haven't had such a day for a very long time, if ever, and at my age these emotional disturbances are a little tiring. I am glad it is over."

No conversational effort was required of her during dinner, for her brother-in-law, who appeared to be in very good spirits, talked throughout, and only polite murmurs of assent were necessary.

Afterwards, when they were sitting in the drawing-room, one on each side of a cheerful wood fire—the evening air grew chill after sunset—and Miss Balfour was knitting peacefully, her brother-in-law said suddenly:

"I expect you have been wondering where I've been all afternoon, Dorothea?"

"Not in the least, Montagu. Why should I?" replied Miss Balfour.

Then, seeing that he seemed dashed by her polite lack of curiosity, she added kindly: "I hope you enjoyed yourself, whatever you were doing."

"Enjoyment was not my aim," he said reproachfully. "But I think I may say that I have succeeded in arranging our affairs satisfactorily—that is, if you approve of my idea, of course." Miss Balfour's knitting needles ceased their gentle clatter, and she looked across at him, her attention and her apprehension roused.

"Where *have* you been, Montagu?" she asked.

"I went back and saw young Ferrier," he said. "And told him what I thought was the fairest way of settling everything. After a good deal of argument, I managed to talk him round."

"Well, go on! Can't you see that it's most unkind and thoughtless of you to keep me in suspense like this?" said Miss Balfour, with most unwonted sharpness. This slow recital was almost too much for her self-control. Her future depended on what he and Mr. Ferrier had agreed upon, and he sat there rolling out his pompous phrases at her!

"I didn't mean to keep you in suspense. I'm sorry," he said, startled. "But—it's a little difficult to put it to you. I—it seemed such a good idea in Ferrier's office, and now I'm not sure it isn't just infernal cheek on my part."

Miss Balfour had herself in hand again. She saw that it was useless to try to hurry him, and she resumed her knitting, though with shaking hands.

"First of all, I want you to believe that I had no idea, no idea at all, that your father had left everything to Belle," he said earnestly. "What I was hoping for was a slice off her half of the estate. It was a frightful shock when I found that the whole thing was hers. I do hope you believe me—"

"Yes. I believe you," said Miss Balfour quietly.

"Thank you, Dorothea. That makes it easier for me to tell you my plan. It is just this—that I should join forces with you, and come and live here permanently. I'd try not to bother you—you'd hardly need to see me except at meals—"

Miss Balfour found his humility both touching and embarrassing.

"If you lived here, I should be glad of your company," she said. "But would you not find it very dull? There is no need for you to tie yourself down. The money is yours—and please don't think that I am blaming you, it is something neither you nor I can help—and you must not consider yourself in duty bound to look after me. Yes, I know that Mr. Ferrier said it ought to be mine by moral right, but that has really nothing to do with it."

She stopped, smiled at him, and went on knitting.

"I made my will this afternoon," said Montagu Milner abruptly. "That was what took the time. I wanted it drawn up, signed and witnessed before I came back here. Of course, I've left everything to you, but it isn't likely to do you much good, for we must both be about the same age."

"I am sixty-eight," said Miss Balfour.

"And I'm sixty-seven, so there's very little in it. I only told you because I wanted you to understand I'm doing my best."

"I understand, and I do appreciate your kindness," said Miss Balfour.

"Then do me a much greater kindness in return," he said eagerly. "And let me come and live here. I've knocked about long enough, I'd like to settle down. We could do very comfortably in this house, on what we've got. And I'm no use with money, it just runs through my fingers. If you turn me out, I'll be broke in a year or two—"

Miss Balfour met the look of his pleading eyes, hungry for understanding, yes, and for affection. She had a shrewd suspicion, backed by his own words, that he was not altogether a desirable character: he was weak and full of failings, but there was something very likeable, even lovable, about him. She knew that she would enjoy having him to share the big empty house with her, so she said:

"Very well. Let us try it, at any rate."

"Six months' notice on either side?" he asked, trying to conceal his immense relief behind a jocular tone.

"It might be a good thing. A sort of safeguard," Miss Balfour agreed, thoughtfully.

"Of course," he exclaimed, in a great hurry. "I was only *joking*, my dear Dorothea."

So she had to assure him that she was joking, too. "But all the same, it was quite a sensible suggestion," she added.

Finally it was arranged that they should review the situation at the end of six months, in Mr. Milner's pompous words, and that Dorothea was to continue to manage the household finances as before.

"For I'm better with just enough for pocket money, you see," Montagu ended with sudden disarming simplicity. "So you must look after the rest."

Then they turned on the wireless and listened to the news, after which Miss Balfour said good night to her brother-in-law and went to bed.

In spite of her extreme tiredness, Miss Balfour was glad of the day that had passed. Because of it she had discovered her brother-in-law's good qualities and found in him a companion. And Willow, though she appeared so selfish and irresponsible on the surface, was really sound when her better feelings were appealed to.

Even Mr. Ferrier had lost his temper on her behalf, and she ought to feel more grateful to him. She would, if he on his side could stop treating Montagu as if he were a black-guard, which, of course, he wasn't. He needed home life, and she would make him so comfortable in the morning-room, which he had asked to have as a bed-sitting-room instead of being away up on the top floor.

That left the rooms up there empty: three of them and a bathroom, besides the little one with the skylight window, hardly more than a big cupboard. Montague had said the top floor would make a good flat, with the little room converted into a tiny kitchen . . . but it would not be very pleasant to have strangers living in the house, meeting them on the stairs or in the hall. . . .

A sudden thought that seemed inspired came to Miss Balfour then, so striking that she sat up in bed the better to consider it. What if she asked Willow and her husband to rent the top flat?

Willow would be independent, which was what her mother wanted, and what Willow needed; and yet her old home was so near that she need never be lonely when her husband was at sea. . . .

"I'll consult Montagu," said Miss Balfour aloud. "And I am sure he'll agree. Then we can ask Willow."

She lay down again, this time thinking that it was pleas-ant to have someone to consult.

Her very last waking thought was how astonishingly nice and good people were when you knew them; and then she was fast asleep.

What she did not know and would not have believed was that the people who knew her could not help living up to her belief in their good qualities, or that their virtues were sometimes no more than the reflection of her own shining honesty and kindliness

CHAPTER 9

ROWAN and Angus Todd had passed under the grey bulk of St. Mary's Cathedral and were heading towards Queensferry Road on their slow homeward way, when he said suddenly:

"It's a lovely evening. Let's take the bus up Ravelston Dykes and walk over Corstorphine Hill. We could catch another bus home on the far side. Come on, Rowan!"

"Too late. I'm tired and I want to get to bed," said Rowan. "And anyhow, it will be pitch dark long before we are over Corstorphine Hill. Banging into trees, and falling over rocks isn't my idea of fun—and suppose we broke our legs, or even sprained our ankles? It would be the end, with the dancing display so near."

"Oh, all right," he agreed grudgingly. "But I can't see why you're always so tired. You're on holiday now, aren't you?"

"In theory I am. In practice it works out that Willow needs so much help that I am doing more than usual."

She fell silent as they walked up Melville Street, its noble breadth free of the day-time ranks of parked cars, the handsome houses looking gravely across at their opposite numbers above the heads of passers-by.

It was quite true that Willow did remarkably little apart from cooking breakfast and supper, and Rowan sometimes felt rebellious. She really was tired, too, it was no idle excuse. She was worried as well. What had happened to Mrs. Baird? She came every Monday, Wednesday and Friday without fail, and yesterday she had never appeared at all, and that was the second day she had missed. Willow had flown into one of her hysterical rages when asked about it. But, Rowan vowed, that if Mrs. Baird didn't come to-morrow, hysterics or not, she would pin Willow down to telling her what was the matter.

"You're very quiet. What's wrong?" asked Angus, and she came to with a start to find they had reached Queensferry Street, with traffic pouring endlessly along it.

"Nothing. I was only thinking," she said. "Why are we standing here? We don't have to cross."

"Aren't you sick of the Dean Bridge?" he said. "I am. It's no longer by Moray Place."

"No, of course, it isn't, and I love Moray Place," agreed Rowan. "Let's go that way. The last bit's rather horrid and slummy, that's the only drawback."

"I like the contrast between the stately classical calm of Moray Place and the draggle-tailed uproar of Havana Lane," said Angus. "It makes me think of myself—my environment, pure Moray Place, and for all I know my heredity Havana Lane, or something very like it."

"You'd be much happier if you didn't think so much about yourself," Rowan told him.

"It's all very well for you to talk. You don't have to think about yourself because you know who you are."

"Well, you may be someone far grander than the Todds, for all you know," said Rowan, rather impatiently.

"That's so likely, isn't it?" he said bitterly.

Rowan's honesty forced her to admit that it wasn't very likely.

"But can't you see it's you *yourself* who matters?" she argued. "Nobody bothers about the rest!"

"You're talking like a child." he said, angrily. "Of course it matters! Do you imagine anyone would like me to marry their daughter, in the circumstances?"

"Oh. Well—you're too young to think about that yet," Rowan said, a little troubled. Then she put her hand through his arm and gave it a little friendly shake.

"Stop moaning and enjoy Moray Place," she coaxed.

The street lamps were beginning to flower delicately

through the gathering dusk, and from the tall dark trees of the shadowy garden in the centre owls were hooting, but still above the roofs of the high houses the sky shimmered with the afterglow of sunset in the west, paling overhead to a chill clear green.

The two, still linked together, stood for a moment on the empty pavement, looking at the sweep of the grey stone houses rising like cliffs on either side, listening to the owls calling boldly to one another against a distant hum of traffic.

The change from this dim quiet to the roar of Havana Lane was almost shocking. Half-way down the steep hill the Three Feathers was disgorging its last reluctant patrons into the street. Unwilling to leave the stuffy, tawdry brightness of the bar, they hung about, talking loudly, adding their share to the noise of crying children, barking dogs and scolding women, and the banging and clanging of the trams shuttling past along the main street below. The air was thick with the smell of chips and vinegar, the ground littered with the newspaper in which it had been wrapped.

"It's a contrast, all right," said Rowan, as they picked their way among the noisy throng.

"I like it," he answered defiantly. "There's life down here—"

"There's life in Moray Place, too, only a quieter kind. Be fair."

He laughed, unwillingly, but Rowan was glad to hear him, for he laughed too seldom, she thought.

"All right. You have your kind, and I'll have mine," he said.

"If you mean Havana Lane by 'your kind' of life, it seems to me you don't know any more about it than I do," retorted Rowan. "What about some chips and vinegar? The place is still open—"

"God, no! I hate the filthy stuff!"

"There you are. I bet I'd fit into the life here better than you!" said Rowan.

Her shining hair and brilliant eyes, her springing walk, had attracted the attention of some men, and as they passed, one shouted after her:

"Hey, hen! Whit aboot a date wi' me?"

"You'll have to ask my boy-friend!" Rowan shouted back, and was hurried on by Angus, who was horrified.

"Good Lord, Rowan! What a thing to do!" he expostulated. "It was just to show you how Vere de Vere you are," Rowan said blandly. "And how *terre à terre* I am!"

"Little wretch!" said Angus with feeling. "I suppose you'd have loved it if I'd had to fight that chap?"

"It would have been very exciting."

"I can't help thinking," said Angus, "that the hazards of Corstorphine Hill would have been nothing compared with those of Havana Lane!"

Rowan chuckled. She was pleased with herself, because she had jolted Angus out of brooding over his woes. He was at his best now, and when he snatched her into his arms on her doorstep as she hunted for her latch-key and kissed her violently, she did not resist.

Only when he released her she said: "That was a—a savage sort of kiss, Angus."

"It's the way I feel about you," he said. "When do I see you next?"

"Well, there's dancing on Friday, of course—"

"Friday seems a devil of a long way off."

Rowan came to a quick decision, and said what she had been meaning to say for several weeks.

"Why not come in one evening and see us all?" she suggested. "Thursday would be nice. Come to supper. Half-past seven."

"All right," he said, ungraciously. Then, over his shoulder

86

as he moved away, he added: "Thanks. Good night."

"Good night, Angus," said Rowan, and turned the key and slipped into the house.

Hazel was coming out of the pantry at the back of the hall, a slice of bread and butter in her hand.

"Hullo, Rowan," she said. "Want anything to eat?"

"Yes, I do. What is there?"

"Precious little," said Hazel, with her mouth full. "The cake-tins are both empty and I can't find any biscuits, but there's a new loaf, and butter and honey."

"Perhaps Willow knows where the biscuits are—"

"I daresay—if there *are* any—but Willow's out," replied Hazel. "Micky Grant rang her up and asked her to make a fourth to go dancing somewhere—North Berwick, I think."

"Micky Grant! That's an old story," said Rowan, in surprise. "I didn't know he was in Edinburgh, even!"

Hazel shrugged. "Well, he is, and Willow went off in a state of dreamy excitement," she said drily. "We might have known he'd turn up again. Lord knows when she'll be home."

"I hope Archie wouldn't mind," said Rowan, rather uneasily. "I mean, it's not as if it had been one of Willow's others. I mean, Micky Grant—"

They looked at one another. There was no need to say any more.

"Well, it's pretty dull for Willow," Hazel said at last. "And she does love a bit of fun. She was always the one who went to parties and things, and had all the boy friends, and now she has to see us doing it."

"It's our turn, and we aren't married," Rowan pointed out. "Willow chose Archie, and she ought to make do with him."

"Archie's away so much, and now that he's on the longer run there are weeks at a time when he can't get home—"

"Do you know what Willow needs?" said Rowan, pausing as she spread honey on a lavishly buttered slice of bread. "She ought to have a baby, and a home of her own. That would keep her out of mischief!"

"Perhaps!"

"You wait and see. I'm sure I am right. Were you out this evening?" said Rowan, with a sudden change from the oracular to the frankly curious.

"Yes." Hazel turned faintly pink.

"When are we going to see this doctor of yours?" Rowan demanded.

"When we see your dancing partner!"

"Well, that will be on Thursday, if you're in. I've asked him to supper."

"Oh, Rowan! And I've asked Adam Ferrier that night, too!"

"Great minds think alike, or there's a singular lack of ideas between two intelligent young women," said Rowan. "I think it's quite a good thing. Look here, why not make a party of it? Fork supper, and ask a few more when we're about it?"

"If Willow'll play." Hazel sounded doubtful.

"Of course she will. She can ask someone too."

"That's almost certain to mean Micky Grant, Rowan."

"Oh!" For a moment Rowan wondered if her plan was a good one. Then she said: "If she's going to see Micky Grant, it's better that she should see him here, where we can keep an eye on her."

"Very well. Will you ask Willow about it in the morning? And I'll put it to Murray when we are walking up the road," said Hazel. She yawned. "Heavens, how sleepy I am! I'm off to bed. Good night, Red Rowan."

"Good night, Witch Hazel," retorted Rowan. "I'm just coming up myself."

*　　*　　*

The idea of a party did not seem such a good one in the cold light of the following morning, with breakfast rather late and a heavy-eyed yawning Willow letting the bacon burn.

"For goodness sake, keep Murray from making one of his acid comments about Willow's housekeeping!" muttered Rowan to Hazel as they met at the dining-room door, Rowan with the marmalade jar in her hand. "I want her in a decent temper!"

Hazel nodded, and they went in, to find Murray scowling at the blackened fragments of bacon on his plate.

"Have some marmalade," said Rowan, setting the jar in front of him and whisking the bacon away.

Murray took a large spoonful in silence, but it was obvious that he was thinking up some really stinging complaint about his uneatable breakfast, so Hazel decided to employ shock tactics.

She glanced at her watch, gave a realistic start of dismay, and announced: "The clock's ten minutes slow, Murray!"

After that there was no more danger. Murray bolted his toast and marmalade, swallowed his coffee, and in a very short time was out of the house, Hazel at his heels, and Rowan and Willow were left with the untidy remains of breakfast to clear away.

"Did you have a good time?" Rowan asked, as Willow continued to sit staring dreamily into her empty cup.

"Gorgeous!" answered Willow. She looked up, her eyes starry. "I'd forgotten what fun a party could be!" she said. "I had a perfectly marvellous time."

It seemed to Rowan that she would never have a more favourable opportunity, so she quickly told Willow of her idea and Hazel's, to have a few people in the next evening.

"Just one of our usual do's," she ended. "Supper and dancing, or singing, or anything we like."

"It *would* be fun," Willow said, slowly, picturing herself as hostess to Micky Grant. "But—well, I've been rather extravagant over the housekeeping, Rowan, and I was thinking I'd have to cut down from now on. I don't see how we could rise to a party."

"Oh, but we'd all pay for the party. It wouldn't come out of the housekeeping money," Rowan assured her. "If that's all—and we could get Mrs. Baird to come and wash up afterwards," she added, knowing that this would weigh a lot with Willow, who hated the aftermath of entertaining at home.

"All right, let's do it!" cried Willow, jumping up with sudden energy. "Mrs. Baird's here this morning—I went round and saw her yesterday—so we can leave everything to her and have a nice long time to make our arrangements."

August is a dull month in Edinburgh, when so many people are away, and the Lenoxes' invitation appeared like a green oasis in the middle of the desert, and was joyfully accepted by all those who were asked.

"Hazel's lot, that's Christine Rennie and Adam Ferrier and his cousin, four counting Hazel," said Willow, calculating on her fingers. "Murray, and John and Pam Drummond and that girl who's staying with them—Susan Somebody, isn't it? That makes eight. Your young man and you, Rowan, ten. And Micky and me, twelve."

"We've got enough of everything except coffee cups," said Rowan. "I don't quite know what we're going to do about them. It's a pity that Holly broke four that time she let the tray fall downstairs. Will you ever forget the yell she gave, and the awful crash?"

The two were standing in the dining-room looking at the table, on which were laid out the dishes for the party supper.

"Well, even if we're short of cups, there's lots to eat," said Willow. "I just hope it will taste as good as it looks. Hazel's done the decorating beautifully."

"Stuffed eggs, chicken patties, sausage rolls, cold ham, salad, peach cream, meringues, fruit salad—I could start in on them now," Rowan said, eyeing the feast hungrily, for the two had only snatched a sandwich and a cup of coffee at lunch, and it was now tea-time.

"Don't you *dare* to touch anything!" cried Willow, alarmed. "Or I'll lock the dining-room door! Rowan, I hope nothing will happen to the good cut-glass bowl. Perhaps we shouldn't have used it for the trifle? Suppose Mrs. Baird breaks it? I'd never be able to face Mummy!"

"Too late now," said Rowan cheerfully. "And Mrs. B. isn't a breaker, luckily. I say, Willow, about those coffee cups. I'm sure Miss Dorothea would lend us some."

She made the suggestion a little nervously, knowing how Willow rather scoffed at their affection for their next-door neighbour, but to her surprised relief Willow thought it a good idea.

"I think we might ask Miss Dorothea if she would like to come," she added, even more surprisingly. "At least for supper. She could go away whenever she liked—and I hope to Heaven we don't break her coffee cups!"

"Why should we? Are you going to ask her?"

"No. I think it should be you," said Willow. "You know her better than I do."

So Rowan, pausing only to untie her apron and throw it down in the hall, ran next door.

She was back in a few minutes, carrying a basket and bubbling over with news.

"Willow!" she called, as soon as she banged the front door behind her. "I've got them. And Miss Dorothea would love to come, and she asked if she could bring her brother-in-law, Mr. Milner, so, of course, I said yes, certainly. Anyway, we'd have been thirteen without him, so it's just as well. But Willow! He's the funny little man I told you about last week—I can't believe he was Mrs. Milner's husband!"

"He must have been," Willow said, unpacking the basket. "But I always thought Mrs. Milner was a widow—what pretty cups!" she added, putting a little pink and gold one on its saucer. "I'm afraid they must be good—yes, Dresden," she ended in a tone of despair, after looking at the mark on the bottom of a cup. "We're *bound* to damage them!"

"Don't be so gloomy, my Weeping Willow," said Rowan. "Miss Dorothea said would we like Edna to help, because it would be a kindness to have her! Edna loves a party, it seems. So I said, yes, please. She'll help with the pouring out and handing round and the washing-up afterwards, so if Miss Dorothea's Dresden china does get broken, which Heaven forbid, with any luck it will be Edna who breaks it!"

"Really, Rowan, it's a good thing you aren't as terrible as the things you say," Willow remarked.

But Rowan only laughed and said they must have some tea at once, otherwise she would not be able to leave the meringues alone.

CHAPTER 10

PARTIES, like pastry, need a light hand if they are to be successful. The Lenoxes had a real gift for entertaining, for much practice had made them all highly skilled in party preparations, from shifting furniture to arranging flowers and making good food. They did everything with much goodwill and apparently little effort, and so were able to receive their guests with unruffled pleasure, instead of looking, as too many hostesses and hosts are apt to nowadays, as if they had been working like slaves until the bell rang.

"It was indeed kind of your young neighbours to include me in their invitation," said Montagu Milner, handing Miss Balfour up the steps of Number Six with solicitous care.

Greatly to his disappointment, Rowan had told him "not evening dress"; but he had compromised by putting on a plum-coloured velvet smoking jacket, his evening trousers, a soft shirt with a pleated front and a black bow-tie. His patent leather pumps shone glossily, and altogether he presented such a dazzling picture of days gone by, as Murray afterwards described it to his sisters, "that I damn' nearly told the old boy he'd come to the wrong house!"

However, as he held the door open, Murray concealed his delighted surprise and handed them on to the reception committee consisting of Hazel and Rowan. Willow, as the eldest and the married one, was waiting in the drawing-room, where the rugs had been lifted, and tables and chairs pushed into corners to leave the floor clear for dancing.

Willow was enjoying herself hugely. Micky Grant, the first to arrive, was standing beside her, giving her the long slow looks which said things utterly at variance with his careless half-mocking remarks.

When Rowan, at the door, said: "Here are Miss Dorothea and Mr. Milner, Willow," Micky muttered, "Why can't we be left in peace for a few minutes? I haven't had a chance to talk to you yet."

Willow gave him a bewildering smile and went to meet the new arrivals. She was feeling elated, thrilled, delighted to think that she had this power to stir Micky, who had always been so wary and off-hand, even with her.

"Miss Dorothea!" she said, holding out both her hands. "I'm so glad you have come! And Mr. Milner—"

She gave Montagu a quick glance from under her long lashes, making him feel a gay dog at once and not a day over forty-five.

The front door bell rang again, and Hazel looked at Rowan in mute appeal.

"You go on down," said Rowan. "I'll come in a minute."

She had guessed that Adam Ferrier mattered far more to Hazel than Angus did to herself. Hazel must be given the chance of meeting Adam downstairs, and if it happened to be Angus who had almost pulled the bell out by the roots to judge from its impassioned jangling, well, Murray and Hazel could deal with him, until she could leave Miss Dorothea and her brother-in-law. They were so much older than anyone else who was coming this evening, and they must be made to feel welcomed and at home. With Micky Grant lowering in the background against a huge bowl of vivid mixed dahlias on a tall stand, Willow could not really be trusted to look after anyone.

Rowan, however, did not know about Willow's visit to Miss Dorothea, and the feelings of liking and respect it had engendered; and she was astonished as well as pleased to see her eldest sister devoting herself to them, though she introduced Micky and tried to draw him into the conversation without much success.

It was only for a second or two, then a babel of voices on the stairs grew louder, and all the remaining guests, together with Hazel and Murray, burst into the drawing-room. Or no, not quite all. Rowan could not see Angus among them, and she was a little annoyed.

"Tiresome creature!" thought Rowan, but comforted herself by remembering that as it was a buffet supper they need not wait for him.

Standing alone behind the upright piano, with her arms resting on its cool polished top, Rowan looked from one to another of the guests whom her brother and Hazel had asked to the house this evening.

Murray's tennis-playing friends, John Drummond and his sister Pam, she knew, and she had met their friend, Susan Rattray.

The interesting ones were Hazel's lot. Christine Rennie, who had been at Greg's and so was an old acquaintance, could be set aside. It was Hazel's Adam Ferrier, the young surgeon, whom Rowan wanted to see. Which of the two strange young men was he? One was tall, with thick fair hair, the other was slight, good-looking, and brown.

Rowan decided that the fair one was Adam Ferrier, he had a shy, abstracted air which seemed to fit what she had heard of him. And just then he raised his head and met her glance down the length of the room.

"Goodness!" thought Rowan, momentarily shaken. "What a piercing stare! It's the sort of look you'd expect from an eagle. Yes, that *must* be Hazel's surgeon. I can just see him in the theatre, scalpel in hand."

She slipped from her vantage point and joined the group at the other end of the room in time to answer a loud cry of:

"Where on earth has Rowan got to?" raised by Murray.

"Here I am," she said, quietly.

"Look, Rowan, your young man's never shown up yet," said Murray, taking her by the arm and leading her aside. "And we can't go on waiting for him."

"No, of course, we can't. I think we should just go down and have supper. Angus can join us when he does come," Rowan answered. "It's very annoying of him."

"Supper, people!" cried Willow, leading the way with Mr. Milner.

Murray followed with Miss Balfour, and they all trooped down to the dining-room.

"The coffee! I've forgotten it! Look after Adam for me!" hissed Hazel, darting past Rowan on the stairs and leaving her beside the fair young man with the piercing eyes.

"I'm Rowan Lenox, the third of us. We're called after trees," said Rowan. "Isn't it ridiculous? But, of course, you must know that already."

"I didn't. Why should I?" he answered, in an amused voice, quite at variance with his shy look.

"Oh, I thought Hazel would have been sure to tell you."

"Your sister Hazel hasn't had much time to tell me anything," he said. "I only met her about a quarter of an hour ago."

Rowan stood still, two steps above him, and looked at him. He was so tall that he was very little below her even so. "You only met Hazel a quarter of an hour ago? But—you're Adam Ferrier, aren't you?"

"No. I'm Charles Ferrier, Adam's cousin. I'd no idea whose house I was coming to this evening when Adam brought me," he said. "And it was still more of a surprise to find an old client of mine here, your next-door neighbour, Miss Balfour."

"Oh, do you know Miss Dorothea?" Rowan was delighted. "Isn't she a darling? We are all very fond of her."

"She isn't very fond of me at the moment, I'm afraid," he said, rather ruefully. "I'm her lawyer, as I said, and I—I spoke my mind to her the other day and she didn't like it."

"I can't imagine Miss Dorothea being angry. Have you done something awful?"

"If you mean, have I been embezzling her money, no, I haven't," he said, laughing, so that his whole face lighted up and the keen eyes almost disappeared. "It's a long story, and, of course, I can't tell it, being business."

"I didn't mean to be inquisitive," said Rowan, with dignity, for she thought he had not known her long enough to laugh at her. "The others are all in the dining-room. Let's go on down, shall we?"

"Please don't treat me harshly," he begged, as they went down the last few steps. "I seem to have no luck with the ladies. First Miss Balfour, and now you—"

The bell rang just then, and Rowan said, "That must be Angus at last!" but before she could go to the door, Edna, in spotless frilled apron and cap, appeared from the pantry and crossed the hall.

"Do go on in and have something to eat," Rowan said to Charles Ferrier. "I'll be with you in a minute, but this is my guest so I must wait for him."

He nodded, and went obediently towards the open door of the dining-room, slowly enough to see the young man whom Edna was ushering in, a dark, sulkily handsome young man in a kilt, with smouldering eyes and a petulant mouth.

"Hullo, Angus," said Rowan coolly, giving him her hand. "So you've got here at last. I began to think you must have forgotten the way."

"I hope you haven't waited for me?" he said.

"Dear me, no! It doesn't matter anyhow, as there are one or two other people here and we are having a cold stand-up supper. Come in, if you're ready."

"You never told me it was a party," he said accusingly, hanging back.

"Oh, Angus! Don't be so difficult!" exclaimed Rowan. "It's only a very small party, and when you do everything yourself it's the easiest way to entertain people. Do come *on*."

" 'Do everything yourself'!" he sneered. "And a maid in cap and apron answering the door!"

"Edna isn't ours," said Rowan, more patiently than she felt. "The people from next door lent her to us for the evening—"

" 'Lent her'—as if she were a slave! And you wonder why the Communist Party has followers?"

"Where you ought to be is at the foot of the Mound on a Sunday evening giving tongue," said Rowan. "Go away if you like, then. I mustn't stay here listening to you."

She turned to go into the dining-room, half-hoping that he would be offended enough to leave. In his present mood he could not be considered an asset to any party—"except, of course, the Communist Party!" Rowan thought angrily.

But after a momentary hesitation he followed her and stood gloomily apart, glaring about him.

"Mercy! Who is the Dark Stranger?" asked Christine Rennie, who was sitting with Willow and Micky Grant, Charles Ferrier not far off.

"It must be Rowan's," said Willow. "She gets to know some very odd types at that country dancing of hers. I don't mean they are *all* odd, but she manages to pick the oddest ones."

"Hamlet in Highland Dress?" murmured Micky Grant with a lazy lift of his eyebrows.

"You're jealous, Micky dear," Christine said. "He's quite fantastically handsome and romantic, I think."

"I must go and speak to him," said Willow. "Rowan shouldn't have left him alone like that."

She flitted away, and after a short silence Christine said, "What a kind heart our Willow has!"

"Little ginger puss," said Micky, looking down at her through half-closed eyes. "Your claws are sharper than ever, aren't they?"

"When I heard that you were to be here this evening, Micky dear, I sharpened them up specially."

"Clever puss! Let's go and lend a hand with the Highland Chief, shall we?"

"All right," said Christine.

It was extraordinary, Charles Ferrier thought, how so many women seemed to prefer bounders, either because they didn't recognize them as such, or because they did and still preferred them. That fellow Grant, for example. It stood out a mile that he was off-key; and another was Montagu Milner, though his was a more restrained type of bounderishness. Any man could tell at once that both Grant and old Milner were potential wrong 'uns—yet the women fell for them with a crash.

To be fair, Charles had to admit to himself that while all he wanted in Micky Grant's case was to land him a hearty kick where it would do most good, he could not help liking old Monty, scalawag though he was.

"It must have taken quite a bit of doing, coming back to the office that afternoon," he thought. "Perhaps all he wants is a home, as he says, and if he doesn't start monkeying with the money too much, it may be all right. And he's company for Miss Dorothea."

"My dear boy! This is the first opportunity I have had of getting near you. I had no idea that you would be here to-night!"

Beaming, dapper and unquenchably friendly, Mr. Milner had bobbed up at his elbow.

"I am equally surprised to see you, sir," Charles replied

politely. "As a matter of fact, my cousin brought me, and until we arrived, I didn't even know I was coming to Kirkaldy Crescent."

"It is a delightful party. Such charming young people," said Monty. "Did you ever see prettier girls than the Lenoxes? The only difficulty is to decide which is the most attractive. A problem even for Paris!"

Charles thought he would give the golden apple to Rowan, and looked across at her, where she stood holding a cup of coffee.

But something had happened to her. She had withdrawn into some secret place of her own, and it was as if a lamp had gone out or a fire died. She was just an ordinary girl with good colouring and rather irregular features, the mouth too big, the nose too short. . . . He had never seen such a change in anyone, and he wondered how the sulky boy in the kilt could go on talking to her as if he had not noticed anything—for Angus had detached himself from Willow and her followers with haste and without ceremony.

"If everyone's had enough to eat, shall we go and dance?" suggested Murray. "Or there's ping-pong in the old scullery in the basement. You pays your money and you takes your choice."

"Dance, please!" said several voices, and with the words Charles saw Rowan come to life again. The shell was occupied, the lamp alight. "Lovely!" he heard her say.

Miss Balfour heard her too, and thought that the word described Rowan herself that evening. Though slightly dazed by the babble of loud young voices and the rapid movement of all about her, Miss Balfour was enjoying the party as much as anyone.

They were all so kind and attentive, and now that she had returned to the drawing-room, a comfortable seat was found for her in a corner where she could watch without any fear of having her toes trodden on.

Since one or two unsuccessful appearances at Edinburgh balls as an awkward girl during the first decade of the century, Dorothea Balfour had not seen any dancing. She found the performance at which she was now looking on monotonous and shuffling, and the dance music sounded harsh to her ears.

"But, of course, it all depends on what one is accustomed to, and I am afraid I am very old-fashioned," she said. "They are all enjoying themselves, and my brother-in-law as much as the younger people."

Indeed, Monty was sliding round the floor most expertly, his plum velvet arm encircling Christine Rennie's waist, his pumps flashing, his face rosy with pleasure and exercise.

"I think modern dancing is more for doing than for watching," said the young man who had come to sit beside her.

It was Charles Ferrier, and he had approached with less than his usual confidence.

Miss Balfour, however, had forgiven him, not, as he would have expected, because she had come to see that he had been trying to guard her interests, but for the excellent feminine reason that he looked so young and shy with his hair a little ruffled.

They talked amicably if impersonally until he went off to dance, and his place was taken by Monty, who lowered himself into a chair with a loud gasp, and mopped his brow with a fine white silk handkerchief.

"I'm getting too old for this, Dorothea," he said. "Short of puff!"

"Nonsense. You were gambading like a boy," said his sister-in-law, knowing that he was longing to be contradicted. "How *well* you dance, Montagu!"

He gave a small deprecatory shake of his head, but he was pleased. Then he said: "I'm not up in these Scottish country dances, though."

Miss Dorothea realized that they were forming a set of two lines, and hoped privately that this would be more interesting to watch.

For all her engrossed appearance, she was not really following the dances themselves, but the movements of two dancers, Rowan and her partner. The others knew enough to do their share without mistakes, but those two, moving like waves of the sea, like flames running through dry grass, were in some way fulfilled and released by this art that they practised with such grave delight. Rowan only became more vivid, more brilliant, but her partner was transformed. Miss Dorothea could see what his attraction was for Rowan; and when, later, he danced alone for them, she understood it even better.

"But, of course, it's *only* his dancing," she thought. "Poor young man!" And she sighed for Angus Todd's sake.

"Tired, Dorothea?" asked Monty, hopefully, hearing the sigh.

This time she answered him, agreed that it was time they left, and after thanking the Lenox girls and Murray, they went quietly home to bed.

CHAPTER 11

THE TWO COUSINS, Adam and Charles Ferrier, walked home in companionable silence to the top flat in one of the windy crescents north of the Haymarket Station where they lived with Adam's mother.

Not even to each other had they ever given, as their real reason for staying on in Lyon Place, their fear that Mrs. Ferrier might die of a broken heart if left by herself. They were mistaken in this, human hearts being a great deal tougher than is generally supposed, but the motive was a good one, and Mrs. Ferrier, who had guessed it almost before they did, smiled and sighed, and said, "Bless them, the silly dears!"

She always thought of them together: the boys, or the dears, she made no difference between her son and her husband's nephew. Charles had been no more than a baby when his parents were killed in a car accident; she had come to consider him as a son, and he and Adam had been brought up together. Besides, it had been Charles' father, Will Ferrier, whom she had loved. Only after he came back from winter sports in Austria engaged to an English girl whom he had met there did she take any notice of Will's brother David. She had married David a few months after Will's own marriage, and the two boys had been born within six weeks of one another. . . . She had been very happy with David, happier, probably, than she would have been as Will's wife. It had been a quiet increasing happiness which did not die when David died, though it had been towards the end of the War, with both the boys away in the Army, and she had been alone.

Somehow David seemed to be not very far from her, just waiting for her to catch up with him, not wanting her to be miserable. So she continued to serve on the various committees to which she belonged, and she went on playing bridge.

And the boys had come back and settled down to work, Adam at medicine and then surgery, which had been his ambition since childhood, Charles to take his S.S.C. and W.S. exams. and go into the family firm of Watson and Ferrier, where he was now a partner.

The boys were dears, Mrs. Ferrier told herself, and if they seemed a little too serious and well-behaved, so that at times they were almost dull, the world they had grown up in and the War they had helped to fight were the causes.

Adam and Charles had no idea that there was anything lacking in the lighter side of their lives, and Mrs. Ferrier's delight on hearing that they were going out to a party made them laugh.

"A pity that Aunt Maud couldn't have gone with us this evening," Charles said. "She'd have loved it."

Adam was not so sure. "Don't you think she might have found it a bit—well—childish?"

"Perhaps. But she likes gaiety and there was plenty of that. I like your Lenoxes, Adam."

"Oh, they're not mine!" Adam began in a hurry. "This evening's the first time I've been to the house—"

"Don't be so infernally literal," Charles begged him. "You know quite well what I mean. What's the name of your one? Hazel? It suits her. She's a real nut-brown maid."

"I wish you wouldn't go on talking about ' my' one like that," growled Adam. "I just happen to know her because she's on the staff in Orthopaedic Out-Patients. She's a sensible sort of girl."

"I doubt if she'd thank you for describing her like that."

"Well, she *is* sensible. You can take her out without giving her the idea that you're crazy about her," said Adam.

"Not like the Rennie. *She* thinks that a visit to the pictures is bound to end in bed."

"It might—with her, though sometimes with those red-heads their hair is the most passionate thing about them."

"What do you know about red-heads?" demanded Adam, suspiciously.

"Not a great deal. My knowledge is largely theoretical," Charles said with regret. "Never mind about them. What I want to know," said Charles, "is—why don't you get cracking and do something about this girl, Hazel? However sensible you think her, she may have hankerings after romance, and some other fellow will come along ready to provide it—and you'll find you've lost her."

Adam said nothing, and Charles was beginning to curse himself for having said too much, when Adam burst out:

"Damn it! I've always meant to steer clear of marriage. It would play hell with my work—"

"Wedded to your scalpel? Well, then, that's all right. You don't need to bother," said Charles. "As long as the girl understands. But it's up to you to see that she does."

"Oh, I know you think I'm a cold-blooded fish!" said Adam, stung by his cousin's carefully expressionless tone. "But since I've got to know Hazel I don't know what to do, and that's the truth. I suppose I'm in love with her—and it's playing hell with my work. You need to be single-minded and single-hearted to be a surgeon, Charles. Or so I believe. And I don't seem to see my way out of this at all."

Genuine perplexity and distress sounded in his voice, and Charles did not know what to say. How could one give sensible advice to Adam?

Between these two was a deep-rooted undemonstrative affection of which they never thought consciously, and which they would have been horribly ashamed to show. Charles could not understand Adam's feelings about marriage

105

and his job, because he could not share them, but he could understand that the problem was a real one to Adam.

Feeling extremely inadequate to the occasion, Charles said:

"If you feel like that, there's nothing for it but to carry on and see how things work out. Only I think you ought to tell Hazel."

"It sounds so—so bloody condescending!" muttered Adam. "As if I knew she was fond of me and wanted to warn her off!"

"Well, that's more or less the case, isn't it? But you can put it on general lines and leave the personal element out," said Charles. "And now, here we are, so you'd better be ready to tell Aunt Maud about the party. I can't say you look much like a returned reveller."

"I don't feel like one," Adam retorted crossly, as they went up the long stairs to their flat.

But he pulled himself together sufficiently to reply to his mother's opening question, "Was it a good party, dears?" so calmly and cheerfully that Mrs. Ferrier knew at once that there was something the matter.

"I think I'll go to bed," Adam said, and having kissed his mother and nodded to Charles, went off.

"Did you enjoy it, Charles?" asked Mrs. Ferrier, hopefully. "Very much indeed, Aunt Maud," Charles said. He went and stood with one arm on the mantelpiece, and looked down at the great sheaf of green leaves with which Mrs. Ferrier filled the sitting-room grate in summer. "It was great fun. I liked the young Lenoxes. The son has just done his National Service and is working for his C.A., and there are three extremely attractive girls. There are four girls all told, but the youngest is away with her mother just now."

"Mrs. Lenox wasn't there?"

"No, but the eldest daughter is married. Willow. She was

doing chaperon—if one is needed nowadays. In any case, Miss Balfour—you know who I mean—lives next door, and was there too. It was all perfectly correct."

"I'm sure it was," said Mrs. Ferrier, stifling a sigh. It sounded just as dull as everything that young people did in these times, dull and decorous!

Presently, Mrs. Ferrier remarked that Willow was a most unusual name, whereupon Charles told her that the others were called Hazel and Rowan. Willow, he said, was the prettiest, but rather empty-headed. The other two were not like that. And he added, casually:

"Hazel is on the staff at the Empress. She was the one who asked Adam to go this evening, and to bring me."

"Oh, is she? Did she? And you liked her, Charles?" murmured Mrs. Ferrier. "Well, I am glad you had such a nice evening, darling."

"And you can't help thinking it sounds terribly dreary and like a Sunday School treat," Charles said teasingly.

"You are far too clever for me, dear Charles," said his aunt, serenely.

"Not I. You can run rings round me, and you know it," he said.

And before she could think of a retort, he had kissed her affectionately, told her not to sit up too late, and gone to bed.

A tune was running through his head as he undressed, and at last he found himself whistling it.

When he recognized it he frowned, remembering. It was the old air called "Whistle o'er the lave o't", to which Angus Todd, the dark, sullen youngster had danced Shean Trews. Charles recalled Willow's saying that Rowan always managed to pick the odd ones. At least, he thought, jumping into bed, Angus Todd was not a bounder like Willow's own boy-friend Grant. He couldn't see Rowan so much as looking at a fellow like that.

107

But of the two, there was no doubt that Grant was the better value at a party.

Charles fell asleep with the words of another old Scots song soothing him like a lullaby.

"Her lips are like rowans in bright simmer seen,
And mild as the starlight the glint o' her een,
Far sweeter her breath than the scent o' the briar,
And her voice is sweet music in bonnie Strathyre."

* * *

"I was a fool to go. A damned fool," Angus said to himself, trudging back alone. "I might have known I'd be out of it. All these others, they speak a different language, they didn't want me. They've all been to the same school, or the same kind of school, and I'm just an outsider. It was all right when I was dancing, even if I had to do it in my stocking feet because I'd no shoes with me. Yes, I could show them something there."

But even their praise, though freely and generously given, was not the sort of praise they would have handed to one of themselves. . . . If he could be a professional Highland dancer! He was good enough, his teachers had all wanted him to take it up seriously, but his parents—or rather the Todds, who had adopted him—were horrified at the suggestion, and so he had to grind away at the University, doing agriculture. Then there would be his National Service to do after he had got his degree, if he got it. The prospect was distinctly gloomy.

This long summer vacation was all very well for those who could enjoy it. He had looked forward to it himself, picturing the pleasure of not having to get up early and rush to classes, of spending days with Rowan, evenings dancing as her partner. It hadn't worked out like that. Things hardly ever did work out the way you wanted them. Lying in bed was not encouraged by Mr. and Mrs. Todd, even if one had nothing to get up for that mattered, and he saw very little of Rowan except at the dancing practices. Perhaps it was just as well that he was going North to work at the harvest whenever the dancing exhibitions were over. Rowan might miss him once he had gone.

But would she? Would she hell, he thought, and laughed sardonically, so that an old lady who was passing him drew aside in alarm and wondered whether she ought to report his peculiar behaviour to the next policeman she met.

Angus never saw her at all. He was already yards away from her in body and miles in mind, brooding still over the certainty that Rowan would not miss him, brooding over his unknown heredity and his undistinguished schooling, brooding over what he would feel when he had to think of Rowan marrying someone not himself. He could not bear to think of her as married. Of course, he didn't want her to be an old maid, but since even in his rosiest dreams he could not see her marrying him, there seemed no other future open to her. Unless she died young, in which case he would go mad and probably kill himself over her tomb. The unwelcome thought that this idea had been used before crossed his mind, but on the whole he felt happier as he stalked along the quiet streets. Reaching the Todds' house just before midnight, he crept up to his room, where he fell asleep comforting himself by remembering that in about nineteen hours he would be seeing Rowan again at dancing.

*   *   *

His insatiable longing to be in the limelight would have been appeased if he had been able to hear the quarrel which developed at Number Six Kirkaldy Crescent during the final tidying-up after the party.

Willow began it. A little above herself because of Micky's devoted attention and Christine's consequent jealousy, she said with a light laugh that *really* Rowan might ask someone slightly less boorish to their next party.

Until that moment Rowan's own feelings had been fairly equally divided between irritation at Angus's inability to mix with other people and pride in his beautiful dancing, but on this attack she took fire at once.

"Angus can't help being shy!" she said hotly.

"Shy?" Willow said with a provoking lift of her eyebrows. "I don't see how you can call him *shy*, my dear. After all, he was only too willing to show off with his solo dancing!"

"He wasn't showing off. Dancing is just the thing he does well," cried Rowan. "Like Murray's tennis, or John Drummond and his piano playing, or Micky Grant's flirting with every female he sees who isn't an absolute gargoyle!"

It was Willow's turn to fly into a rage, and she did it dramatically as always, stamping her foot and shrieking.

"How dare you be so beastly about Micky? I believe you're jealous because he doesn't pay any attention to you!"

"As it happens," retorted Rowan, her eyes sparkling. "He has tried his well-known charm on me more than once, but I've succeeded in making him understand that as far as I'm concerned there's nothing doing."

"I don't believe it!" cried Willow.

Rowan said nothing. She had far more self-control than Willow, and was already sorry she had lost her temper. But Angus, poor Angus, was not fair game, she had to defend him.

"For Heaven's sake, Willow, stop making that ghastly din!" said Murray, coming into the drawing-room, where this scene was taking place.

Hazel, rushing up from below, went straight to her elder sister and shook her.

"Stop it at once!" she said sharply. "Or I'll pour a jug of water over you."

"I must say," remarked Murray, lighting a cigarette, "I've never met anyone so completely uninhibited as our Willow. Did you ever hear anybody but a small child make such a row? It was like pigs being killed."

"You're all beasts to me!" Willow wailed, but on a lower note, for Hazel had looked meaningly at the largest bowl of flowers. "Why don't you go for Rowan? Why do you always pick on me?"

"Well, for one thing, Rowan seems perfectly quiet and sane," answered Murray. "But if she's been tormenting you, poor persecuted creature, we'll deal with her. Come on, Red Rowan. What have you been at?"

"I lost my temper," Rowan confessed at once. "But she was horrid about Angus."

"I'm sure he isn't the kind of person Mummy would like you to know, or to ask to the house," said Willow priggishly.

Rowan's mouth opened, but before she could make an angry reply, Murray said:

"What rot! There's nothing the matter with him that I could see, except that he *is* a bit Byronic, you know, Rowan. Hardly the life and soul of the party."

When Murray looked at her like that, with a twinkle, and spoke so reasonably, Rowan never failed to respond.

"I know," she said, nodding. "He is a gloomy creature. But he's unhappy by circumstances as well as nature. You see, he's an adopted child, and the Todds told him he was when he was quite little, so he's never felt the same as other people with proper parents."

"Oh, poor fellow!" Hazel said softly.

But Willow cried: "There! Isn't it just as I said? We don't

111

know who he is or where he comes from—"

"I don't suppose he escaped from Borstal to come here this evening," Murray said, drily. "Pipe down, Willow. Rowan can ask her friends to the house without all this from you."

"I'm the eldest. I'm *married*," began Willow.

"Then you'd better start behaving like the eldest," said Murray, losing patience. "And if you want to have the say in who's to come to the house, you'd better set up house for yourself. I don't know why you and Archie haven't done it long ago."

Willow burst into tears in earnest, and sobbed that they all hated her and wanted to get rid of her.

Hazel and Rowan exchanged glances of dismay. Murray had allowed his sharp tongue to run away with him for once, and Murray, though he was not going to acknowledge it, was a little sorry he had spoken. But he only said disgustedly: "If this is the way a party ends, for God's sake don't let's have another. Good night, girls, I'm going to bed."

"We're tired and cross. It's time we were all in bed," said Hazel. "Come along, Willow, dear, and do stop crying."

Characteristically, Willow wrenched herself from Hazel's arm and turned to Rowan, with whom she had been quarrelling violently.

"Rowan! I'm so *miserable*!" she sobbed.

Rowan nodded to Hazel. "You go on," she said. "We'll be up in a few minutes."

What means Rowan used to calm Willow the others never knew, but she had always been able to do it from the days when she had been in the nursery and Willow a temperamental schoolgirl.

At breakfast the next day Willow appeared composed and cheerful, but treating Murray with a dignified reserve which made him want to laugh.

He said so to Hazel as they walked up the Crescent to their bus stop.

"The truth is that Willow thrives on scenes," Hazel answered. "Rowan's the one who looks a rag this morning. All the same, Murray, my pet, I wish you hadn't said that to Willow about finding a house of her own."

"I rather wish I hadn't, myself," he said, with a rueful grin. "But it's true, Hazel. She and Archie *ought* to be on their own."

CHAPTER 12

MONTAGU thought Miss Balfour's scheme of asking Willow if she and her husband would like to rent the top floor of Number Four, once it had been converted, an excellent one, and told her so.

"It was really your plan in the first place, Montagu," said Miss Balfour. "But I didn't care for the thought of having strangers living in the house. It would be quite different in the case of the Harpers."

"It certainly would be a great deal more agreeable," he said. "But it was you, Dorothea, with your wonderfully practical brain, who saw at once where you might find someone to occupy the little flat."

Miss Balfour reminded him that they did not know whether Willow and her husband would want to live at Number Four.

Mr. Milner's buoyant optimism refused even to consider such a possibility. In his imagination the top floor was already a model flat and the young Harpers installed as tenants.

"The only thing is, Dorothea, we shall have to consult Ferrier," he said.

"Oh, dear, shall we?" Miss Balfour's face fell.

"Now, my dear Dorothea, don't look so downcast as soon as I mention young Ferrier," said Montagu. "It makes me feel very guilty, for I know you found him a pleasant young fellow until I appeared on the scene and he, quite rightly, had suspicions of me. We shall have to tell him about this project of making a flat because it is bound to cost something, though I hope not a great deal."

"I've thought it all out, Montagu," Miss Balfour said rather nervously. "Perhaps it won't be practicable, but I think it might."

She told him about it, diffidently at first, but with growing confidence. The little room with the sky-light would be the kitchen, with a small electric cooker and a sink, for which the water could be heated by "one of those electric immersion things". The big room to the back would be the sitting-room and dining-room combined, and they could have another electric water-heater in the bathroom so that the main hot-water supply of the house, run off a stove in the basement, would not be affected.

"Then there would be two bedrooms for them, or they could use one as a sitting-room if they liked. It has a divan bed which would do for a sofa," said Miss Balfour, her cheeks pink with excitement, her brown eyes shining. "And really, the biggest expense would be the new sink, and the piping from the bathroom to it. And the electric contrivances, including the stove, of course."

"I am lost in admiration, Dorothea," Montagu said. "You are a wonderful woman. I'm sure young Ferrier will see that the expense involved will be reasonable, and ought soon to be covered by the rent."

Once again Miss Balfour, though pleased by his praise, felt that she must remind him that so far they had not got a tenant for the flat-to-be.

"Ask young Mrs. Harper, then," was Montagu's advice. "And if she doesn't want it, we don't need to go any further in the matter. If she does, we can approach Ferrier with the news that we have a tenant ready for the flat."

This was sensible, and Miss Balfour said gratefully, "You are such a help to me, Montagu. You always know just what to do."

He looked pleased enough to purr, thought Miss Balfour, looking at him with mild affection, and with his round face and neat features he was not unlike a cat. A large contented cosy cat.

Miss Balfour was not a real cat-lover, but she had sometimes thought that a nice strokable cat would have been agreeable to have about the house. Belle, however, would not hear of it, even on the grounds that the cat would catch mice in the wine-cellar.

Of course, there was nothing to prevent Miss Balfour from having a cat now, only she no longer seemed to want one. She had Montagu instead.

Their conversation took place at breakfast, and Miss Balfour, getting up from the table to go about her household duties, was struck suddenly by the dinginess of the dining-room.

"Montagu!" she exclaimed. "We have quite forgotten papering and painting!"

Mr. Milner, who had also moved and was now standing by one of the windows looking at the *Scotsman*, started and lowered the paper.

"Eh? What's that? Oh, of course, my dear. You mean for the flat. Yes, it will have to be done."

"When or if it is done, I really will not be able to endure the rest of the house as it is. The contrast will be too shocking," said Miss Balfour in tragic accents. "Just *look* at this room! Have you ever seen anything so hideous? Except perhaps the drawing-room?"

"Not often," he admitted, smiling to soften the blow. "But I supposed that you liked the house as it is. If you don't—and I am thankful to hear you say so—there is no reason why we shouldn't have it all done up. It will cost a good deal, but we can afford it. The furniture is good and handsome, if it had a proper background."

"Could we get it done before the winter? Or at least this room and the drawing-room and the hall and stairs?" demanded Miss Balfour.

"I don't see why not."

"Then we must see Mr. Ferrier at once. Will you ring up and make an appointment, Montagu?" asked Miss Balfour.

"Certainly," he said, in his obliging way. "But you will remember, won't you, that having painters in the house will make it very uncomfortable?"

"Then we must stay in an hotel, and Edna can have her holidays. Her room could be done, too," Miss Balfour declared. "Yes, that would be best. An Edinburgh hotel, of course, so that we can come in and see how the men are getting on."

"My dear Dorothea!" said Montagu, throwing aside the paper and gazing at her in astonishment. "You are inspired this morning. I have never heard you make so many decisions before. And all at once!"

Miss Balfour laughed, a soft, youthful-sounding laugh all too seldom heard. "I know," she said. "I *have* thought that some re-decorating ought to be done, but I've always pushed the idea aside. Now— I don't know what has happened to me. I think the worm has turned at last." She gave him a quick, shy glance. "It never would have turned without your help," she added.

Then, as the grandfather clock on the stair cleared its throat and began to strike: "Ten o'clock. I must go down and see Edna about the meals at once. You *will* ring up and ask Mr. Ferrier to see us soon, won't you?" she begged.

She was gone, and Montagu Milner took a long breath.

"Well, I am—blest!" he muttered. "And she's grateful to *me*!"

He sank into the chair by the window, conscious of its comfort, and stared at the ugly room. It was comfortable, too; the whole ugly house was comfortable, and he was as fond of his comforts as the cat he resembled. He owed it all to Dorothea. The money might be his, but if she had not agreed to let him live with her, it would not have done him much good. . . .

"She shall have what she wants if I can manage it," he vowed to himself. "She is a really *good* person, the only one I've met who has been kind to me. I won't let her down."

Meanwhile Miss Balfour was in the kitchen, seated at the round table which overlooked the back-green, and on which was an aspidistra in a pot, greatly cherished by Edna. In her hand she held a slate-pencil, and she was writing, with many nerve-jarring squeaks, on a child's slate, the menu for the day's meals.

Edna stood beside her in silence during this time-honoured ritual, making no suggestions.

"Have you any ideas for a pudding, Edna?" asked Miss Balfour, hopefully.

Edna frowned in an agony of concentration, moistened her lips, and said: "No'm."

"Oh, dear! Well, what about a tart? Mr. Milner likes your pastry—and you make very good pastry."

"A jam tart,'m?" said Edna.

"Well—I did think a plum tart, or an apple one would be nice—"

"There's no plums,'m, nor apples."

"I'll get some when I go out." Miss Balfour wrote "Plum (or apple) tart" on the slate so firmly that the pencil broke, and she stood up with a sigh of relief.

"Do you never look up some of the puddings in the cookery book, Edna?" she asked.

"Oh, no'm!" said Edna, in shocked tones.

Miss Balfour gave it up, smiled and said not to over-boil the potatoes, and left Edna to her work.

It was one of those mornings which look quite pleasant from inside the house, with the sun shining in a hard, almost colourless sky. But outside there was a dry wind blowing grit into the faces of everyone who walked down Linden Terrace towards the shops.

Miss Balfour, purse in hand and basket on arm, walked along with her head lowered, trying to avoid the dust. The streets were quieter and emptier than they had been for several weeks, and she realized that the children must have started school again. How frighteningly quickly time passed as one grew older! It seemed only yesterday that the children began their holidays, and yet it was two months, the beginning of July, and now it was the beginning of September. A great deal had happened during those eight weeks: Belle dead, herself making friends with the Lenoxes, Montagu appearing. It was not given to many people on the threshold of old age to discover themselves with new friends and a place in the world for the first time, and needed by somebody, as she was by Montagu.

Full of humble gratitude, Miss Balfour raised her head, heedless of the flying grit, and looked down Linden Terrace to the dark squat shape of the church where she worshipped every Sunday. She had a great deal to be thankful for.

At this moment a piercing scream brought her to a sudden stop.

Down the steps leading from the house beside her a perambulator was hurtling, while the woman who had let it go stood with her mouth open screaming at the full pitch of her voice.

Miss Balfour had never moved so fast. She was not even conscious of moving at all, but she had sprung forward and caught the crying baby as the perambulator turned over, bounced across the pavement into the street, and was smashed to matchwood by a passing van.

A small crowd appeared as if by magic. The driver of the van, white and shaken, was calling everyone to witness that it was not his fault. Several message boys were peering at the wreck of the perambulator in ghoulish curiosity. The mother, now weeping hysterically, was being comforted by two friends in carpet-slippers and overalls, while neighbours were flocking out of their houses, full of pleasurable excitement.

Miss Balfour, with her hat over one ear, still held the baby. They both seemed completely forgotten, until an earnest young constable, pushing his way through the gaping throng with good-natured authority, spoke to her.

Excitement and shock must be making her peculiarly stupid, thought Miss Balfour, for the policeman seemed to be admonishing her in a fatherly way for being careless.

"Ye should keep a hold o' the pram," he was saying. "And not let it run away like that. The bairn might easy have been killed."

"Let her alane!" shouted a voice, and a large woman wearing a man's cap askew over a head bristling with hair-curlers, burst between two of the enthralled bystanders. "Let the wumman alane! If it hadna been for her the wee one wad be lyin', bashed to bits in the prawm!"

She squared up to the constable in a menacing manner, and the female element in the crowd at once began to agree with her.

The most unconcerned person of the whole gathering was the baby, which, ignorant of its narrow escape, lay quite contentedly in Miss Balfour's inexpert grasp, gazing up at her out of beady dark eyes like a young bird's.

"Somebody'll need to give me the facks," said the perplexed constable. "The incident will need to be reported."

He looked at Miss Balfour, and she, clutching the baby and feeling decidedly shaky, started to tell her short story, enlivened by a running commentary from her well-wishers.

"I was walking down the street, officer, when I heard a—a cry. . . ." ("Dod, ay! Ye never heard sic a yell as Maggie Dunlop let!") "And the pram ran away. It came down the

120

steps—" ("Silly bizzom, she should've kept a hold o't!") "And as it overturned I managed to catch the baby—" ("She was *that* quick! Ye'd never think a wee old body like her could ha'e done it!") "And—and that's all," finished Miss Balfour. "But I do think the baby should be given to its mother. I'm afraid she thinks it was still in the perambulator when the van—" she broke off, shuddering.

Willing hands now seized the baby, which promptly set up a wail, and handed it to its mother, and both then wept in chorus.

"Thank you, madam," said the constable. "It's a mercy you were passing."

"Ay, ye've changed yer tune now!" cried the lady of the hair-curlers.

The constable, wisely ignoring her, proceeded to take a statement from the driver of the van.

Miss Balfour, hoping that she would not faint, but aware that her legs felt very queer, set her hat straight and looked about for her basket.

"Here's yer purse, hen," said someone, thrusting it into her hand. "An' yer basket."

"Oh, thank you. Thank you so much," murmured Miss Balfour, wishing they would all go away.

"Miss Dorothea!"

"Oh, my dears!" Miss Balfour, seeing Rowan and Willow hurrying towards her, held out her hands. "I am glad to see you!"

"What's happened?" asked Willow, taking the basket, while Rowan put her arm round Miss Balfour protectingly.

A chorus of voices took up the tale, and the hair-curlers said: "She's a hee-royne! But she's got a shake, an' no wonder!"

"Perhaps if she could sit down for a minute," said Rowan. "I'll put this paper on the steps, and—"

But they would not hear of it. She must come into the house—any house—and "get her breath"; and before Miss Balfour knew what was happening, she, with Rowan and Willow, was swept into the nearest ground-floor flat and pressed into a basket-chair. She had no idea whose flat it was, the little room was full of women who all seemed equally at home; but it was her defender, the wearer of the cap and curlers, who handed her a cup of tea so strong that it looked black as treacle. Timidly sipping it, Miss Balfour became aware that it closely resembled treacle in its sweetness also.

Nauseous though it was, she drank it rather than hurt the feelings of her hostess. Such goodwill and real kindness were being shown her that she would almost have swallowed poison to please them.

"What kind souls!" she said, as they went on their way down Linden Terrace, Miss Balfour privately thankful that the girls were with her.

Willow said: "But, after all, Miss Dorothea, if it hadn't been for you, that baby would probably be dead!"

"I did so little, and at no risk to myself," said Miss Balfour.

"Well, I think it was wonderful of you," Willow said firmly. "I wish I could be sure I'd have done the same in an emergency."

"Of course you would, my dear. And now, *do* let us talk about something else," implored Miss Balfour. "I wonder if they have cooking apples or plums at the Fruit Mart this morning?"

"I'm going there for vegetables," Willow said, prompted by a look from Rowan. "Perhaps we could go together."

For an instant Miss Balfour was faintly disappointed because Willow and not Rowan was to be her companion. Then she remembered the flat, and her conversation with Montagu, which the stirring events of the past hour had driven from her mind, and thought that here was the opportunity to sound Willow on the subject.

So she agreed that it would be delightful if Willow could come with her, because her stupid knees were still rather wobbly. Rowan, saying that she would go and change the library books, ran swiftly after a tram, sprang on board and was carried away up the hill and round a bend out of sight.

Miss Balfour and young Mrs. Harper did their shopping very happily together. The Fruit Mart had both apples and plums, and Miss Balfour turned to Willow for advice about them.

"I should think plums," said Willow. "You see, there will be cooking apples all through the winter, but the plums will soon be over."

"Of course. How *sensible* of you," said Miss Balfour. And to the bored assistant: "Two pounds of plums, please."

Willow was pleased to be consulted and told she was sensible. "If only Mummy weren't so terribly competent," she thought, as she looked at cabbages, marrows, and the late French beans. "I'm sure I'd be cleverer at housekeeping. I could do it for Archie and me because I wouldn't have to wonder all the time if Mummy would approve."

She bought a large cabbage and a small marrow, and the two went out into the glare of the street again.

"Are you going to stuff the marrow?" Miss Balfour asked. "It is very good like that—you stuff it with minced cold meat flavoured with a little onion and a pinch of herbs, and then bake it and serve a good brown sauce with it."

Willow had not really thought what she would do with the marrow. It was cheap and she required a vegetable, so she had bought it. This suggestion of Miss Balfour's offered a welcome change from the everlasting shepherd's pie to which the ragged remains of the joint were doomed week after week.

"That sounds good," she said. "I'll try it for lunch tomorrow. Thank you, Miss Dorothea."

Miss Balfour smiled and said she supposed that Willow was becoming a very good cook.

"Oh, we can all cook, even Holly," said Willow. "It's the housework and the—the organizing, that I'm so bad at. I expect it's partly because I try to do things just as Mummy does them."

"We are thinking of turning our top floor into a flat," said Miss Balfour, carelessly. "Of course, whoever took it would have to use the front door and stairs, so I am not at all anxious to have strangers as tenants. But my brother-in-law is quite right when he says the house is far too big for us. Are you going into the baker's?"

"No. He's sending—Miss Dorothea!" cried Willow. "Do you really mean that about the flat? Could Archie and I have it? I'd have to ask him, but I know he'll say yes. He comes home for a few days the week after next."

"Ask your husband by all means, my dear. I should be delighted if the top floor would be of use to you."

Miss Balfour went on to speak of the alterations she and Mr. Milner proposed to make, of the number of rooms and the furniture available, but it is doubtful if Willow heard anything of these details.

Murray's hasty words had stayed in her mind as irritatingly and painfully as a rose-thorn in a finger, but against the advantages of being independent in a flat of her own she weighed the fear of loneliness and boredom during Archie's absence at sea. If she were at Number Four, the family would be next door and she would have Miss Dorothea and Mr. Milner and Edna actually in the house. It would be wonderful!

Miss Balfour, who had a pretty good idea of what was in Willow's mind, left her to her thoughts, made her own

124

purchases and gave various orders to the butcher and fish-monger. Then, conscious of feeling tired, and of a sudden wish to sit down quietly in her drawing-room, she turned homewards.

Willow, still in a trance, went with her. As the two turned into Kirkaldy Crescent, going rather slowly now, for Miss Balfour found her basket unexpectedly heavy, Willow woke up.

She looked at Miss Balfour with a radiant smile, and said in her pretty, exaggerated way: "You've saved my life, Miss Dorothea, really you have! I'll write to Archie by air-mail and catch him at one of the ports on his way home, so that he'll have the news about the flat before he gets here. I'm *certain* that he'll want us to have it, when he sees how much it means to me. It's terribly sweet of you!"

"It is Mr. Milner, too, you know," said Miss Balfour, gently. "But it was you who thought about us!" cried Willow. "I feel so happy! This has been a wonderful morning!"

And though Miss Balfour, creeping wearily up the steps of Number Four, did not entirely agree—she could have dispensed with that business of the baby and the perambulator—she had to admit that it had not been ill-spent.

CHAPTER 13

"IF YOU PLEASE,'M," said Edna, hovering in the drawing-room doorway. "The young man that was here the other evening when you and Mr. Milner was out's come again and says can he see you a minute."

"Was that the fellow who called that night we went to see Rowan at her dancing show?" asked Mr. Milner, who was playing patience at a small table under the standard lamp and near enough to the wood fire for comfort.

"Yes, it must be. I can't imagine who he is or what he wants."

"The easiest way to find out is to go and see him," said Monty, carefully laying a red six on a black seven.

Then he glanced up at her as she moved slowly to the door. "Would you like me to come with you?" he asked.

"Oh, Montagu, I *should*! It would give me much more confidence if you were there, too," said Miss Balfour.

For answer Monty put down the pack, went over to the door, and held it open.

"Come along then, and we'll get it over," he said cheerfully. The young man standing in the hall staring respectfully at an old engraving was tall and thin, dressed in the tweed jacket and grey flannel trousers which are almost a uniform for men nowadays. As he turned, he revealed a distressingly loud shirt of multi-coloured checks, and a red tie.

"Good evening," said Miss Balfour.

"Pleased to meet you," responded the young man, seizing her hand and shaking it with a violence due as much to embarrassment as heartiness. "Dunlop's ma name. Jems Dunlop."

"How do you do?" said Miss Balfour.

It was quite plain that she was none the wiser, and Mr. Milner now came forward.

"Suppose we go and sit down?" he suggested. "And then Mr. Dunlop can tell us why he came."

He led the way to the dining-room, saw them comfortably seated, and said:

"Now let us hear why you have come to see Miss Balfour." The young man called James Dunlop took a pull at his beer, and replied, speaking to Mr. Milner:

"I wanted to thank her. An' to say if there's any wee job I can do for her she has just to say the word. I'll be real pleased."

"That's very good of you," said Mr. Milner gravely. "Er— why do you want to thank Miss Balfour?"

Miss Balfour herself, having refused refreshment, was leaning back in her chair, quite content to leave the unravelling of the mystery to her brother-in-law.

She still had not the slightest idea who this Dunlop was, or why he felt he had to thank her. Realization broke upon her as she heard the words "Linden Terrace", "pram" and "the bairn". This must be the baby's father, and how very good of him to feel that he ought to come round and thank her. . . .

She wondered what Montagu was thinking, for she had never told him about her adventure. There had been the call on Mr. Ferrier and his tempered approval to the scheme for doing up the house and renting the top floor; and then there had been the evening spent in watching Rowan dancing in her exhibition team, never to mention the difficulty of trying to find accommodation in an Edinburgh hotel during the Festival. . . .

Montagu listened attentively and in silence until the story had been told.

"Miss Balfour was too modest to tell me this herself," he said. "So I am most grateful, personally, to you for coming here this evening."

His sister-in-law looked at him. "There was so little to tell," she said. "And we had a great many other things to discuss. Of course, the baby was important. It would have been terrible if anything had happened to the baby, and I am so glad to have been of use. But what I did was very simple, and anyone else who was passing would have done as much."

She turned to young Dunlop. "I'm afraid it was rather an expensive business, having the perambulator smashed like that."

"Och, never heed the pram!" he exclaimed, his accent broadening in his feeling. "Whit does it matter? It was the bairn! An'—an'—onyway, it was no sma' thing to us, an' I'm verra greatly obliged tae ye, an' the wife says the same, an' I'd like fine if there's onything I could dae for ye, just to show what we think o' it."

"Thank you, Mr. Dunlop," said Miss Balfour. "But I really I don't think there's anything. It is exceedingly kind of you—"

"Wait a minute, Dorothea," Montagu interposed. "What were you thinking when you said you would like to do something for Miss Balfour?" he added, to their visitor. "Was it something in the odd job line?"

"Weel—that, if it's what ye want," said Dunlop. "I'm a painter to trade, and I thought maybe there might be some bits o' painting ye'd like done in ma spare time—a Setterday afternoon, or an evenin'?"

"Oh, but that is *far* too good of you! We couldn't dream of taking up your spare time!" began Miss Balfour, hastily.

Again, Mr. Milner, begging her pardon for interrupting, took charge of the situation.

"We are going to re-decorate the top floor," he said. "If you and perhaps a friend in the same trade would be willing to do the papering and painting in your free time—at the usual rate of pay, of course—we should be most grateful."

"I'll just take you up and let you have a look round. Then you can see whether it would be too much for you to tackle," said Montagu, and they went away, talking eagerly.

"Dear me!" said Miss Balfour, mildly, a trifle put out by this cavalier treatment. Then she smiled, and at last laughed. They had been exactly like small boys rushing off to look at some new treasure.

When Mr. Milner, some time later, came back to the drawing-room, having seen James Dunlop off, he found Miss Balfour quietly reading her book again.

"Please forgive me, Dorothea," he said, sounding much too pleased with himself to feel in need of forgiveness. But I could see the young man really *wanted* to do something for you, and it seemed such a good opportunity of getting the top floor done. You know we can't get rooms in an Edinburgh hotel for at least a fortnight, but we don't have to turn out while Dunlop and his pal are painting upstairs of an evening. The only trouble was to get him to agree to being paid, but we have settled that. Now all we need is to hurry the plumbers and then he can start."

"I hope he is a good painter," said Miss Balfour, not without mild malice.

"Good God, Dorothea!" cried Montagu, bouncing half out of his chair at the mere thought. "I hope so, too! I never thought—"

Miss Balfour relented. "I expect he knows his job, Montagu," she said, soothingly. "He struck me as a capable and sensible young man. I very much doubt if the other kind would ever have made the offer."

"Good. So now all we have to do is make the plumbers get a move on."

Mr. Milner's new occupation of harrying—and hurrying—plumbers, kept him employed, and Miss Balfour, helping Edna to get the rooms on the top floor ready for painters, found herself with very little spare time, so that neither noticed how quiet Number Six had become.

They knew, of course, that Rowan had gone to join her mother and Holly at Kersland, because she had come to say good-bye to them. Murray, too, was on holiday. He had received a graciously worded invitation from Susan Rattray's mother in St. Andrews', and had decided to go there. Good tennis and golf, neither of which he could get at Kersland, were the reasons he gave for accepting; and if Susan were a greater attraction, he never mentioned it.

Willow was left alone at Number Six, except during the evenings after Hazel came home; but she was so full of the prospect of her flat that she made no complaint either of being lonely or having too much to do.

"What's Willow up to? She looks like the cat after it's eaten the canary!" said Murray, but as he was on the point of departure for St. Andrews', the question was never answered, or even thought about.

Rowan, dismissing Angus and dancing from her mind, was anticipating the joys of Kersland, and Hazel was too heavy-hearted to bother about anything except her own troubles.

Not as pretty as Willow, less vividly attractive than Rowan, Hazel suffered from a slight inferiority complex about her own looks. She had no opinion at all of her power to appeal to men.

So when Adam, notorious for his indifference to the female staff, began to notice her existence, she continued to behave with her normal impersonal friendliness. It was the remarks made by Christine Rennie and the other girls that awakened her not only to the fact of his attentions but to her own growing fondness for him.

After that Hazel was lost. With the abandon of the single-hearted she fell headlong in love, and until the day after their party had cause to hope that Adam cared for her.

But since then everything had gone wrong. Adam had hardly spoken to her, certainly had made no attempt to arrange a meeting outside the Hospital, and Hazel was in such a state of bewildered misery that she did not know how to bear it.

The only redeeming feature was that Christine was on holiday, which meant that Hazel was spared her searching looks and sharp comments. She thought herself lucky for this, but she was more fortunate in being a conscientious person, for it meant that no matter how unhappy she might be, she worked hard and well.

She had schooled herself into never glancing up when she heard his quick step across a hall or down the passage outside her office; she had succeeded in returning his hasty "Good morning" with calm politeness, and then, suddenly, he stopped beside her desk one afternoon, put down a little pile of forms for her to file, and said:

"Could you come and have tea with me on the way home?"

For a moment the whole office, the desk with its forms and cards, all whirled so madly that she had to put out a hand to steady herself by the back of a chair. The feel of its cold round bar, more than the actual support, helped her. She was able to reply quite composedly.

"It will be rather late for tea, won't it, by the time we leave?"

"Well, coffee, then, or a drink. It doesn't matter, does it?" he said, impatiently. "I'll meet you at the bus stop."

Hazel nodded, and he went away. She set to work on her files, wondering why she wasn't wild with delight. Adam had come in and said he wanted to see her. Yet she was conscious only of feeling very tired and stupid, and unaccountably heavy-hearted.

The bus was crowded, it always was at the rush-hour, and there was no opportunity for talking until they had found seats in a corner of the lounge in the Caledonian Hotel.

"Why the Caley? Aren't you being rather grand?" asked Hazel, trying to sound gay, but with a quiver in her voice.

"Why? Oh, it's handy for both of us," he said, vaguely. "What will you have? Sherry or a cocktail?"

A waiter came noiselessly up and, took Adam's order. Hazel, from her place, could see, through one of the long windows, the grey mass of rock and the Castle crowning it. She sat staring as if she had never seen this well-known, well-loved landmark before. Somehow she could not think of anything to say, and Adam seemed equally dumb.

There was nothing companionable about their silence. It hung over them like a thick dark blanket, choking thought and speech.

When their drinks came, Adam took a gulp at his—it was a double whisky, with only a splash of soda, as Hazel noticed with uneasy surprise—put down his glass, and said:

"I've been slaving these last few weeks."

"Yes. I—I thought you were pretty busy," murmured Hazel.

"You see, there's a chance that old Prentice may take me on as his assistant, and that would be a tremendous lift for me."

Hazel turned to him then, honest delight and pride in her eyes. "Oh, Adam, it would! It would be splendid! I do hope he will!"

"Old Prentice," spoken of in this familiar manner, but thought of with admiration and awe, was one of Edinburgh's foremost surgeons. To be chosen as his assistant at the Empress meant real recognition to a young surgeon.

"I think he will," Adam was saying. "It's what I've wanted and worked for ever since I went to the Empress."

"Of course," Hazel agreed.

132

"I—my whole life is in my job," he went on speaking quickly and avoiding her clear gaze. "It must be like that if one means to be a really good surgeon. There isn't room in one's life for anything else—anything else at all."

"I see," said Hazel, very quietly. "I hope you will succeed in what you want to do, Adam. I wish you the best of luck in your career, always."

She was on her feet, she was smiling at him, and then she was gone, walking away across the big lounge, leaving her sherry almost untouched on the little table.

"Hazel—!" he began, starting up.

Then he sat down again. After all, this was what he wanted, wasn't it? He ought to be pleased, indeed, he *was* pleased, that she had taken his meaning so quickly. And yet he wished it hadn't happened quite like this. He had meant to tell her that she was beginning to mean too much to him. . . . All he could think of now was the smile on her lips, and the stricken look in her eyes.

Pride carried Hazel through the big swing-doors, held open for her by a hall-porter, and took her as far as the crossing to the West end of Princes Street.

There, suddenly, it deserted her, to be replaced by stunned incredulity. That *any* man should have thought it necessary to warn her off seemed impossible. Yet Adam, *Adam*, had just done so.

Speeding across the Dean Bridge, Hazel was overcome by a fine heartening rage, which flamed in her like fire and made her pale cheeks glow. "How dared he? Oh, how *dared* he?" she said, over and over again as she hurried homewards. "How *dared* he?"

Then misery rose like a lump in her breast, almost choking her. She stood beside the scarlet pillar-box wondering how she could go on living like this for years, until she was old enough not to care any more. She did not see the beautiful curving row of tall pillared houses, or the trees lifting their dusty autumn foliage to the clear sky; she did not hear the screams of children playing in Linden Terrace and the dull roar of distant traffic. For the moment she was blind and deaf to everything except her own unhappiness.

"Oh, Adam!" she thought. "How could you? Why didn't you leave me alone? I was all right before you came—"

She went on down the Crescent and let herself in to Number Six.

A piece of paper lay on the hall table, covered with Willow's sprawling writing.

"Hope you don't mind getting your own supper, but have been asked out—theatre and so on. Don't wait up for me. Fish baking in oven. W."

"Micky Grant, I suppose," thought Hazel, crumpling the message up.

She was rather relieved not to have to be cheerful in company, but the thought of the evening alone was less agreeable.

"Well, you can't have it both ways," she told herself aloud. "And you'd better go and see what the fish is doing. It may be cooked until it's like a brick by this time."

But on investigation the fish proved to be just ready.

Hazel did not feel hungry, but if she didn't eat it, the fish would still be there to-morrow, and even the self-absorbed Willow would notice and ask questions. So she made a slice of toast, decided that as she was alone she would have her supper in the kitchen, and spread a cloth on the table by the window.

The meal took a very short time; far too short from the point of view of helping to fill the hours until bedtime; and washing-up for one was an affair of five minutes. Hazel went out by the back door and wandered round the garden, shoving the thought of Adam firmly back when it intruded.

She was rather startled to see how badly the borders required weeding, and realized guiltily that none of them had touched the garden since Mrs. Lenox left for Kersland, more than five weeks earlier.

With sudden decision Hazel fetched a basket, a broken knife used for digging out obstinate weeds, and the gardening gloves, and set to work. At first she did not get on very fast. Her eyes kept filling with tears, and she could only blink them away as she dug and prodded with the knife-blade. But she stuck to the job, and after a while the smell of earth and grass combined with the satisfaction of seeing the cleared patch growing bigger to soothe her.

When it got too dark to do any more, she was amazed to find that it was time for bed. She tidied everything, left a thermos of hot milk on the hall table for Willow, had her bath and crept to bed, where, to her surprise, she fell asleep quite soon.

Waking the next morning with a sense of impending doom, and remembering at once what had happened, was bad. Trying to appear perfectly normal at the Hospital was worse, but somehow Hazel got through the day, and those that followed, and by night was too tired to lie awake.

Adam was duly appointed as assistant to Mr. Sidney Prentice, and disappeared from Orthopaedic Out-Patients in a cloud of glory, congratulated by everyone, and Hazel was glad to know that she would no longer have to see him at frequent intervals during the long working day.

Her own holiday would begin on Christine's return to duty, and she was now looking forward to going to Kersland as eagerly as she had formerly dreaded it, and for the same reason. It would take her away from Adam Ferrier.

She made no mention of her unhappiness to anyone, but went about in her quiet self-contained way. The only hint she gave was in a letter to Rowan, when she wrote that Adam was now working in a different part of the Hospital and she never saw him at all. Rowan would know what she meant without further explanation, and would spare her any allusion to him.

So the days dragged on. Archie came home from sea and Murray from St. Andrews', and Hazel packed a suitcase and took the train to Kersland.

CHAPTER 14

ROWAN, when she read Hazel's letter, was very sorry. Something must have happened, but if Hazel did not want any questions asked or sympathy offered, then she should not be troubled by either.

Rowan had a problem of her own just at the time. It annoyed rather than distressed her, but it took something of the gold from the warm harvest weather.

When Angus Todd had gone North to do a month's work on an Aberdeenshire farm with other agricultural students, he had said: "I suppose you won't bother to write to me?" in his resentful fashion.

"Of course I'll write if you write to me. I always answer letters," Rowan had said.

A picture postcard giving his address had come, and Rowan, who felt that this could not be considered a letter, sent him a postcard in return, a picture of Melrose Abbey, which she and Holly had visited by bus.

The response to this was startling. Writing savagely enough for his pen to make holes in the paper, Angus accused her of caring so little about him that she could only send him a picture postcard. In fact, she did not care for him at all, having said that all that mattered to her was his dancing; and for his part he hoped never to see her again.

Rowan read this effusion as she walked slowly along the little dusty road between high hedges nodding with purple-black elderberries.

"Goodness gracious!" she exclaimed aloud. "What an idiot Angus is! I wonder what's bitten him now?" Then she laughed. "Midges, poor dear, I expect!"

All the same, she thought, Angus really could not be allowed to get away with this sort of thing. When she wrote back, it was very coolly, and she made no comment on his hope that they would never see one another again.

"What a nuisance men are!" she said to Hazel, one morning after the latter's arrival. "I sometimes wish all the inhabitants of the globe were women."

Hazel laughed and told her to stop talking nonsense; and as Rowan's main object was to amuse Hazel, she laughed too and changed the subject.

The Lenoxes were staying, as they always did, at a big farm, Muirhouse, which faced south across a wide expanse of rolling ridges to the distant Cheviots. Mrs. Roxburgh, the farmer's bustling, capable wife, was their friend, and made them feel as free as if they were at home, but without any household cares and tasks.

This last fortnight of country days and cool, quiet nights drifted by, more quickly now that the holiday was coming to an end. The four Lenoxes spent them each in her own way.

Mrs. Lenox, who had a few old friends in the neighbourhood, went out to comfortable talk and tea, with an occasional mild game of bridge. Hazel and Rowan wandered about the fields and side-roads, or picked plums for jam if they felt energetic, or lay in the orchard grass reading Victorian romances. Holly helped with the harvest, getting browner almost hourly, and for some unknown reason larger, unless it was her bursting health which made her look as if she were liable to split every garment she possessed.

The results of the Highers were out, and Holly, though without distinction, had obtained a reasonable number of credits. She seemed to consider that this justified her going about like a tramp from morning till night and said so every time her appearance was criticized, until Mrs. Lenox lost patience.

"I can't see what passing your Highers has got to do with it," she said one evening when Holly had sat down to supper wearing a pair of grey flannel trousers so tightly stretched over her exuberant form that they looked as though she had been poured into them, and a faded yellow shirt with a large rent under one arm. "And in any case, Miss Beadnell said in her letter to me, that you could have got distinction in several subjects if you had worked a little harder."

"For a product of higher education," said Rowan, laughing, "you do look a bit uncouth, I must say, Holly."

"I don't bother about what I look like," Holly answered, unnecessarily. "I'm going to be a *nurse*, so my looks don't matter."

"Holly dear, when you talk like that you sound as if you were twelve years old," said her mother, and went on rapidly: "And it will be at least a year before you can start nursing, so I have arranged for you to go to classes this winter."

Mrs. Lenox, thankful that she no longer had this announcement hanging over her, hurried on before her youngest daughter could break into loud expostulation.

"I know this may come as rather a surprise to you, Holly, but please *think* before you begin to make a fuss about it."

Holly bent her face, on which the crimson of mortification joined with sunburn to produce an alarming purple effect, over her plate, and muttered sulkily: "Think? How can I think? All I know is it's *beastly*. I've left school. Why should I go to another one?"

"This isn't school," Mrs. Lenox said with patience. "You are going to classes in a private house, with Madame Perrot, the wife of one of the professors at the University."

"*French?*" cried Holly, in tones of scorn and loathing. "It *would* be! I hate French worse than anything—"

"French conversation," said her mother. "It will be quite different from learning irregular verbs. And Madame Perrot will take you to concerts and theatres too. She is a charming and cultured woman, and I am sure you will enjoy being with her."

Hazel said suddenly, "I think you're jolly lucky. We never had anything like this."

If one of the others had spoken, Holly would have retorted angrily without hesitation; but somehow Hazel could say these things and not give offence, perhaps because she attached no hidden meaning to them.

Mrs. Lenox snatched at this life-line, with a grateful look at its thrower.

"I couldn't manage it for you older ones," she said, with real regret. "Holly just happens to be lucky because she is the youngest."

"*Lucky!*" growled Holly, twisting her round face horribly in an attempt to sneer. But the first fury at the proposal had left her, and her mother and sisters recognized this as a conventional expression of disapproval, and prudently began to talk of other matters.

Holly cut a generous slice of fruit-cake, and with it in her hand, mumbled a perfunctory " 'Scuse me, please," and crashed out of the room.

A moment later they saw her pass the window, cramming cake into her mouth as she went, and slouching along in faithful imitation of the ploughman's stride.

"Off to the stackyard again, I suppose," Mrs. Lenox said, despairingly. "If Madame Perrot could see her now she would never have accepted her as a pupil!"

"Oh, Holly's all right, Mummy," said Rowan, with the easy confidence of youth. "She's at the awkward age. She'll tone down."

"It is to be hoped so," replied Mrs. Lenox.

Loud and long were Holly's lamentations when the day of their return to Edinburgh came. She wanted to stay on at Kersland and work on the land; she hated town and didn't want to go to Madame Perrot's stuffy classes; she liked Muirhouse, where at least she had a room of her own.

"Rowan's quite decent, but I don't like having to share a bedroom with her," she announced, as Mrs. Lenox was packing.

"I don't suppose Rowan likes sharing a room either, though she is very good about it," said Mrs. Lenox. "—No, Holly, I am *not* going to take those dreadful trousers home. I shall give them to Mrs. Roxburgh for the first tramp who comes to the door—and it is worse for Rowan, not only because she is older, but because you are so terribly untidy."

"I'd keep a room of my own tidy. At least, I'd try to," said Holly.

Mrs. Lenox agreed that Holly had some grounds for grievance in this respect and was too honest not to admit it.

"I know it is very awkward," she said. "And I am truly sorry about it, Holly. I mean to try to do something, if you will just have a little patience."

She spoke as she would have spoken to Rowan or Hazel, and Holly, feeling agreeably mature, said, "All right. I didn't mean to *bother* you."

But it was high time that she did do something definite about the crowded condition of Number Six, Mrs. Lenox thought. She must harden her heart and tell Willow and Archie to look for somewhere to live, and with this resolution as her companion she walked into the hall of her house and greeted her married daughter.

Everyone knows what a shock it is to think that there is one more step than really exists on the stair, and having the floor come up with jarring suddenness underfoot. Even worse is to lift some object which one expects to be heavy, and which rises and hits one in the face because of its lightness. Mrs. Lenox felt as if either or both of these

141

things had happened to her, when, as she kissed her, Willow said rapturously:

"Oh, Mummy! Archie and I have got a flat! Isn't it marvellous? The top floor at Miss Dorothea's!"

It was like an answer to prayer, in Mrs. Lenox's opinion, but the surprise left her without a word to say.

"You don't mind, Mummy, do you?" Willow sounded a little dashed. "We shall only be next door, after all—"

"Of course not, my dear," said her mother, heartily. "I think it's a splendid plan. How clever of you!"

"It was Miss Dorothea's idea, and partly Mr. Milner's," Willow answered. "You haven't seen Mr. Milner yet, of course."

Before Mrs. Lenox could speak, Holly, who had gone in search of something to stave off the pangs of hunger until supper, emerged from the pantry with a handful of biscuits.

"Who's Mr. Milner?" she asked.

"Miss Dorothea's brother-in-law," said Willow, rather impatiently. "I told you about him in my letters."

"You never told *me*," said Holly, with her mouth full.

"Well, never mind," Mrs. Lenox said. "Here's something much more interesting. Willow and Archie are going to live next door, on the top floor of Number Four."

"You've made a poem, Mummy, or at least a rhyme," said Holly, interested. "Live next *door*, on the top *floor*, of Number *Four*." Then she suddenly grasped the significance of Mrs. Lenox's rhyme.

"I *say*!" she exclaimed. "Then I'll be able to have a bedroom of my own!"

Willow was offended. "That's all you think about," she said, crossly. "I don't believe you're a bit sorry that I'm going away."

"What is there to be sorry about?" asked Holly, opening her eyes wide. "Married people always have houses of their own. And anyway, you're only going next door."

It was exactly what Willow had just said to her mother, but somehow it sounded quite different when Holly said it in such a matter-of-fact way.

"Please don't start quarrelling the moment you see each other," said Mrs. Lenox rather wearily. "Holly, you can spend the time until supper unpacking, and please put your things away tidily. Willow dear, come with me and tell me all about the flat and how you have been getting on, while I unpack my own cases."

What Willow had to tell pleased her mother very much. Miss Balfour had evidently proved a most kind and helpful neighbour; and this offer of the flat had come just at the right time.

"You have managed wonderfully, dear," said Mrs. Lenox, when Willow had reached the end of her account. "I think you have been extremely clever and hard-working."

"I didn't do such an awful lot of work. Hazel and Rowan helped—more than their share," said Willow, impelled to confession. "And I—I was very extravagant to start with, Mummy. Miss Dorothea helped me or I wouldn't have managed well at all."

"You didn't have to borrow money from Miss Dorothea, I hope?"

"No, Mummy."

"And you aren't owing the shops, are you?"

Willow shook her head. "No. I got out of the mess once Miss Dorothea talked things over with me."

Again Mrs. Lenox felt a wave of gratitude to her neighbour sweep over her. She had no intention of probing further into Willow's difficulties. They were over—Willow would never have said they were if this had not been the case—and the child might have said nothing about them at all if she had chosen.

"Tell me more about the flat," she said, sitting down in

143

front of her dressing-table, once more covered with her familiar tortoiseshell brushes, combs and boxes, and beginning to tidy her hair. "Will it be long before it's ready for you?"

Willow was only too pleased to embark on a detailed description of the flat—"all pale grey and pale yellow and white"—and she didn't think it would be long now, because two painters were doing the work in their spare time. "I don't know why," she ended. "They seem to want to pay Miss Dorothea back for something she did. She does do kind things, you know, Mummy."

"I know she does," said Mrs. Lenox, and meant it.

She lost no time in going next door to see Miss Balfour. When supper had been eaten and washed up, and the younger members of the family, all at home for once, had sat down to play Canasta, Mrs. Lenox took the dozen new-laid eggs and the pat of fresh butter churned that morning by Mrs. Roxburgh, and went to Number Four.

Miss Balfour welcomed her with evident pleasure, and was full of regret that "Montagu" was not in; but Mrs. Lenox, however curious she might have been to see this brother-in-law who had so suddenly and it seemed mysteriously appeared on the scene, was glad to know that she could talk to Miss Balfour undisturbed.

Miss Balfour accepted the eggs and butter very gratefully, and asked how Kersland was looking with interest, but not at all wistfully.

"As lovely as ever," said Mrs. Lenox. "I don't think there can have been much change there since you saw it."

"Ah, my dear! The place may not have changed, but the people must have. I doubt if I would know a soul there now."

"Some of the old people have died, of course," said Mrs. Lenox. "And a few—surprisingly few—of the younger ones have left. But I'm sure you would find some there who were children when you used to stay at Kersland."

And she leaned forward and said, as impulsively as any of her daughters might have spoken, and with the same eager friendliness:

"Miss Dorothea, do forgive me, but why do you always talk as if you were eighty?"

"Montagu asked me that the other day," said Miss Balfour with a smile. "And what I said to him was that I had no idea I did. After all, sixty-eight is quite a good age."

"Sixty-eight? Why, it's *nothing*! You are so well, and your mind is so clear and young, and you aren't a bit old-fashioned in your outlook! It's just—don't be angry with me! —it's just your clothes and your hair that make you look like an old lady, and that's why you talk as if you were one."

"My sister was always very severe about mutton dressed as lamb," said Miss Balfour.

"Yes, and she was right. But there is a happy medium," suggested Mrs. Lenox hopefully. "I wish you'd let me help you to choose some nice clothes, Miss Dorothea, to make the best of yourself."

Miss Balfour was silent long enough for Mrs. Lenox to fear that she had offended her, and to remember that this was not what she had come to talk about at all.

"Do you know, I think it would be great fun," said Miss Balfour suddenly. "I mean, to buy some nice clothes with you to advise me. But one thing I am absolutely *determined* about," she added, so firmly that she sounded quite fierce. "I will *not* have my hair chopped about and given a 'perm' or whatever the thing's called. I have no wish to look like an elderly Jezebel."

"I didn't know that Jezebel had a perm," said Mrs. Lenox.

"Possibly not, but you do know perfectly well what I mean," replied Miss Balfour in a stately manner. "After all,

145

I wonder if I really would care to go shopping with you when you make a mock of me like this?"

"Of course you would! We'll have a lovely time, and I'll give you lunch somewhere really good and much too expensive," Mrs. Lenox said.

The grandfather on the stairs began to strike, and Mrs. Lenox, with a glance at the little French gilt clock ticking fussily on a marble-topped table, exclaimed in horror: "Ten o'clock! And I've never even begun to say what I really came for! I must do it now, and then fly home to my neglected family. Dear Miss Dorothea, I do thank you so very, very much for your goodness to Willow. I know you helped her over the housekeeping, for she told me so, and now the flat! What would Number Six do without you? I am most truly grateful."

"There is no need, my dear," said Miss Balfour. "You and your family have brought so much gaiety and brightness to this dull house and to me, that the boot is on the other foot."

"Let us agree to be one another's benefactors, then—or should it be benefactresses—or we shall never stop arguing about it," said Mrs. Lenox. "Oh, dear! They'll be sending out a search party for me. I must go!"

She hurried home, to find them all a little indignant over her desertion of them, but easily smoothed when she told them about the prospective shopping trip with Miss Balfour.

"Well, I can quite see you and Miss Dorothea having a tremendous day," said Murray, standing with his hands in his trousers'-pockets looking down at the five feminine members of his family in lordly male superiority. "But I thought charity began at home. What about going shopping with your youngest daughter? She looks to me more in need of it than Miss D."

"I know she does," Mrs. Lenox agreed. "But this is to be an *outing*, Murray darling. Shopping for Holly is a penance. It ought to be kept for Lent."

146

"Oh, *Mummy*!" shrieked Holly.

"Well, my dear lamb," said her mother sadly. "Just think what we always endure when I have to buy clothes for you! How you wriggle and writhe when you are being tried on—"

"Well, they stick *pins* into me! Anyone would wriggle with *pins* being stuck into them! And those were *school* clothes," said Holly, with such vehemence that Murray removed himself ostentatiously out of the line of fire, remarking that as far as he knew spraying ought to be carried out only in the garden or the field.

Holly turned a contemptuous shoulder on him and continued loudly to assure her mother that she was perfectly willing to be fitted with ordinary decent clothes, promising to stand as still as a statue, and suggesting that she should make a third on Mrs. Lenox's and Miss Balfour's expedition.

"No, Holly dear. Certainly not," said Mrs. Lenox so firmly that Holly gave up, and announced in the voice of a tragedy queen that she would go to bed, and would Rowan please try not to waken her when she came in.

"*Misunderstood*, by Florence Montgomery," said Murray, whereupon Holly rather spoiled her exit by making a hideous face at him. "Never mind, old Prickles!" he called after her. "I'm not proud. I'll take you to a movie to-morrow evening, if you like."

Holly's face, wonderfully restored to good humour, reappeared round the door.

"Oh, Murray! Will you, really?" she cried. "Oh, you are an *angel*! Thank you!"

"Go to *bed*, Holly," said Mrs. Lenox, and Holly disappeared once more.

"Something will *have* to be done about that child," remarked Willow.

Mrs. Lenox murmured, "Don't be unkind, Willow," automatically; but she, too, thought that something would

147

have to be done about Holly, and wondered just how it was to be accomplished. Even Madame Perrot, she felt, might find herself hopelessly discouraged by her new pupil.

CHAPTER 15

WHEN Holly first saw Mr. Milner she wanted to giggle wildly.

By an unfortunate coincidence the film which Murray, true to his promise, had taken her to see, had included in its cast a dapper little elderly gentleman who had provided a good many of the laughs. He was so like Mr. Milner that Holly had some excuse, especially as she was still at the latter end of the giggling age.

Home upbringing and the honour of the school (a term much used by Miss Beadnell) prevailed. Holly did indeed turn absolutely purple and appeared to swell in her efforts not to laugh, and her reply to Mr. Milner's greeting was a mumbled growl, but her mirth was invisible and inaudible.

Mrs. Lenox observed her child's demeanour, and not knowing its cause or realizing that she had much to be thankful for, felt despairing.

Montagu merely supposed that Holly was shy, and as he had a kindly nature, he tried to set her at ease by talking to her without waiting for more than the minimum of reply.

After a few agonized minutes during which she was sure she would burst, Holly began to yield to Montagu's spell.

With her mother, she was having tea at Number Four, to meet Miss Balfour's brother-in-law, and also in order that the two older ladies might fix a day for their "outing" together.

It was misery to Holly to have to balance a sandwich or piece of cake in her saucer. Her hands felt far too large for the delicate china, and at the same time she seemed unable to hold it without slopping tea or letting crumbs and larger pieces fall on to the carpet by way of her lap.

Mr. Milner unobtrusively provided her with a little table, saying that he liked to be able to put his cup down, and gave her a plate as well, so that she was quite comfortable, and soon ceased to bother about the stream of crumbs which kept on dropping.

When they got up to go, her gloves slid off her knee, and he picked them up and restored them to her with a little bow, in the most grown-up manner possible.

Once again, Holly felt that she might burst, but this time with pride and gratitude. Never before had any man stooped to pick up something she had dropped. Indeed, as the youngest, she was more accustomed to being the picker-up of the family herself.

Though she was so overcome that she could only reward him with a wide grin, Holly had no inclination to giggle now. With one stride she had stepped out of the giggling stage. She would have many lapses, of course, but no longer would she feel impelled to giggle on every occasion.

The only grudge which Monty Milner's easy-going nature had allowed him to harbour against Belle had been her refusal to divorce him, and so prevent him from re-marrying and having a family. He had always cherished a longing for daughters, and he would have made a very pleasant father to his girls. He had taken a fancy to all the Lenoxes, especially the girls, and something in Holly's gawky puppy-like youth made a particular appeal to him. Now, as he held the drawing-room door open for Mrs. Lenox, he said on impulse:

"I wonder, Mrs. Lenox, if you would allow me to give Miss Holly lunch, on the day when you and my sister-in-law are shopping? It would be a great pleasure to me."

"How very kind of you, Mr. Milner," said Mrs. Lenox, rather doubtfully, glancing at her crimson-cheeked daughter, who was twisting her only good pair of gloves into a kind of suede rope in her emotion. "But do you really think you can be bothered with her?"

"Oh, *Mummy*!" muttered Holly. She knew now why girls left home.

But Mr. Milner smiled at her very kindly before turning to her mother to say: "If Miss Holly can be bothered with an old fogy like me is the question. But I hope—"

"Of course I can!" Holly broke in, finding her voice with a roar. "I mean, you're *not* an old fogy! Oh, Mummy, do please say I may!"

"Certainly you may, my dear," said Mrs. Lenox, surprised but acquiescent.

Miss Balfour, who had taken no part in this discussion, but had watched and listened with interest, now remarked placidly that she was very glad to think that Montagu would also be enjoying himself while she was.

"That was a good idea of yours, Montagu," she said, when Mrs. Lenox and Holly had gone. "But wouldn't you have preferred to take one of the older girls out instead of Holly?"

"None of them would want to come so much," he answered. "In any case, aren't Hazel and Rowan working? I like Holly, and it will be good for her to lunch out by herself."

"I daresay it will," agreed Miss Balfour, and said that they might go upstairs and look at the top floor's progress before James Dunlop and his friend arrived to put the finishing touches. They expected to complete the job that evening.

Holly could hardly wait until they were home before attacking her mother on the subject of clothes.

"Mummy, I can't possibly go out to lunch with Mr. Milner in my navy-blue suit!" she exclaimed in the hall. "It's terribly babyish and far too short and tight and—"

"We'll go and look for a suit for you to-morrow," Mrs. Lenox promised recklessly.

For the first time in her life Holly was not only patient but wonderfully reasonable as she and her mother toiled in and out of shops seeking a ready-made suit for her. She even showed enough interest to make the business, tiring though it was, much less so than usual.

Perhaps as a result of this, they returned to Kirkaldy Crescent exhausted but triumphant, and very late for tea, in a taxi, surrounded by parcels and boxes.

Murray, who was just putting his latch-key into the lock as their cab drew up, ran down the steps to help them.

"Good Lord!" he said, when he saw the boxes. "You've bought up most of Princes Street!"

The taxi-driver, handing out parcels, grinned broadly and winked at Murray.

"Thae weemen! They're a' the same when they get amang the shops!" he remarked.

Murray paid him, adding a handsome tip, and followed Mrs. Lenox and Holly into the house.

"No, it's far too late for a nice cup of tea," he said, as Willow offered to make some. "What Mummy needs— and what she's going to have—is a whisky and soda, and not too weak."

"What about me?" demanded Holly.

"I think a glass of sherry," Murray prescribed gravely. "As you are no longer a schoolgirl."

"Murray! She is only sixteen—" began Mrs. Lenox weakly.

"She's had sherry before this, even if it's only been in trifle," said Murray. "It won't do her any harm. We'll all have some. It isn't every day that Holly gets an outfit to go out to lunch with her boy-friend!"

Mrs. Lenox murmured that they really should not go putting silly ideas into Holly's head, but she was too tired to do anything but lean back and sip her whisky and soda, while the others drank sherry and asked when they were going to see the results of the shopping.

"After supper," Mrs. Lenox roused herself to say. "And not a moment before."

Accordingly, after supper, Holly paraded up and down the drawing-room under her family's critical gaze, intensely self-conscious, but not giggling, as her mother noticed with pleasure, and trying her hardest to hold herself well.

"I must say," said Murray. "I would never have believed that old Prickles could look so decent! It's miraculous!"

"That really is a very good suit," was Willow's contribution.

Hazel and Rowan were kinder to the wearer of the suit. "Holly looks quite pretty," said Rowan, and Hazel added, "She has height, which Willow and I haven't got, and her feet are so neat in those brown pumps."

"Yes, Prickles, if I'd met you in the street I wouldn't have recognized you," Murray concluded.

"I think you ought to drop that silly nickname," said Mrs. Lenox.

"See what comes of indulging your fancy and calling your daughters outlandish names," said her undutiful son. "Holly really asks for 'Prickles'! Thank Heaven, there are no trees suitable for a man's name."

Holly turned from the round mirror over the writing-table in which she was vainly trying to see her feet, and said with a slow considering look at her brother's elegant form:

" 'Spruce' would have suited you nicely."

"Well done, Holly!" cried Rowan, while Hazel and Willow laughed loudly, Murray's care for his appearance having always been a joke.

"Ungrateful chit," said Murray, who had joined in the laugh against himself with complete good humour.

"Do you really and truly think I look all right?" Holly asked anxiously.

"Not bad at all," Murray assured her.

"Yes, dear, you look very nice indeed," said Mrs. Lenox. "And now please go and take them off, and *do* hang the suit up carefully and put the other things neatly in drawers."

"Wait a minute," said Willow, suddenly. "I know what will give just the finishing touch."

She ran out of the room and was back again in a minute, carrying something in her hand.

"Mummy, you know Archie gave me a pearl string when we were married," she said. "Do you mind if I give Holly the little culture pearl necklace I got from you?"

"No, Willow dear, of course I don't mind," said her mother. "It is a very kind thought and I'm sure Holly appreciates it."

"Oh, Willow! You don't mean to *give* it to me?" said Holly, breathlessly, for Willow hated parting with her possessions. "Oh, it's *sweet* of you, truly it is!"

"There you are," said Willow, pleased and excited. "Let me fasten it for you. Now look, isn't that just what was needed?"

Holly stood facing them in the suit of soft brown tweed and the coral-red jersey of thin wool, the plain brown felt hat on her dark brown hair, the glossy brown court shoes on her nylon-covered feet, the pale hogskin gloves on her hands, and the little string of cultured pearls round her neck.

"You—you're all so—so awfully nice to me!" she blurted out, and huge tears suddenly began to roll down her flushed cheeks.

"Too much excitement, and tired out," remarked Mrs. Lenox briskly. "Now, Holly, don't cry all over your new clothes, my pet. Come and I'll help you to change. In fact, I think you'd better go straight off to bed."

She led Holly, still weeping silently into her handkerchief, away, and the four older ones stared at one another, uneasily conscious that they were not always "awfully nice" to their young sister.

"Poor Prickles! I've never seen her so overcome," exclaimed Murray, lighting a cigarette to hide the fact that he himself was not untouched by Holly's unexpected tears.

"Prickles or not, Holly has a heart as soft as—as *butter*," declared Hazel.

"The pearls *did* add the finishing touch, just as you said. She's terribly pleased with them, Willow, and I do think it was nice of you to give them to her," said Rowan.

"Oh, it wasn't anything, really," Willow protested. "After all. I've got the real ones that Archie gave me."

"All the same," as Rowan said later, when Willow was not in the room. "A little time ago Willow would never have thought of lending those pearls to Holly, far less *giving* them! Willow's got much nicer since she knew she was going to have Miss Dorothea's flat. Don't you think so?"

Murray and Hazel, to whom she was speaking, agreed.

"I expect it's because she feels happier and more settled. It's much easier to be nice when you're happy," said Hazel, stifling a sigh.

Rowan, the only one to guess that Hazel was not happy, said quickly. "That applies to a lot of us, but people like you are just the same whether you're happy or not."

"Hullo! Haloes being dished out?" Murray said with lively interest. "What about one for me? I'm sure I'm always sunny and sweet."

"You, you stony-hearted ruffian!" Rowan cried, dealing him an affectionate thump; "I don't believe anything makes you really unhappy."

"Well, I'm sure I hope not. I'd just as soon be happy," said he.

Then, as Hazel quietly left the room, he looked at Rowan, "D'you mean Hazel's unhappy?" he asked, uneasily.

Rowan nodded. "I'm afraid so. But *don't* let her see that you know it, Murray, please. She would simply hate that, and she's battling on—"

"A young man?"

"Yes," said Rowan, and now it was her turn to sigh. "First and last, your sex causes us poor females most of our troubles."

"Here, not you too, my Rowan-tree?" cried Murray, in alarm.

"Not badly like Hazel," Rowan admitted.

"What's wrong? Lord Byron cutting up rough?"

"Poor Angus! He is being terribly difficult."

"I must say if I knew my young woman was calling me 'poor Murray' in that smug pitying way I'd be difficult myself," said Murray, severely.

"You don't know anything about it," Rowan told him. "And I'm *not* Angus's young woman."

"I'm hubbled, I'm bubbled, bamboozled and bit," declared Murray. "I thought you were."

"So does Angus, that's the trouble."

"Well, do you want to tell me about it? Bring all your little problems to Auntie Heartsease, and she'll solve them for you."

"Murray, you are an idiot!" said Rowan, laughing, but thinking how much easier Angus would be to deal with if he could only fool like Murray now and then. "I don't mind telling you, but it's all so *silly*!"

"It always is," replied the oracle austerely. "Go on. Cough it up."

"Murray, I don't know where you collect all these—these out-of-date vulgarisms! Yes, well, I'm going to tell you. . . . When the dancing team was picked," began Rowan, "Angus and I were made partners, and the girl he used to dance with wasn't picked at all. I think she was jealous, for she said some rather nasty things about Angus to me, and I said that as long as he was a good dancer, nothing else about

156

him mattered much. I'd only seen him that one evening, and I didn't know him at all."

"Fair comment. The dancing *was* what mattered," said Murray. "Go on."

"After I went to Kersland Angus met this girl somewhere and she told him what I'd said."

"Good Lord, what a storm in an egg-cup! Is that all?"

"It would be nothing," Rowan said, sadly, "if it weren't that Angus has this inferiority complex or whatever it is, and I daresay she made it sound as bad as she could."

" 'Nor Hell a fury', etc. All right, go on."

"Angus wrote me an absolute stinker," said Rowan. "It made me simply furious. One of the things he said was that he hoped he'd never see me again."

"So the first thing you did when you got home was to ring him up and arrange for a meeting," said Murray. "In order to quarrel."

"No. I didn't. He did," Rowan answered simply. "I said I thought we'd be better to keep away from each other—at least for a bit. Only—you see, the dancing classes begin soon, and we've enrolled in the Mixed Advanced as partners, so it's very awkward."

"Well," said Murray. "My advice to you is—don't turn up at it."

"Murray!" Rowan was aghast. "But it would mean Angus couldn't *dance*! "

"What of it? Perhaps it would teach him not to be such a baby," said Murray, hard-heartedly. "Anyhow, that's what I'd do if I were you. Trust your Auntie Heartsease, ducky. Auntie *knows*."

"Auntie Fiddlesticks!" said Rowan, and suddenly yawned. "I'm sleepy. I must go to bed or I'll never be able to cope with my brats in the morning. Good night, Murray. Thank you for listening to my tale of woe."

"I hope you are going to take my advice," he said, quite seriously. "The fellow needs a lesson, you know, Rowan. It would do him a power of good."

"I'll consider it," said Rowan, and blew him a kiss from the door.

"Queer," thought Murray, flinging himself into a chair which groaned protestingly at this brutal treatment. "Queer how girls spend all their time bothering about men! I'm blowed if I'd like it."

"Stony-hearted," Rowan had called him in fun, earlier this evening. But he didn't think he was. It was just that he had so many other things to occupy his mind, and girls were only one among the rest. He did think about Susan Rattray, and sometimes he wondered if she thought about him. If she was like other girls, then she did.

Of course, Susan and he were just friends. They had talked it all out as they trailed round the golf course pretending to play, but more often than not walking slowly on with their clubs slung on their backs, to the scorn and disgust of those devotees of the Royal Game who happened to be following them, and who wondered audibly why people came on to the course at St. Andrews' if they did not mean to play golf.

"We are far too young to get married, or even to be engaged," Murray had said. "I'm only twenty-two and a half, and you're just nineteen; we both ought to have a good look round first before we think of settling down."

"People our age do get married, Murray," Susan had pointed out.

"More fools they!"

"I'd like it," Susan had said, dreamily. "A dear little house, and a baby, or two babies—"

"Yes, yowling all night, and strings of nappies airing in front of the fire all day. No, thanks. I'm not ready for that yet."

Then it had struck Murray that perhaps he was being selfish, and not seeing her point of view.

"Look here, Susan," he had said, dropping the bag of clubs and taking her hands in his—they had reached a deserted hollow —"if you don't want to wait, go ahead. Only it will have to be someone else, not me. I *know* I don't want to marry and settle down for a bit."

"I—I thought you were fond of me!" Susan had looked like the hurt child she was.

"I am. Very fond. I don't expect to meet anyone I'm fonder of than you. But don't you see we ought to give ourselves the chance?"

He had talked her into unwilling agreement in the end, just as an infuriated cry of "Fore!" made them snatch up the clubs and hurry on.

He had felt rather a brute, but certain that he was right.

He still felt a brute, and he was still quite certain he was right, but he had not taken into account this feminine absorbedness in men and their own hearts. Rowan's hint that Hazel was unhappy, her own worry over the ridiculous Angus, her rueful accusation: "It's your sex that causes most of our troubles," had disturbed him.

"Murray! I thought you had gone to bed," said Mrs. Lenox, coming into the quiet drawing-room, all shadows except for the little pool of light cast by the lamp on the table beside him.

"I'm just going," Murray said. "Why are you still up?"

"I'm never very early, as you know. I do *hope*," said Mrs. Lenox, twitching a chair-cover straight, "I *do* hope this affair, Holly going out to lunch with Mr. Milner, will be all right. And I really must get the summer covers off these chairs and have them laundered and put away."

Murray, accustomed to his mother's habit of making two totally irrelevant remarks in the same breath, ignored the

159

chair-covers, and replied: "Why shouldn't it be all right? Do you suspect old Milner of lecherous designs on Holly?"

"Certainly *not*," said Mrs. Lenox, with great dignity. "There are times, Murray, when I think you really have a very nasty mind."

"Oh, I don't expect it's a patch on yours, darling," Murray assured her cheerfully. "I just say things, but you think them."

"I don't do anything of the kind."

"Then why are you agitating about Holly and Papa Milner?"

"Only because I'm afraid that Holly may giggle dreadfully or knock things over," said his mother. "You know how clumsy she can be when she's excited or nervous."

"She'll be all right," Murray said. "Without your eagle eye on her she won't be nervous, and if she does spill anything, you won't be there to see. Don't worry, Mummy, your duckling has turned into a very creditable cygnet. Let her try her nice new wings."

CHAPTER 16

MRS. FERRIER was putting on her hat in a pleasurable flutter. Charles did not take her out very often (though more frequently than Adam did), and she liked to look her best for him.

To-day she was meeting him for lunch at L'Apéritif. It was a fine autumn morning, one of those days when Edinburgh is especially beautiful, and she thought she would start early and walk quietly eastwards along George Street.

Mrs. Ferrier had been no more than ordinarily good-looking as a young woman, tall and with rather a high colour. Now, the fine modelling of her bones could be seen, her colour had gone, and her slim height gave her an air of great distinction. As she walked along in her quiet well-cut coat and skirt, using a long-handled umbrella as a cane, not because she required support but because she considered, quite rightly, that it suited her to do so, she matched the wide street in elegance.

"Mr. Milner," said Holly, who had been placed by her host in the seat which commanded the whole room, while he had his back to it, "I know it isn't polite to make remarks about people, but a lady has just come in who looks like what I think a duchess ought to."

"Then she is almost certainly not a duchess," replied Mr. Milner. "I'm sorry I can't see her, but if I turn round it really would not be very polite."

"She's coming past our table," hissed Holly.

Even his short acquaintance with the youngest Miss Lenox had taught Montagu that he had better look at once, in case she made her interest too marked. So he glanced quickly up at the tall woman who was being led past by the head waiter, inwardly commending Holly's taste, and in the same instant a young man following in the wake of the "duchess" caught his eye.

"Good morning, Ferrier," said Mr. Milner, with a smile. Charles Ferrier halted, wondering who the schoolgirl could be that the old rip had got hold of.

"Good morning, sir," he said, politely.

"Allow me to introduce you. Holly, this is Mr. Ferrier. Miss Holly Lenox, Ferrier. I think you know her elder sisters and her brother."

"I'm afraid I must join my aunt. She's having lunch with me," Charles said, but he lingered.

"Perhaps you would both care to have coffee and a liqueur with us?" suggested Mr. Milner.

"If my aunt says yes, we'd like it very much, sir," said Charles, and made his way towards his own table, where Mrs. Ferrier was already sitting.

"Tell me who you were talking to, Charles," she said, with lively interest, almost before he had sat down. "I've ordered sole for myself, by the way."

"Good, if that's what you want. Fillet steak for me—sauté potatoes, and lots of 'em," said Charles to the waiter. "And spinach or something green. And a carafe of *vin rosé*."

"*Now* tell me. Who are they?" demanded Mrs. Ferrier.

Charles began to laugh. "It's old Milner. Miss Balfour's mysterious brother-in-law, the chap who turned up about six weeks after his wife died in the summer. I'd never heard of his existence before—thought he'd died years ago. And the girl is the youngest Lenox daughter. Holly, her name is."

"Dear me, how interesting. And Mrs. Lenox and Miss Balfour are having lunch here, too, on their own. I wonder if either party knows that the other is here," said Mrs. Ferrier.

"Don't suppose so," said Charles. "By the way, would you like to drink your coffee with old Montagu Milner and his protégée? He's asked us to."

"Oh, yes, do let us. I love meeting people, and I'd like to see something of your Miss Balfour now that the grim sister isn't there any longer, poor soul," said his aunt.

"Mrs. Milner was calculated to freeze anyone's blood who dared to call on her, but Miss Balfour will like to see you," Charles said.

"I liked Mrs. Lenox," murmured his aunt. "I wonder if we could ask her and some of her family to the flat one evening?"

To her surprise, Charles seemed a little dubious about this.

"I don't know," he said, hesitatingly. "Adam's so dashed unsociable, Aunt Maud."

"Well, we could have them on an evening when he's working late at the Hospital, though I think it's ridiculous for him to live like a hermit. He *ought* to meet people— young people—"

"Meaning girls?" enquired Charles.

"Why not?" said Mrs. Ferrier.

"Oh, well, Adam's a bit of a misogynist these days."

"Then he must stop being one," said his aunt with determination. "Oh! Here comes our food. How good it looks and smells! It's heaven to eat a meal without having to deal with its ingredients in the raw first."

"You must come out to lunch again with me soon," said Charles.

"Well, Charles, you know I come every time you ask me," said Mrs. Ferrier. "Yes, *all* the sauce, please," she added, to the waiter, who was helping her to sole.

When he had served Charles and was gone, Mrs. Ferrier looked at her well-filled plate with a sigh of satisfaction.

"I think one of the greatest advantages of having reached my age is that one does not mind being greedy," she observed.

"I should never have called you greedy," Charles said. "You enjoy your food, which is so much nicer for the person you are lunching with."

Lunch proceeded very pleasantly, and Charles, who found his aunt in this mood particularly good company, was not over-anxious to join Montagu Milner and his fledgeling Lenox for coffee.

His Aunt Maud, however, seemed to think she would like it, so Charles, after going across to tell Montagu, came back and escorted Mrs. Ferrier to Mr. Milner's table.

Once he had made the necessary introductions Charles relapsed into amiable silence. There was no need for him to talk, and not much chance either, he thought, with Aunt Maud and old Monty chattering nineteen to the dozen, and the child Holly joining in as well.

He was immensely amused by Holly's open disappointment when she heard that her mother and Miss Balfour had also been lunching at L'Apéritif. Aunt Maud, bless her, was soothing the child by saying negligently that two women lunching together was not at all the same as being given lunch by a man.

"I suppose you have involved yourself in all sorts of social activities with the Kirkaldy Crescent households, Aunt Maud?" he said, as they walked westwards again, he to go back to his office, Mrs. Ferrier to drop in at her bridge club for a quiet rubber before tea.

"If by that you mean have I said that I should like to call on Miss Balfour and Mrs. Lenox, Charles, you are right," answered his aunt serenely. "I can't say that it seems exactly a *whirl* to me."

"It's the thin end of the wedge."

"You know perfectly well that whoever I ask to the flat it doesn't interfere with you and Adam in the least. If you want to meet them, you can. If not, you don't need to," replied Mrs. Ferrier.

"Rather different when they happen to be my clients, Aunt Maud!"

"Well, it will do you no harm to see more people, dear. Yes, I know you are going to say you see more than enough in your office, but you ought to have some social life as well."

Charles laughed. "In fact you are engineering all this to give Adam and me a social life, aren't you?" he asked.

"Partly," his aunt admitted. "And partly because I like Miss Balfour and I think I should like to know the Lenoxes."

They had reached the corner where their ways diverged, and they stopped for a moment while Charles thanked his aunt for lunching with him, and Mrs. Ferrier thanked him for having asked her.

Then they separated, Mrs. Ferrier pleased with her plan for introducing some young life into the quiet flat in Lyon Place, Charles wondering how Adam would feel when he found that he had to meet the Lenox girls again in his own home.

*   *   *

Mrs. Ferrier did not believe in letting the grass grow under her feet, but she happened to be rather more occupied than usual with committee meetings, and it was almost a fortnight later when she went to call on Miss Balfour in Kirkaldy Crescent.

Edna, answering the door with a pleasant assurance which had grown on her under Miss Balfour's gentle rule, said that she was very sorry, but her mistress was out. "She's gone to tea at Number Six'm," she added.

"Oh, well, I was going to call on Mrs. Lenox in any case, so I shall find her there," said Mrs. Ferrier.

She rang the bell of the house next door, and this time it was not a maid in cap and apron who opened to her, but a girl dressed in a red jersey and dark green skirt, a slim young creature as vivid as her clothes.

"You must be one of Mrs. Lenox's daughters, I think," said Mrs. Ferrier, smiling at her. "I am Mrs. Ferrier. I have come to call on your mother, and I hear that Miss Balfour is with her."

"Do come in," said the girl, hospitably, and holding the door wide open. "I'm Rowan. Mother will be so pleased to see you, and Miss Dorothea, too."

Mrs. Ferrier was accustomed to feeling at ease no matter where she found herself, but she could not remember ever being so instantly at home anywhere except in her own house as she was in Mrs. Lenox's drawing-room.

Rowan and Holly went away at once, one to make fresh tea, the other to fetch an extra cup and saucer. To Mrs. Ferrier's protest that she was being a bother Mrs. Lenox merely replied that, of course, she must have tea.

"How can we enjoy our own last cups if you haven't had any?" she asked. "And a fresh pot will be an excuse for Miss Dorothea and me to have a *last* last cup. We are both what Mrs. Baird, my daily, describes as 'Tea-Jennies'."

Mrs. Ferrier wanted to hear about Murray and the girls, and their mother was quite happy to talk about her family, which she did in her usual impersonal manner, except in Murray's case. She could not help the warmer note in her voice when she mentioned him, Mrs. Ferrier noticed, and wondered if she herself sounded like that when Adam was the subject of conversation. She fancied not; she thought that she probably spoke of Charles and Adam in exactly the same tone.

What a busy, happy family they seemed, Mrs. Ferrier thought, and as she said so, wondered inwardly if they ever quarrelled.

166

As if in answer to this Mrs. Lenox said: "Oh, yes, we *are* happy. Of course, there is a good deal of wrangling at times. I suppose it can't be avoided when there are four girls in the house. But it is usually just a flare-up and then it is over until next time. And Murray has a sharp tongue, like his father, which sometimes makes for trouble." But she sounded rather proud of this than otherwise.

Mrs. Ferrier, herself the mother of one son and almost the mother of her nephew, was more interested in the girls than in Murray. If she had had a daughter it would probably have been the other way about, she supposed.

In the kitchen Holly hung about while Rowan waited for the kettle to boil, refusing to face the drawing-room alone, but very willing to babble about Mrs. Ferrier.

"Don't you think she's just like a duchess, Rowan?" she asked for the fifth time, leaning against the kitchen table so heavily that even that massive piece of furniture moved a trifle. "Don't you?"

"I've hardly ever seen any duchesses, except the royal ones, and Mrs. Ferrier isn't a bit like them," answer Rowan, adding obligingly: "But I know what you mean, and she is very good-looking and elegant."

"Elegant!" breathed Holly. "Yes, she is. She's *elegant*."

"And Mr. Ferrier, her nephew, you know the one, he's Miss Dorothea's and Mr. Milner's lawyer—"

Rowan was pouring boiling water into the tea-pot with care. "Yes, I know him, at least, he came to a party we had while you were at Kersland."

"Pigs to have it when I wasn't here," said Holly dispassionately, and returned at once to her original topic. "I think Mr. Ferrier is like Rudolf Rassendyll," she announced.

"Red hair and a beard?" murmured Rowan. "I must say I hadn't noticed—"

"Now you're just trying to be clever and awfully grown-up.

167

I didn't mean red hair, of course," cried Holly.

"All right, all right. You meant that if Charles Ferrier had red hair, etc., he would be like Rudolf Rassendyll, or if Rudolf had not had red hair he'd be like Charles Ferrier."

"Do you call him Charles?" asked Holly.

"I don't call him anything," Rowan said. "Come on, for goodness sake and don't forget the cup for your duchess! I've only met the man once, but as he has a cousin called Adam Ferrier I—well, I said Charles to—what does it matter, anyhow?" she ended, wondering why she had entered on this lengthy explanation to her young sister.

Galloping upstairs in Rowan's swift wake, the cup and saucer rattling ominously in her hand, Holly gasped: "What's the Adam one like?"

Rowan slowed her pace a little. "Better-looking than Charles Ferrier," she answered fairly. "But I don't think he's so nice."

"I don't believe he *could* be," said Holly, fervently.

"He's your duchess's son, remember," said Rowan, but as she opened the drawing-room door while speaking, Holly had no chance to reply.

They found the three ladies so engrossed in discussion that they had not noticed how long the tea had been in making its appearance.

Rowan and Holly exchanged eloquent glances, and sat down quietly, a little in the background, to listen.

"Of course, they are very comfortable and most beautifully looked after," Mrs. Ferrier was saying. "But they do miss a little *life*, poor old dears. That is why the Committee asked me if I could get up an entertainment for their amusement, something of their very own. I thought an all-Scottish programme would please them best, and I have got two good singers and a violinist, but I would like something rather less static as well. A dance or two would be good."

"Perhaps Rowan could help you with that," suggested Miss Balfour.

Mrs. Ferrier turned her long grey-blue eyes on Rowan and smiled at her.

"I wonder if you could tell me how I can get some people to dance for my old folks?" she asked.

"If a team from our class would do, I could easily ask our instructor," said Rowan.

"Rowan's class is jolly good!" Holly burst in rather too loudly. "It's the advanced—"

"Holly, dear, don't interrupt," said her mother.

Holly glowered, and wished she had not spoken, if she was going to be pulled up like this every time she opened her mouth, and in front of Mrs. Ferrier too!

But Mrs. Ferrier was looking at her now, out of those beautiful eyes, and saying gently: "I'm sure she is good, and I think, Holly, that a team from your sister's class would be just right."

Rowan then promised to ask if her class could provide a team of four couples to dance at the Old People's Home, concealing any qualms she might have at the prospect of asking Angus to take part. He would have to be asked, naturally. He was by far their best dancer; he was in the Edinburgh team; and if he would only agree to come, he might be persuaded into doing one or two solo dances as well.

"How good of you all to take such a practical interest in the old people's entertainment," said Mrs. Ferrier, as she got up to go. "I am accompanying the singers, and we are having one or two practices in my flat in Lyon Place. If you, my dear," this to Rowan, "would like to come one evening when they are there, we could arrange the programme." She turned to Mrs. Lenox. "Perhaps you could spare Holly too? I think she might like it."

"That would be delightful," said. Mrs. Lenox.

Holly, crimsoning, muttered, "Thank you."

"And I hope, Mrs. Lenox, that you will have tea with me one day soon, when Miss Balfour can come. We will have a quiet talk—"

All these invitations having been accepted, and days and hours fixed, Mrs. Ferrier said good-bye to her hostess and Miss Balfour, and was taken downstairs by Holly.

"Rowan dear, why didn't you go down with Mrs. Ferrier?" asked Mrs. Lenox, as the drawing-room door shut behind her departing visitor.

"Holly was dying to do it, Mummy," said Rowan. "It seemed a shame to spoil her simple pleasures."

In the hall Holly, holding out her hand and giving Mrs. Ferrier's gloved fingers a shake that made their owner wince, said hoarsely: "My sister Hazel can sing."

"Can she?" Mrs. Ferrier, who had her own reason for wanting to meet Hazel, rescued her mangled fingers, and smiled at Holly's eager anxious face. "I'll ring her up, then, shall I?" she said. "And ask her to come with you and Rowan."

"Oh, yes, please do! That will be lovely. Thank you, duchess," said Holly and, Mrs. Ferrier by this time being halfway down the step, banged the front door on her retreating figure with a crash that shook the house. She was happily unconscious of having addressed her idol of the moment by the honorary title which she had given her, but Mrs. Ferrier, walking up the Crescent, wondered if she had heard aright. Certainly it had sounded as if Holly had said "Thank you, duchess". Perhaps it had really been something else.

She dismissed it from her mind, and began to think out her entertainment for the Old People's Home, which she was anxious should be a real success. All the details must be very carefully planned. It was no good thinking that the old people in the home would be delighted with whatever they were given. They picked out an inferior performer and commented on the performance freely and fearlessly—and unfavourably.

Mrs. Ferrier knew that the man and woman whom she had already asked to sing were good and could suit their songs to their audience; the violinist would not be too high-brow and would certainly include a selection of reel tunes to set the ancient feet tapping. And they loved to see nice-looking young people, so they would enjoy Hazel, whatever her voice might be like, and the dancing was sure to go down well.

So brooding and planning she walked homeward, through the quiet grey streets where lights were showing in windows and lamps cast circles of pale radiance on the flags of the pavements.

CHAPTER 17

ROWAN was brooding too. She had taken Murray's advice and stayed away from the first of the Mixed Advanced dancing classes, but Angus had given no sign that he had noticed her absence. The second class was on the following evening, and she did not know whether to go or not. Now that she had promised Mrs. Ferrier to collect a dancing team she would have to attend, if only to ask the instructor about it.

In a state of disgust with the world most unlike her, Rowan went off to spend the day looking after her small charges. At least if the telephone rang while she was leading the three little Tinkers through the mazes of their infant lessons, she need not bother, for it would not ring for her. . . .

"So. Pat. And. The. Pussy. Sat. On. The. Mat," intoned the middle Tinker, Viola.

"That's wrong! Isn't it wrong?" squeaked the elder sister, Rosalind. "It's Cat, not Pussy. Silly *thing*! "

"Is a Pussy," said Viola, sticking her lower lip out and preparing to cry.

The youngest, Orlando, who only had a book by courtesy to keep him quiet—vain hope—while his sisters did their reading, roared with laughter.

"Silly Vi! Silly Vi! It's CAT!" he shouted.

"Please be quiet, Orlando, or I shall take your book away," said Rowan, calmly. "And Rosalind, don't be so dreadfully clever. Now, Viola. It *is* a Pussy, but when the book calls it a Cat, you must read Cat. If you don't, people will think you can't read at all."

This reasonable explanation produced a lull, and Viola continued laboriously to read her sentence.

The telephone, which had been ringing madly during this short passage of arms, had evidently been answered by

Mrs. Tinker, for she now put her head round the door and said: "It's for you, Rowan."

"For me?" Rowan jumped up, told the children each to draw a picture of anything they liked until she came back, and followed Mrs. Tinker into the dark untidy hall, where the telephone lived in an even darker and untidier cupboard.

She supposed it must be her mother, wanting her to do some urgent errand on her way home, and as she disapproved of her family ringing her up at work, her voice was chilly when she said: "Hullo. This is Rowan."

Then she almost dropped the receiver, for the voice at the other end was Angus Todd's.

He sounded extremely surly. "What a time you've been," was his opening remark.

"I'm at my job, which you seem to have forgotten," replied Rowan. "Do you want me for anything in particular?"

"Yes, of course I do. I wouldn't have rung if I didn't," he said crossly. "Are you coming to dancing this evening or not?"

Rowan's heart jumped up, but she steadied her voice and said as carelessly as she could: "Oh, I expect so. Why?"

"Why?" he exploded, so that the receiver crackled at Rowan's ear. "*Why?* You seem to have forgotten that you were supposed to be my partner. A fine fool you made me look last week! I'm not going to stand for—"

"I thought you hoped you would never see me again?" Rowan said very gently.

There was silence at the other end, and Rowan wondered whether he was completely taken aback, or merely too angry to speak.

At last he said quite quietly: "So you're holding that against me? I might have known. But I wrote in a rage, and—"

"I don't hold things against people," said Rowan. "And I *must* stop speaking to you. I can hear the infants raising Cain, and I'm not paid to neglect them. I'll see you this evening."

"May I come for you?"

"No, Angus. But if you'll try not to be quarrelsome you can see me home. Good-bye."

And Rowan put down the receiver and flew back to her charges, who were each loudly deriding the others' pictorial efforts.

Viola, as usual, was in tears, Rosalind looking smug, and Orlando had snatched this heaven-sent opportunity of covering the end pages of the big atlas with a spirited battle-scene in some bright red substance which Rowan recognized as lip-stick. Orlando's pudgy hands, his round, intent face and the front of his jersey were all smeared with it as well, and he was blissfully happy and absorbed.

Rowan dealt briskly with the situation, praised Viola's picture and thus stopped her copious weeping, told Rosalind that as she was the eldest her drawing ought to be better than her sister's, and turned to Orlando.

"Little man," she said. "Show me what you've been drawing, and give me your drawer."

It was useless to ask Orlando for a pencil. In his simple, practical vocabulary anything that drew was a drawer, just as a pen was a writer and a spoon or fork an eater.

Orlando was always perfectly ready to fall in with Rowan's wishes, even when he found them a trifle difficult to understand. With everyone else he was quite intractable.

He unclenched his fist now, displaying a scarlet palm, and let Rowan take the mangled remains of the lip-stick from him.

"Bloody picksher," he remarked conversationally, gazing with admiration at his work.

"Orlando's naughty," said Rosalind. "That's Mummy's lipstick, and he's been eating it too, and now he's said a Bad Word."

"I don't know why you didn't ask him not to," said Rowan. "Orlando, you will have to come and wash. Keep your hands off the table-cloth and the books just now, please. It's time for your rest, anyhow. Rosalind, you can draw a map, and leave Viola alone. And Viola, here's the history book. See if you can tell me what the pictures are about when I come back. Now, Orlando—"

"Picksher!" said Orlando, hanging back.

"Oh, of course. I haven't looked at it yet, have I?" Rowan picked up the atlas. "We'll take it with us and look at it while you're washing your hands and face."

While Orlando performed his unwilling and perfunctory ablutions, Rowan glanced at his gory picture.

Young though she was, and in sympathy with the children, especially Orlando, whom she considered worth a dozen of his sisters, the look she gave his work of art was the indulgent, half-amused look of an adult.

Then she blinked and looked again, neither amused nor indulgent but frankly bewildered. Her technical knowledge of drawing and painting was almost nil, but she could not help seeing that Orlando's "bloody picksher" was not the production of an average child at all.

None of his former scribblings with a pencil on small pieces of paper had looked like this. He had needed the softer, broader medium of his mother's lip-stick and the space afforded by the double end pages of the atlas to express himself in this extraordinary representation of a horse fighting a man. The drawing was crude and faulty, of course, but the figures were perfectly recognizable. It was as lively and full of rough movement as the prehistoric scratchings on the cave walls of Combarelles or La Moute, which it resembled.

175

Orlando, having transferred most of the lip-stick to the towel, came to stand beside her, his untidy brown head bobbing about below the open atlas, which Rowan was holding up.

"You won't tear it up, will you?" he asked, anxiously.

"Certainly not. I'd like to keep it and look at it while you are having your rest, if I may," said Rowan.

He nodded. "Awright. Was it bad of me to do it?"

"Well—you mustn't go on drawing in books, Orlando. But I'll get you a proper drawing-book, a big one, and some chalks," Rowan promised, and he allowed himself to be tucked up under his quilt without protest.

After looking in on the little girls and seeing that they were peacefully occupied, she sought out Mrs. Tinker, whom she found preparing lunch in the kitchen.

"May I speak to you for a minute, Mrs. Tinker?" she said.

"If it's about your pay, Rowan, I'm terribly sorry, but I just haven't got it!" exclaimed Mrs. Tinker, dropping a spoon with a clatter on to the unswept floor.

"No, no! It's not that at all!" cried Rowan, flushing and far more embarrassed than her employer.

Her pay was more often than not in arrears, and she knew that if her mother had any idea of the hugger-mugger household in which her daughter was employed, she would insist on Rowan's leaving the Tinkers and finding another job. But Rowan did not want to leave, because of Orlando. She would have parted from Viola with very little regret and Rosalind with none at all, but Orlando was a darling. Until he went to school she wanted to look after him.

"No," she said again. "It's just—look at this!" And she laid the atlas down on the table among a clutter of dishes and crumbs.

"Who did it?" asked Mrs. Tinker, after a pause.

"Orlando," said Rowan, with pride. "And he's only

just four."

For answer Mrs. Tinker burst into tears. "I can't *bear* it!" she cried.

Rowan could not understand. "Do you mean—the atlas and your lip-stick? I'm sorry about them, and it won't happen again. But aren't you glad that he's inherited his father's talent? At least, it looks to me as if he has."

"Glad? No, I'm not glad. How can I be? One artist in the family is more than enough!" said Mrs. Tinker, tears pouring down her thin cheeks. "I want Orlando to be a doctor or a stockbroker or a lawyer. Oh, I know you think it's frightful of me, and, of course, I am proud of Martin's work. But being proud of him doesn't pay the milk bill, or the rent—or you!"

"Well, never mind about me. I can wait," said Rowan. "And you're taking part in a radio play this evening, aren't you? That will mean ready money for milk and things. Now sit down quietly and I'll go on getting lunch. The girls are quite good and happy."

Mrs. Tinker gasped, blew her nose, and sank on to a wooden chair.

"I feel ashamed of myself," she said. "But—honestly, there are days when I don't see how we are to carry on. Martin is good, but he doesn't sell enough to pay for his paints and canvases. The real truth is that artists shouldn't marry unless they have private means. What a good girl you are, Rowan! You ought to leave us, you know. It isn't fair on you, pigging along here teaching the infants for next to nothing—and that in arrears."

"I like it, so unless you are giving me the sack, please don't say any more," Rowan begged, finding a ragged apron and tying it round her waist.

"It's Orlando, isn't it? Not Rosalind and Viola," said Mrs. Tinker, and Rowan nodded.

"Poor Orlando, I wonder what will become of him," went on Mrs. Tinker dreamily, as she watched Rowan's quick assembling of the meal's ingredients. "He isn't mine, you know. Martin's, but not mine. The girl died when he was born. I've tried to make no difference between him and the girls—indeed, I'm very fond of him, funny little boy—"

Rowan, though shaken badly by this disclosure, gave no sign. She guessed that it was doing Mrs. Tinker good to talk, so she continued her work, hardly listening, her mind full of Orlando, her opinion of Martin Tinker lower than before. If he had been worth anything as a man, she thought, he'd teach drawing in a school or something, not sit back and say he'd sooner starve. He ought to consider his family and work for them instead of shutting himself up in his studio painting pictures which never sold, while his wife tried to make a little money at the B.B.C. And the children should be at the local school, and would be if he weren't such a snob.

The stress of the day left her tired and limp, and she went to her dancing class feeling quite unequal to coping with Angus if he was in a bad mood.

The thought of the wretched Tinkers lay on her heart like a real weight pressing her down. From remarks made by Rosalind, she had gathered that the family affairs were much worse since the end of the summer term. Rowan had silenced Rosalind instantly, of course, but she could not help remembering what the horrid child had said.

The "painting holiday" so airily alluded to by Mrs. Tinker, the children's "nice long stay with my relations" assumed darker colours in the new knowledge Rowan had of the situation. Because Martin Tinker refused to remain in Edinburgh during August and September, he dragged his wife away from her B.B.C. work to the country. There they took a temporary job for her as cook or housemaid or both, while he painted when the spirit moved him and spent money they did not possess in the local pubs.

Nor were the children much better off, dumped on a reluctant aunt of Mrs. Tinker's, who had grumbled about the noise and mess they made all the time they were with her.

What on earth was going to happen to them, wondered Rowan, as the bus carried her towards her dancing class. It was obviously impossible for them to go on getting deeper and deeper into debt, until they were turned out of the squalid house they rented furnished. The disagreeable aunt, if appealed to, would do something; but not very much, and only for the girls.

Yes, the girls would be all right. It was Orlando who worried Rowan almost sick. He was a practical and sensible little boy, quite different from any of the other Tinkers, but he liked stability. If she left the wretched house, Orlando would feel lost, and worse, he would lose confidence; and Orlando was a worth-while person already. He *mattered*, Rowan thought. For his sake she must stick to the Tinkers as long as Mrs. Tinker's conscience would permit.

After that—but Rowan could not bear to think of it. She sat clutching her dancing shoes, tense and pale.

The familiar sights and sounds of the big hall, filling with chattering couples, steadied her. By the time she had hung up her coat, changed her shoes, and met Angus just inside the door, she was able to greet him with a faint smile.

"Hullo," he said. "I've got places for us in a decent set at the far end. Come on."

"Just a minute, Angus," said Rowan, suddenly remembering something. "I must speak to Miss Mackintosh. I won't be long."

He frowned a little, but nodded, and Rowan flitted across the floor in her ballet flats to where Miss Mackintosh, the instructor, stood beside the piano on its platform, discussing the evening's programme with her pianist.

"Yes, Miss Lenox?" she said, smiling. Rowan was a favourite of hers. "What is it?"

Rowan explained about Mrs. Ferrier's entertainment, and Miss Mackintosh listened with careful attention.

"Of course," she said finally. "We'll pick out a team for your friend. You and Mr. Todd will be one couple, naturally—"

Rowan, quite forgetting that she had not had a chance to sound Angus, said yes, and with the instructor's promise of choosing a team and some suitable dances, and practising them, she went off to join her set.

She had an opportunity, just before the class began, of saying to Angus that a friend of her mother's had asked her to produce some dancers for a show she was organizing.

"A charity affair?" asked Angus, without enthusiasm.

"Not exactly. It's for old people living in a Home."

"Oh, Lord! They won't know dancing from performing elephants. It's a waste of time and trouble doing it for people like that."

"Not if it gives them pleasure," said Rowan. "But you don't need to do it if you'd rather not."

There was no time for him to say any more then, and he found himself not wanting to argue with Rowan this evening. She seemed rather subdued and out of spirits, not like herself. He made a sudden resolution, tremendous to him, that he would be gentle and do as she asked—only for this evening, of course! He was not going to give up any independence of thought or action even for Rowan; but just this once he would acquiesce.

Being Angus, however, he could not make this concession gracefully, and for the remainder of the class was so gloomy and grumpy that Rowan wished heartily that she had not said he might walk home with her.

"It will act as a counter-irritant, I daresay," she told her-

180

self as she changed her shoes. "Squabbling with Angus demands the whole of one's attention!"

As they went out into the crisp exhilarating night air, Angus took her dancing shoes from her without a word, and rammed them into the pocket of his shabby waterproof. He remembered these little courtesies so seldom that Rowan was touched, and when he drew her hand through his arm yielded without protest.

In front of them the street ran downhill in a sweeping curve between the tall cliffs of houses. The overhead lights, strung up among the tramway wires, were like gold beads on a black thread. Far ahead, the few points of light from windows in the Castle shone as if in mid-air.

Forgetting the Tinkers for the moment, Rowan said softly: "How lovely Edinburgh is! There's no town in the world like Edinburgh!"

"Horrible slums, and vile suburbs," replied Angus at once.

"Yes, I know all that. But in spite of the slums and the mess they have made of the High Street, and the nasty rash of little bungalows all round," said Rowan defiantly, "you can't really spoil Edinburgh."

"The only reason I can stand the place at all," said Angus, in a strange stifled voice, "is because you're here."

"Oh, Angus!" Rowan felt touched again, but uneasy. "I may not always be here, you know——"

He seized the hand that lay in the crook of his arm and swung her round to face him, heedless of passers-by. "You—you're not going away?"

"Not that I know of," said Rowan, trying to speak lightly. "But I don't think my job is going to last much longer, and I might not get another in Edinburgh."

"I knew there was something wrong with you to-night," he said, still standing looking at her. "You are worried about your job, aren't you?"

"Yes, I am," said Rowan.

"They aren't going to sack you, are they?"

"Oh, no." Rowan could not help smiling at this. "But I know they can't afford to pay me. In fact—" she broke off.

Angus could be uncomfortably quick in guessing what was left unsaid. Now he said sharply: "You mean they don't pay you regularly? Well, then, you'd better leave at once. It's no good staying in a job like that."

"But I'm fond of them. I couldn't just leave them," Rowan began. She was going to say that she couldn't bear to desert Orlando, but she was afraid Angus would never understand her feeling for the little boy. "I'm fond of them," she finished lamely.

"Oh, of course, if you're going to be sentimental about your employers—" said Angus, and seemed to lose interest.

"What about this dancing you're arranging for the Lost Pussies' Shelter, or whatever it is?" he asked, as they walked on.

Rowan told him about it, adding that she thought Mrs. Ferrier would probably ask him to her house one evening. "I hope you'll come," she said. "Hazel and Holly and I will be there."

"All right. You let me know the day," Angus answered quite mildly, and without any of his usual sneers at her "snob friends". He seemed to have forgotten his quarrel by letter, too. Rowan had no intention of reminding him about it. To be amiable was as near to an apology as one could ever hope he would reach.

She wished he had been a little kinder over the question of the Tinkers and her job, but perhaps he was right and taking the sensible view, and she was, as he said, sentimental about them.

"Then I'll *be* sentimental about them, or at least, about Orlando," she thought, suddenly rebellious.

Her colour rose, her eyes began to sparkle. The crusading spirit was burning in her. She would do something, when the time was ripe. Aloud, she said: "Tell me about your harvesting in Aberdeenshire, Angus. What was it like?"

So Angus told her about it all the rest of the way home, and walked away feeling less out of tune with life than usual. Rowan went to bed with a little nagging thought for company. Perhaps she had not done Angus any good by allowing him to complain so much about his hard lot, perhaps she ought to have taken a different line altogether, and told him he was lucky to have been adopted, even by the Todds, and not left in his orphanage.

She had been sorry for him. She was still sorry for him, but he was very selfish and his own troubles had not made him any more understanding of other people's. And yet, he could be so attractive when he liked, and she remembered how he had carried her shoes for her this evening.

Then she remembered something else.

"Oh, dear! The silly creature has gone off with them in his pocket! How like him!"

CHAPTER 18

"YES, I'll go with you. Why not?" said Hazel, when Rowan gave her Mrs. Ferrier's message asking her to come with her sisters and bring some songs.

"Oh—thought perhaps you might have something else on, that's all," Rowan mumbled in confusion.

Hazel smiled. She never had anything else "on" nowadays, and was growing accustomed to it. Life was a succession of dull grey days with nothing to lighten them, but what of it? Thousands of people must live like that, so why not Hazel Lenox?

"You *will* be wearing your new greeny-browny dress, Hazel, won't you?" Holly asked anxiously.

"I'm going to wear my black georgette, as it happens," said Hazel.

Holly wailed. "Oh, no! Don't wear that, it doesn't suit you a bit, and besides, it's so old! Do wear your new dress, Hazel."

The new dress was a brown taffeta shot with green, and it made Hazel's eyes green too, and showed up the lights in her soft brown hair. She knew it suited her; she had bought it to wear when Adam asked her out, and it had never been needed.

"Very well. Anything for peace," said Hazel, and Holly beamed.

"You'll be glad you listened to me," she remarked smugly. Rowan, who heard all this, turned away to hide her amusement, and met Hazel's eyes in the mirror.

It was too much. They both gave way to laughter, and Holly, flouncing from the room with the dignified but obscure remark that it was a funny thing a person couldn't tell another person what dress she should wear without people behaving like laughing hyenas, only made them worse.

"Poor old Holly! It's a shush-shame!" Hazel said, hiccuping with mirth and wiping her eyes. "But I cuck-couldn't help it!"

"Holly is funny," Rowan agreed. "All the same, she is right about that dress, Hazel, and black doesn't suit you."

"All right, all right. Don't *you* start," Hazel implored her. "Or I won't come at all."

Holly had better cause than she knew to plume herself on persuading Hazel to wear the new dress. First impressions, rightly or wrongly, mean a good deal, and Mrs. Ferrier might have seen Hazel looking like a stick of blanched celery, the effect of wearing black, instead of a dryad in bronze-green.

"What an enchanting creature!" she thought, feeling more annoyed than ever with Adam for saying that he would not be at home that evening.

Charles had been quite ready to stay in and listen to music. He was making himself agreeable to Lavinia Browning, the violinist, at this moment, and from the way that rather prickly, difficult woman was smiling at him, appeared to be a success.

A personable young man was a great help on these occasions, and Mrs. Ferrier was grateful to Charles. But two personable young men would have been even better. Two pretty girls in party frocks were another asset, and Holly, though she could not yet be described as pretty, was a handsome stalwart young thing with a capacity for hero-worship, and John Marshall, the baritone, would like her.

Altogether, apart from Adam's defection, Mrs. Ferrier was pleased with her party, in spite of the preponderance of women. This reminded her of something, and she turned to Rowan.

"I thought your dancing man was coming, my dear?" she said.

185

"Yes, he is, Mrs. Ferrier, but I'm afraid he is going to be late. Angus is rather vague. I hope he doesn't get cold feet at the last minute."

"Is he likely to?" asked Mrs. Ferrier, with interest.

"It's very difficult to tell with Angus," said Rowan doubtfully.

But at that moment Mrs. Ferrier's daily woman, who was obliging for the evening in a highly unsuitable light blue dress and a small frilled apron, opened the door and ushered in a kilted figure.

"Here he is," exclaimed Rowan, much relieved, and introduced Angus to his hostess.

Mrs. Ferrier welcomed him so warmly that Charles, approaching, grinned sardonically and said to himself, "I knew she wouldn't be able to stand the fellow, poor brute."

He didn't mind much if Angus saw through this—it was more than unlikely that he would—but he would be sorry if Rowan noticed and was distressed. It was really very wicked of Aunt Maud, and he meant to tell her so when he got her to himself. In the meantime, as she was leading Angus away to introduce him to Ellen Fairweather, the plump good-natured little soprano, and as he himself considered that he had done his duty by Mrs. Browning, who was pretty heavy going, Charles said to Rowan:

"They'll be starting soon, and we aren't performers, so let me find you a good seat where you can listen comfortably."

Rowan liked Charles. Though she had only met him once before, she felt as if she knew him quite well. He was the kind of person who was dependable without being dull. But she hesitated, glancing towards Angus, for whom she felt responsible.

"Oh, he'll be all right. Aunt Maud doesn't neglect her guests," said Charles, easily.

To demur would be foolish, and she did not want to behave as though Angus were incapable of looking after himself, so Rowan smiled at Charles and took the chair he had kept for her.

It was in a little alcove with a rounded top, at the corner of the wall next to the window, and farthest from the door. From it the whole room could be seen, with the black boudoir grand along the wall opposite. An old-fashioned sofa, very long and with a high back, fenced it in.

Charles pulled a second chair forward and sat down beside her.

"What a good place you've chosen," said Rowan, approvingly. "I like this."

"Before the house was made into flats this was the main bedroom, with a dressing-room off it, reached by a door in this very alcove," Charles explained. "My aunt had the door walled up. When there isn't a party she has a little table in here with flowers on it. I've always liked this corner. You can see and hear better than anywhere else in the room, and no one can come shoving in beside you."

"It would be difficult, certainly," said Rowan.

"Very. That's why I chose it," said Charles tranquilly. And as she looked at him, a little taken aback, he added: "I hate to be disturbed when I'm listening to music. Don't you?"

"Oh! Oh, yes, I do," replied Rowan, annoyed with herself for turning pink, and sure that she could read amusement in his cool grey eyes.

"I wonder if you'd come and have lunch with me one day soon?" he asked next.

"Well, I'm at my job, you know. I have lunch there every day except Saturday and Sunday," said Rowan, regretfully. "I'm sorry."

"We could make it a Saturday," he suggested. "Tell me about your job."

Rowan, beginning with the bare statement that she taught three small children, found to her own surprise that she was telling him all about the Tinkers, and especially about Orlando, her certainty that the family was going to crash, her fears for Orlando's future.

"What a rotten show," he said, when she ended. "He sounds a nice little chap, too. I don't wonder you're worried."

"Oh!" Rowan's face, vivid with pleasure, was turned to him again. "Oh, you *do* understand!"

Before he could answer, Mrs. Ferrier, who had seated herself at the piano, began to play, and silence fell over the big softly lighted room.

Charles was not sure whether he was sorry or relieved. Sorry, because his sympathy had lighted that blaze in her eyes, but relieved as well, for honesty would have forced him to tell her that her shiftless employers would have to be left to fend for themselves, and she could not make herself responsible for the small boy with the absurd name, no matter how fond she was of him. On the whole, relief predominated. Cool and level-headed though he was, Charles did not want to see the light in Rowan's brilliant eyes quenched, nor to know that she had withdrawn her sudden step towards him.

Glancing round the room, he became aware of a hostile gaze fixed on him and their corner. It was the gloomy Angus, who had seated himself alone on a straight-backed chair alongside the door, as if to ensure his escape, and was glaring at them morosely.

Angus was as gloomy as he looked. He felt defrauded, brought here to the house of people he did not know and did not want to know. Rowan might at least have sat beside him instead of being penned in the far corner of the room, cut off from everyone and especially cut off from him, with that supercilious fair-haired brute of a lawyer close by her.

If he had had the courage, he would have gone. Nobody would have missed him, of that he was bitterly certain.

Rowan wouldn't. She didn't care a straw for him, though she was the only person he looked for or thought of. Nothing seemed to touch her except things like the plight of that crazy artist's family where she worked. She could get into a grand stew over *them*. "Fond of them," she said, but somehow Angus had been sure she was going to mention one by name. Could it have been the painter himself? Had she fallen in love with Tinker? Angus had let this thought creep into his head, and like all disagreeable thoughts it lay, apparently forgotten, in some recess of his mind, ready to appear again when its moment came. . . .

All this time the music had been going on, piano alone, then violin and piano. Angus was not paying any attention to it, but the waves of sound, flowing out into the still room, had their effect on him.

Now John Marshall was going to sing. He had a fine voice, beautifully trained, flexible and sympathetic.

" 'My faithful fond one'," he sang, the notes ringing out with exquisite tenderness:

" 'My faithful fair, wilt not come to me?
    On bed of pain here, who remain here,
With weary longing for a sight of thee!' "

'My fair and rare one. My faithful fair' . . . Angus, hearing the words, thought of Rowan. Fair and rare, yes, she was; and she would come flying if summoned to his bed of pain . . . but she would come for anyone who asked her, not only for him. He sighed impatiently, and did not notice that people turned their heads reprovingly at the slight sound.

Now the singer was asking if anyone had a favourite in the old book. He would be delighted to sing it for them.

189

Charles Ferrier said clearly: "Could we have 'Bonnie Strathyre'?"

John Marshall looked over at him and nodded, smiling, and Charles sat back to listen to the song that always brought to him the memory of warm summer afternoons in Perthshire, honey-smelling heather and heather-tasting honey, white-stemmed birches and running water, blue hills and a blue sky. Now it made him think of Rowan too. He would like to wander with Rowan through one of those golden days, through all the golden days.

The music took its toll of each of them in one way or another.

The crystal-clear soprano of Ellen Fairweather was soaring effortlessly as the lark's she sang about. It was a song that Mrs. Browning liked, though for her part she was never so deeply stirred by singing as by an orchestra or her own instrument.

Angus was not paying much attention consciously to the pure sparkling voice, or the air, though it was to haunt him later. The words were what struck him. Something about the lark finding repose in the full waving corn, and the bee on the rose though surrounded with thorn. Lovers were just like the silly larks, going over and over again to the place where they lost their happiness or their nestlings. The bee must go where honey was, thorns or no. . . . He was a muddled thinker, too intent on seeing everything from the angle of its effect on him, for clarity; but he realized suddenly that it was stupid and unjust to blame either the waving corn or the thorn-set rose, and therefore he could not blame Rowan for being Rowan. If she hurt him, she did not mean to. She had given him her friendship, frank and generous, and he was lucky to have it. Of course, he loved her. How could he help it? Could any man with blood in his veins know Rowan and not love her?

"Thank you, Ellen, that was delicious, as usual," said Mrs. Ferrier at the piano, as Miss Fairweather gathered her songs together.

"Have we come to the end of your programme? I *have* enjoyed it," said Ellen Fairweather. "But are none of the youngsters going to perform at all?"

"Bless me!" exclaimed her hostess. "I'd quite forgotten One of the girls sings—the little brown one with the big eyes. I don't know what she'll be like, but I must ask her."

So Hazel, who had found herself soothed and comforted by the music and had almost lost sight of the dread fact that she might have to sing, was startled by hearing Mrs. Ferrier say:

"Miss Lenox, won't you sing for us now?"

It never occurred to Hazel to protest or refuse. They had all been taught by their mother that it was rude to make a fuss when asked to do anything. With her heart somewhere in the soles of her little green shoes, she went across to the piano.

"I'm afraid I'll sound very rustic and untrained after those lovely voices," she said to Mrs. Ferrier. "And I can only sing very ordinary things."

Mrs. Ferrier, ruffling through the little bundle of songs, murmured: "Surely you don't call these Hebridean songs ordinary? Will you sing one or two of them?"

She chose them because Ellen did not sing them particularly well, so that the contrast might not be too cruel, and she set them on the music-rack with an encouraging smile.

Hazel gave a hunted glance round the room, certain that when she opened her mouth nothing but a squeak would come out, with all these eyes on her.

Then she saw Rowan in the corner, not looking at her, rapt away into some secret place where she heard notes falling like a shower of diamond-bright drops from a branch. She could sing for Rowan, who liked to listen to her.

It was a blackbird's voice, small, but mellow and true, and Hazel sang simply and without affectation. "The Wild Swan," she sang, and "The Fairy Hill", and last, "Land of Heart's Desire".

This was what Adam Ferrier heard as he let himself noiselessly into the flat, and something kept him standing there in the hall, unable to go to his room until it was ended.

Even when the singing voice had died away and a buzz of conversation took its place he still stood there thinking. "Heart's desire!" Well, he supposed he had got it, but there was something wanting. He was working harder than ever, the work was as interesting as before, and yet he felt that he was getting stale. He must be, or Old Prentice would never have told him to take things a bit easier, and urged him to go out more.

"All work and no play, Ferrier!" he had said. "You know how it goes on. You need some outside interests if you are to do your best work. Take it from an old stager, who has been at it since before you were born."

Was this what the life he had planned was going to be like—standing alone outside the warm room where other people laughed and talked?

On a sudden impulse he decided to join his mother's party. Charles had told him that Rowan Lenox was going to be there. He could ask her casually how Hazel was, say that he never had a chance of seeing her nowadays. . . . It would be no good, of course. He had finished himself with Hazel, and even now he reddened as he remembered how he had—well, warned her off. He had been incredibly stupid, priggish and conceited, and if he ever had an opportunity, he would tell Hazel so.

He opened the drawing-room door and walked in.

"I found I could get away earlier than I expected, Mother," he said to Mrs. Ferrier.

"You have missed all the music," she told him. "But you are in time to hand round coffee and drinks. I wish, though, that you could have heard Hazel sing."

"Hazel! Does she—was she singing?" he asked, looking round the room in search of her.

"Indeed she does, and was. I thought you would have known," said Mrs. Ferrier. "She was singing last of all. Ellen Fairweather and the others were delighted with her. Ellen wants to give her some lessons. It is a charming voice, and just like her, somehow."

Adam nodded vaguely, but he hardly heard. So it was Hazel whom he had listened to singing "Land of Heart's Desire". He seized a plate of sandwiches and walked about the room with them, looking for her.

"I wish Adam would let us have some of those sandwiches he is carrying round," observed Miss Fairweather plaintively.

Charles, watching his cousin's relentless progress towards Hazel, whom he had seen in a far corner talking to Holly and John Marshall, laughed.

"I'll rescue them for you," he said, and followed Adam. Hazel had seen him come in, and so was armoured in composure by the time he reached her.

"Good evening, Adam," she said, pleasantly. "I don't think you know my youngest sister, Holly."

"Have a sandwich?" said Adam, holding out the plate.

"I think I'd rather wait until we have some coffee, thank you. Wouldn't you, Holly?" said Hazel.

"I'll have one now," remarked Holly, and helped herself. "They're frightfully good," she added to John Marshall with her mouth full. "You'd better have one too, Mr. Marshall."

Charles arrived at this moment and took the plate from Adam.

"I'll deal with this," he said. "Holly, you come with me and try some of the other eats. They're on a table over near the door. There's whisky and soda," he said, to John Marshall, "Will you just go and help yourself?"

And so, in a few seconds, Adam and Hazel were left in a little backwater of their own out of the main stream of talk and light laughter.

"Look here, Hazel," he said at once, before she could think up a remark. "I want to tell you that I'd like to kick myself hard for—for the rotten things I said to you the last time I saw you to speak to. What a prig and a cad I must have sounded!"

Hazel's hurt had gone deep. She would be wary of letting herself be hurt like that again, although seeing him, hearing him stammering his awkward apology, her heart turned over. But she was too vulnerable where he was concerned. She would never, never let him, by the wildest flight of imagination, be able to think that she was running after him.

"Oh, no. Not in the least," she said, rather quickly and breathlessly. "You were perfectly right, feeling as you do, to tell me that you had no time for anything outside your work. I hope you are getting on well with Mr. Prentice."

"Damn my work and Old Prentice, too," said Adam savagely, and turned away without another word.

"You've deserted Hazel very suddenly, haven't you?" said Charles, catching Adam by the arm as he pushed blindly past him.

"It's no good. I've done for myself with her, and serve me right. Don't say any more, Charles, there's a good chap," muttered Adam.

Charles raised his eyebrows, but said nothing.

"What a lovely, lovely party it was," Holly remarked with a loud sigh of satisfaction, climbing the stairs ahead of her sisters when they got home a little later. "I enjoyed every minute of it—no, every second. Every single second!"

"So did I, but you needn't waken Mummy and Murray," said Rowan.

"Didn't you think it was lovely, Hazel?" insisted Holly.

"Yes. Lovely. Good night," said Hazel.

As she opened her bedroom door and went in, both Rowan and Holly could see the tears trickling down her cheeks.

"Good *Gracious*!" exclaimed Holly, her eyes like saucers. "What's wrong? Do you think it was the music, Rowan?"

"Yes—no—I expect it was. Don't say anything about it, Holly, like a dear," Rowan besought her. "Not to Mummy or *anyone*. You won't, will you?"

"No, I won't, truly." Holly was sobered, not only by Hazel's tears, but by something in Rowan's voice.

Being grown up, she decided, as she threw her clothes off and promised herself that she would put everything away in the morning, was very strange, and on the whole, rather sad.

"But terribly interesting," she added to herself, and fell asleep at once.

It was a long time before Hazel slept that night.

CHAPTER 19

FOR SOME TIME after Willow had moved into the flat next door, Mrs. Lenox had been so busily and happily employed in changing the rooms in her own house, so that Holly and Rowan should each be comfortable on their own, that she did not notice how little she was seeing of her eldest daughter.

After some thought, for she had made a vow to herself not to interfere with Willow and her establishment, Mrs. Lenox went to Number 4 to call on her married daughter without invitation.

Edna, opening the door to disclose a vastly improved hall—the decorating of it, and the stairs, dining-room and drawing-room had been carried out, and Number Four was now fresh and light—said that she thought Mrs. Harper wasn't in.

"But I could take a run up and make sure, if you like,'m," she added, obligingly.

However, Mrs. Lenox said she would go up herself, and did so, only to find the rooms on the top storey empty.

Everything was extremely neat and well-kept, she was pleased to see, but the whole flat seemed desolate, as if it were not lived in. Absurd though it was, she felt that by being up here alone in Willow's absence, she was prying, and she hurried away down the long stairs, her feet making no sound on the thick carpet.

Later in the day, when Rowan and Holly had come in, Mrs. Lenox asked them if they had been round to see Willow recently. Holly, whose classes were now occupying her to the exclusion of every other interest, shook her head.

Rowan hoped she did not look startled as she also said that she had not seen Willow for four or five days, but she felt it. A recollection of the dark windows on the top floor of the next-door house was troubling her. For some reason which she could not explain and had no grounds for, she thought that Willow was away from home. If Willow had been foolish enough to go off somewhere with Micky Grant, which was what Rowan feared and dreaded, it would be better that Mrs. Lenox should not know.

Rowan intended to deal with the situation so forcibly that Willow would be frightened into promising good behaviour. But no drastic measures had to be taken since Willow, with more sense and courage than she was given credit for by her younger sister, had settled her own affairs.

On a dismal November afternoon Miss Balfour's drawing-room door opened a little and Willow's voice said: "May I come in, Miss Dorothea?"

"Of course, my dear, do."

Miss Balfour put down her book of travels and smiled a welcome. She was quite glad of company, but she was also rather surprised, because Willow very seldom came to see her.

"I hope there is nothing wrong—with the cooker, or the light, or anything?" she asked.

"Oh, no. Everything is all right," said Willow, coming farther into the room so that Miss Balfour could see her.

She did not look as if everything were all right. Her pretty face was pale and her eyes looked as though she had been crying.

"I—I just thought I'd like to come and see you," she said. "But if I'm interrupting you I'll go away again."

Miss Balfour was conscious of a cowardly desire to say that she was a little tired and if nothing was wrong perhaps Willow could come and see her later.

She knew that Willow had been away from the flat for three days before she had reappeared yesterday, it was impossible not to know, when someone lived in your house and used your stairs and front door.

This flashed through her mind so quickly that she had told Willow to come and sit down near the fire in much less than a second.

"You look chilled, Willow dear," said Miss Balfour in her kindly way. "I hope you keep a good fire in your sitting-room."

"I haven't lighted it yet. I've been out all day," Willow said listlessly.

She sat in the big chair with her whole slender body drooping, a weeping willow, indeed, Miss Balfour thought.

"You must light it the moment you go upstairs," she said, firmly. "I believe you have caught a chill. I'll get Edna to bring you a hot drink."

"No, really I haven't, Miss Dorothea. Please don't bother," said Willow. "I sound snuffly because I've been crying such a lot, that's all."

Miss Balfour picked up her knitting and continued unobtrusively with the socks she was making for Montagu; those which he bought were, in her opinion, far too thin for a man of his age to wear during winter in Edinburgh. She knew that it was often easier to talk to someone who did not appear to have her whole attention concentrated on what was being told, and knitting looked peaceful and commonplace.

"It's funny, you know," Willow went on, staring into the fire. "I cry very easily, and as a rule I rather enjoy a weep. But after to-day I feel as if I'd never be able to cry again. It hurt, to-day. I hope you don't mind if I tell you about it, Miss Dorothea. The girls are too young, and Mummy, poor darling, would never understand. She'd be horrified. I don't believe she ever looked at another man except Daddy."

If it occurred to Miss Balfour to wonder why she, an elderly spinster, should be expected to understand, without being horrified at, whatever Willow's revelation might be, she gave no sign of it. With a placid-sounding murmur she went on knitting, and Willow, never taking her eyes off the fire, continued in a low voice hoarsened by tears.

"It's Micky. Micky Grant. I never knew he was really fond of me before I married Archie. Micky's one of those people who has to make love to every girl whose looks he fancies. He said he was an education for girls. I didn't think I cared much to be educated that way, so I never let him know if I was fond of him or not. I didn't really know myself. And then I married Archie, and Micky went away on a job. He came back to Edinburgh this summer, and he wouldn't behave as if I were married, and it was so difficult to be stand-offish and staid with him! You see, he's always attracted me, always. I can't help it. I love Archie, I do, really, but Archie's away such a lot, and even when he's at home, he isn't—isn't exciting. He's so sort of *colourless* beside Micky. Of course, Murray says Micky's 'nothing but a doggone pest', and I daresay he is, but he makes everything seem so thrilling, and Archie doesn't.

"Archie's far too quiet and gentle," Willow said. "If he would shout at me when I scream at him in a rage, it would be much better! I'd pipe down then. But he just leaves me alone to get over it, and that isn't any good—"

As she pictured the uproar that would be created by the young Harpers shouting and screaming at one another in her top flat, Miss Balfour could not be too thankful that Archie was quiet.

"But I wouldn't have paid any attention to Micky," Willow was saying. "Truly I wouldn't, if he hadn't told me he wasn't fooling, and that he'd always cared for me, and it had been the most frightful shock to him when I married Archie."

At that Miss Balfour let the half-knitted sock drop on to her lap, and sitting very straight, said severely: "He had no business to tell you that. It was most heartless and un-scrupulous of him to do so."

Willow turned her head to look at her, and said with a wan smile: "Of course it was. But it's the sort of thing the Micky type of person does do, Miss Dorothea. I'm the same kind myself, so I know. And when he said it was better for one person to be unhappy than three, I listened. But I told Micky I must have three days to think it over, and that's why I went away. I had to be somewhere that had no associations with Micky or Archie, and so I went to one of the little seaside places in Fife where I'd never been before. It was funny to see the sands quite empty, and the ice-cream booths and bathing-huts all boarded up, and big waves lashing on the shore. I stayed in an old-fashioned hotel that smelt of very old cabbage and roast mutton, and I walked miles along the shore every day, all alone, without another soul in sight. I was able to think and not be interrupted. It takes me a long time to think, and I don't believe I'd ever have got it sorted out, only the day before yesterday when I got in, I felt rather queer and faint, and had to sit down in the hall.

"And the landlady told me I ought to take more care of myself—of course, I should have known that I was going to have a baby! I can't think why I didn't, except that I was too muddled over the Micky business—" She broke off, and looked at Miss Balfour's troubled face.

"It's Archie's baby, Miss Dorothea. You needn't look like that!" she exclaimed. Then she sighed. "After all, it's not surprising that you should be shocked. I've behaved very badly, though not as badly as that. Anyhow, when I realized about the baby, I knew I couldn't possibly leave Archie. And so I came back, and to-day I've been walking about the Queen's Park and the slopes of Arthur's Seat in the mist and rain, having it out with Micky."

"You told him?"

"Not about the baby. That's none of his business," said Willow. "I told him that I was going to stay with Archie. It took a long time."

And tears began to fall from her eyes and roll down her pale cheeks.

She brushed them away impatiently. "Oh, Lord! I thought I'd stopped *that*!" she said, angrily. "I must have a far bigger supply of tears than most people. I'm—sorry, Miss Dorothea."

"My dear child," said Miss Dorothea. "You are tired out, and cold and hungry. You are going to lie down on the sofa here, where it is warm."

"I don't want to argue," said Willow, wearily. "I've been doing that for hours and hours."

She found it very comforting to lie on the old sofa with soft cushions under her head and a warm light rug over her. When Miss Balfour brought a hot-bottle in its bright blue cover and put it at her feet, Willow caught the elder woman's hand.

"I hope you aren't going to hate me for this?" she said.

"You have been very foolish, Willow, and very naughty," said Miss Balfour, but her tone was much gentler than her words. "Try to rest, and I will go and see about some soup for you."

She could not bring herself to sympathize with Willow over the loss of this most undesirable young man, or to condone her behaviour, and she went away, leaving Willow, exhausted with emotion and distress, lying with closed eyes. A tear or two trickled from under her eyelids, but she lay still, content not to think any more for the moment.

Downstairs, Miss Balfour found Edna in the dining-room, and explained briefly that Mrs. Harper was tired and was lying on the drawing-room sofa as her own fire was not lighted.

"If you will heat up some of the chicken soup, Edna, and make a piece of thin crisp toast, and bring it up, it will do her good," she said.

Edna, willing and obliging creature that she was, was only too ready to do it, and was on the point of going down to the kitchen when the front-door bell rang.

"Oh, dear! I don't want Mrs. Harper disturbed," said Miss Balfour. "If it is a caller—though I don't see how it can be at seven o'clock at night!—show them into the dining-room, Edna."

She went in there herself and waited. Presently Edna came in to say it was a gentleman asking for Mrs. Harper.

"Ever so handsome he is'm," she said, with thoughts of film stars surging in her head.

Miss Balfour felt certain that she knew who this handsome gentleman was.

"Show him in here, Edna," she said. "And remember, handsome is as handsome does."

"Yes,'m," replied Edna, dutifully, but with regret, and in a moment a tall undeniably good-looking young man came into the room.

"I'm sorry, I'm afraid there's been some mistake," he said, pleasantly. "I didn't want to trouble you. I asked for Mrs. Harper. Is she in?"

"She is in, Mr. Grant, but I think you had better not see her," said Miss Balfour, calmly.

She was suddenly and irrationally glad that she was wearing one of the new dresses chosen with Mrs. Lenox's help, a soft wool garment of excellent cut and a becoming deep purple in colour. The young man, though they had met at the Lenox girls' party, obviously did not recognize or remember her.

"I think she will want to see me," he persisted, not quite so pleasantly, for he was unused to being thwarted.

"No. She is much too tired, and in her present condition she ought not to be worried," said Miss Balfour. She had no scruples about mentioning the baby, she found.

He stared at her, angry and perplexed.

"Perhaps you didn't know that Mrs. Harper is going to have a baby?" said Miss Balfour.

"A baby! Good Lord! No, I didn't know. I—I—well, perhaps after all, I'd better not disturb her," he stammered, for once shaken out of his easy self-assurance. "Just say good-bye to her from me, will you? I'm off to-morrow, you see."

"Mr. Grant," said Miss Balfour. "I believe you have already said good-bye to her, have you not? I am sure you don't really want me to give her any message."

"No. You're right. I don't," he said, hurriedly. "I'll be off. Good night."

And he turned and dashed into the hall, dragged open the heavy front door and was gone.

"A good riddance," observed Miss Balfour.

As she went upstairs again, she suddenly thought how appalled Belle would have been if she could have heard her coolly telling a young man about Willow's baby, and she chuckled.

"Poor Belle," she murmured. "She would be horrified by a good many things about me if she could see me now!"

She found Willow sitting bolt upright clutching the rug to her and looking scared.

"It was Micky, wasn't it?" she said, as soon as Miss Balfour opened the door. "Oh, don't let him come up! I really couldn't bear to see him!"

"It is quite all right. He has gone away," said Miss Balfour, firmly. "Now lie down again and don't be silly, my dear. He won't come back, I promise you."

"How did you get him to go?" asked Willow, but she lay down and let Miss Balfour tuck the rug round her.

"I just told him about the baby. That settled it," said Miss Balfour cheerfully.

"He—he fled?"

"He fled," agreed Miss Balfour, with an emphatic nod.

"I'm not surprised," Willow said, mournfully.

"Nor was I. He really isn't worth making yourself ill over, my dear," said Miss Balfour. "Your husband is worth six of him."

"Oh, I know. Only—only it's hard to put him out of my mind all in a minute," Willow said, rather piteously. "I am trying."

"Think about the baby," was Miss Balfour's advice. "And don't think about men at all, not even your husband, just now."

"I expect the baby will be twin boys," said Willow, but she smiled, though faintly, and Miss Balfour felt that it would not be very long before her spirits recovered.

CHAPTER 20

THE news that Willow was going to have a baby was received by her family with much pleasure and excitement.

Mrs. Lenox was relieved as well as delighted. Now Willow would settle down properly at last, and there would be no more mysterious absences from her flat. The only thing that troubled her was the very practical consideration that a baby in a top flat would be rather difficult.

"Such a long way down to the green with all the washing every day," as she said. "And though I'm sure Miss Dorothea will let you keep the pram in the hall, it will mean carrying the baby up and down all those stairs."

Willow only smiled. She had gained a serene composure during the past few days, and if there were faint blue shadows under her eyes and a slight hollowing below her cheekbones, this was merely put down to the baby.

"Don't worry, Mummy," she said. "We have a long time to think about it still! And these rooms up at the top are so light and airy, I think it's worth the stairs. We can see what Archie says. He'll be home for Christmas."

The younger Lenoxes each took it differently. Murray professed himself to be highly diverted, but privately, and after making some careful calculations, he opened a Savings Bank account for his future nephew or niece, into which he intended to pay a certain proportion of his salary each month.

Rowan started to knit a trousseau for the baby which would surpass anything that a baby had ever had.

Holly appeared to be completely overwhelmed with amazement that such a thing should be going to happen in her family.

"It's quite a common occurrence, you know," as Murray said, breaking in on her loud exclamatory remarks.

"Mummy will be a *grandmother*!" Holly went on, paying no attention to her brother. "And Murray will be an *uncle*! Oh, and I'll be an *aunt*!" Her voice rose to a triumphant squeal. "And so will Hazel and Rowan. Aunt Hazel, Aunt Rowan, Aunt Holly! Doesn't it sound silly?"

"Not half so silly as you do, Auntie Holl," said Murray, unkindly. "For Heaven's sake, stop yelling and be your age. You're enough to make Willow have a miscarriage."

"Murray, *dear*!" exclaimed Mrs. Lenox, but the others only laughed, and Willow, by asking Holly if she would like to be a godmother, reduced that young person to a silence of stunned gratification.

"Aunt Hazel's keeping very quiet about the Happy Event, isn't she?" said Murray.

"I haven't had a chance to get a word in edgeways," Hazel said, mildly.

"It's a blessing there's one quiet one in this noisy family," said Willow. "I must go, Mummy. Come in and see me, all of you, any time."

When Mrs. Lenox had gone to the door with Willow to give her some final injunctions about not doing too much, and the others had scattered on their own various affairs, Hazel remained sitting on the low stool beside the fire, thinking.

She wasn't envious of Willow, but she wondered if her own fate was always to be "Aunt Hazel" to the others' children. It looked very like it, she thought. In her own mind she was quite certain that she would never love anyone but Adam Ferrier, and therefore she would never marry.

The worst of it, to her mind, was that her job had become a grind. She had no interest any longer in the chatter of the other girls, in Christine's devastating affairs of the heart, or even in the patients.

Everything was disagreeable, including the weather, for it was a horrible grey afternoon, with a "haar", that east coast sea-mist, creeping in from the Forth and blotting out all the familiar landmarks.

"Me for an evening by the fire with a good love story and a bag of peppermint creams," said Christine Rennie, after a shuddering look at the gloom outside. "I shan't go out to-night no matter who asks me!"

"I suppose by that you mean that no one has," said one of the others.

Christine tossed her fiery head. "That's all you know," she answered.

The prospect of sitting at home until bed-time suddenly filled Hazel with boredom. She decided to go to the pictures, and having rung up her mother to say she would not be in to supper, powdered her nose, put on hat and coat, and left with the rest.

Instead of eating in one of the tea-rooms along Princes Street as usual, she went boldly into a small restaurant which was half a bar, and ordered a gin and lime before her meal.

"If I've got to go about without a male escort," she told herself, defiantly, as she sipped her drink. "I'd better get accustomed to coming to this sort of place alone."

It was a strange little place, with red plush seats against the walls, weary palms in pots too small for them, and a good many fly-spotted mirrors, but the fried fish and chips came piping hot and very well cooked, and there was a large rack of freshly made toast and plenty of butter. Hazel shut her eyes to the defects and ate a good meal.

She enjoyed the film too. It was *How to Marry a Millionaire*, and was so wildly improbable that she forgot real life and her job and Adam, while she laughed at it.

A wind had risen and blown away the haar when Hazel emerged, blinking, into Princes Street. Stars were pricking the dark sky, and against it the great mass of the Castle on its rock rose black. Tower and wall and battery were out-lined clearly, all the buildings which by daylight looked commonplace were lent a strange beauty.

There were not many people about. She met one or two elderly men giving their dogs a bed-time trot, and a little knot of girls in Guide uniform, talking about the meeting they had just left. In a dark entrance a boy and girl stood close together, her head on his shoulder, his arm round her waist. An occasional car purred past like some enormous jungle beast, its lights searching the street before it. The air was chill and had a smell of frost, and even Hazel's light tread made the pavements ring as she walked.

When it seemed to have reached the bottom of the hill the road divided, and Hazel's way lay to the left, round a sharp bend and plunging down a farther slope between dark gardens. Behind them on either side of the road lay terraces of quiet houses, but a stone's throw down the hill light and noise streamed up to meet and bewilder the oncoming walker.

Hazel had almost reached the bridge spanning the Water of Leith, when she caught up with an elderly man who was having some difficulty in walking straight.

As she passed him he collided with her, and at once raised his hat, saying with drunken gravity: "Thousand— 'polologies, m'dear. A little giddy this evening."

"Mr. Milner!" said Hazel.

"Call me Monty," he replied, staring at her owlishly, his hat on the back of his head. "All frien's call me Monty."

Hazel did not hesitate. She took his arm, and saying firmly, "You must see me home, Mr. Milner," tried to urge him on across the bridge.

It was not an easy task. Mr. Milner, though only an inch or so taller than Hazel, was solidly built, not to say rotund, and his legs described such peculiar circles as he progressed that she felt she was arm in arm with Humpty Dumpty himself.

Fortunately they had not far to go, but she did wish that he would not stop so often to assure her of his intention to see her safely home.

This had happened for the fifth time, when a young man came up at a great pace, seized Mr. Milner by the coat-collar, and tried to detach him from Hazel's arm.

"You old blackguard! What do you mean by annoying this young lady?" he exclaimed, in a low but furious tone. "I've a good mind to hand you over to the nearest policeman!"

"Oh, *Adam*!" cried Hazel. "Please let him go! It's only Mr. Milner, and I'm trying to get him home! Don't shake the poor old thing like that!"

Adam Ferrier, still retaining his hold on his victim, looked at him closely.

"Good Lord! It's the old boy from next door to you, isn't it? Charles's client—"

"'Thank you to take your handsoffme, young man," said Mr. Milner, in a rush. "Ol' boy, indeed! Seeing young lady home, an' you come bombarging in—"

"That's a good word, bombarging," said Adam, and re-leased him, so that, deprived of support, Mr. Milner had to cling to a convenient lamp-post. "Well, what are we to do with the old so-and-so?"

"If you *could* help me to take him home to Number Four?" said Hazel, doubtfully.

"Of course. I'll do it myself, and you can go on ahead," Adam said.

But Hazel would not do this. She wanted, she explained, to try to get Mr. Milner into the house and if possible to his own room without disturbing his sister-in-law.

"Right. Let's get under way," said Adam, briefly. "An arm each, that'll be best."

So with Mr. Milner sagging between them, the two went on towards Kirkaldy Crescent.

Now that Hazel had some of the responsibility for Mr. Milner, not to speak of his weight, taken off her, she had time to wonder why Adam was in this part of the town at all; and because the whole evening had turned into such a strange adventure, she was able to ask him point-blank.

"What are you doing down here, Adam?"

"Oh—I—well —" he began, glancing at her above their charge's head.

Then he seemed to make up his mind. "All right, I may as well tell you just what a fool I am," he said. "I was looking at your house. I didn't know you were out."

This, though spoken in a tone of savage self-mockery, sounded to Hazel like all the great lovers of history talking together.

"Oh, Adam!" she said, softly. "You weren't really, were you?"

"I was. And I know you've done with me, and I don't blame you," he said. "But I want you to know that I can't do without you and be either happy or useful. I daresay I'll get along somehow, but—"

"Why are you so sure that I've done with you?" asked Hazel.

"I thought you were finished with *me*."

"Could we start again?" he said, "Would you, Hazel? Hazel, my darling, would you?"

Hazel shook her head. "I'd rather just go on from where we left off," she answered, amazed at her own boldness.

"Oh, Hazel!"

"Oh, Adam!"

"Oh, for goodenssake, lesh get home!" muttered the third member of the party, startling them considerably, since they had forgotten his existence for the time being.

"Whatsh use slip-slopping an' Oh—ing, eh?" continued Mr. Milner, now stumbling forward almost at a run. "Why dontcher k-kish her, silly fool?"

"Because you're in the way, old boy," replied Adam. "Just wait till we've got rid of you, that's all."

Hazel, pink to the roots of her hair, hurried along, half-longing for, half-dreading the moment when she would be alone with Adam. The dark sky and houses, the lamp-lit street, the rather dirty pavement and the drab passers-by were all alike invisible to her. She was walking in a magic forest with Adam, and everything had been put right with hardly a word said.

"If it hadn't been for Mr. Milner, poor dear old pet, we'd still be unhappy," she thought, and hugged the arm she held.

Adam, being a man, did not rate Montagu's assistance quite so highly, but he was willing to concede that having to lug the old rip home like a sack of potatoes had certainly broken the ice.

"We'll have to be awfully quiet," murmured Hazel, when they had manoeuvred Mr. Milner up the steps of Number Four Kirkaldy Crescent at last. "Miss Dorothea hasn't gone to bed, there's a light in the drawing-room."

"Where's your key?" said Adam to Mr. Milner, in a low voice.

"Key? Key? Aha, you'd like to know, wouldn't you?" said Mr. Milner, roguishly, and to their anxious ears much too loudly.

"Oh, Lord! He's going to be troublesome," muttered Adam. "Don't you want to go in?" he went on. "It's pretty cold out here, isn't it?"

"Cold, cold. Poor Tom's a-cold," said Mr. Milner, mournfully.

"I don't believe he's got a key at all," said Hazel, suddenly, and this proved to be the right line to take, for Mr. Milner, sitting down on the stone doorstep, pulled a mass of small objects from his overcoat pocket. There was a slight metallic sound, and the key fell down into the area.

Adam, with a groan, went and retrieved it, after which it was simple enough to open the door.

To induce Mr. Milner to enter, however, was another matter altogether, and was only achieved in the end by Adam's taking him under the arms and heaving him bodily into the hall.

"His room's on the ground floor," whispered Hazel.

"Go ahead and open the door for me," was Adam's reply, as he prepared to heave again.

"Oh, darling, don't hurt yourself!" Hazel breathed, anxiously.

The endearment so inspired Adam that he hoisted Mr. Milner to his feet, and half-guiding, half-dragging him, got him across the hall to the door which Hazel had flitted ahead to open.

"I'll put him to bed if you'll stand guard in the hall," was Adam's next order, and he shut the door, leaving Hazel to go and sit on a large oak chest and wait for him in a happy daze.

He reappeared in a wonderfully short time, and the two tiptoed to the front door and let themselves quietly out.

"I found some alka-seltzer and gave him a dose. Old brute, he must have drunk a devil of a lot," observed Adam. "But never mind about him. What about us?"

Hazel was all at once overcome with shyness. "What about—us?" she repeated, looking everywhere but at Adam. "I—I don't know what you mean."

"Come over under that tree and I'll tell you," he said, leading her across the street to where an old hawthorn obligingly hung its branches over the garden railings.

There, without another word, Hazel was folded in a close embrace and kissed most satisfactorily until she had no breath left. Just at first she stiffened instinctively against his arms, but soon Adam found that she was returning his kisses with an innocent ardour that made his heart pound.

212

When at last he released her he said, rather shakily: "Look, darling, don't let us have one of these long engagements. It would drive me mad."

Hazel, with her face buried in his tweed-covered shoulder, made a muffled sound which he took for assent.

"I'll come and see your mother to-morrow evening," he said. "And I'll tell mine to-night."

"Oh, Adam! Will she mind?"

"Mind? She'll be overjoyed," he said. "She has wanted to get me off her hands for ages. Now, good night, my precious one. I'll wait here until I see you are in, and then I'll go home."

There was a last kiss, prolonged into several more, and then Hazel ran lightly across to her own door, opened it, turned to wave, and vanished inside.

Adam, after staring at the door's blank unfeeling oblong in a besotted way for several seconds, walked away in the direction of the West End.

In spite of all their care and the extremely solid structure of the house, Miss Balfour, sitting alone in her drawing-room, had heard sundry bumps and a strange scuffling noise from the hall below.

Once or twice recently she had heard Montagu come home late and have some difficulty in finding his way to his room. Until this evening she had left him alone, knowing how ashamed he would be if she saw him like that. But to-night he seemed worse than usual. She put down the book she had been trying to read, and crept silently out to the dark landing, to be nearer at hand if he should need help.

Unseen she watched Hazel open the door and then leave Adam Ferrier to take Montagu into his room.

"How good of them!" she thought, though she was very sorry that they should have discovered poor Montagu's little weakness, and especially that Hazel should.

She waited until the two had gone out, then went back to do the small tidyings of the drawing-room which she performed each night before going to bed.

The books were laid straight on the little table by her chair, the footstools aligned, the cushions plumped up. Finally the curtains were drawn back and looped in regular folds by their tasselled bands of the same material.

It was while she was doing this that Miss Balfour saw the two figures standing in the old hawthorn's shade against the garden railing.

The merest glance told her who they were, though she turned away at once.

"Bless them both!" she said, under her breath, switching out the light by the door, and went downstairs to see that her brother-in-law was all right.

Never in her life before Montagu came had she been in contact with anyone the worse for drink, but her attitude was as matter-of-fact as Adam's, and she was less horrified than Hazel.

Of course, she disapproved, and, apart from other and perhaps more important considerations, she was sure that what Montagu drank in that dreadful public-house at the corner near the bridge must be bad for his health. Somehow he would have to be discouraged from this habit.

But when Miss Balfour thought of the drunken men she had seen in the streets on Saturday nights, not very many of them, but still a few, she could congratulate herself on Montagu's behaviour. She could not picture him either truculent or tearful—"fechtin' drunk or greetin' fou", as her neighbours in Linden Terrace graphically described these conditions— In fact, even when under the influence of alcohol, Montagu remained a gentleman.

"What a horrid way to have to put it," Miss Balfour thought, as she opened Montagu's bedroom door very gently. "But I can't think of any other that means the same."

Mr. Milner was sound asleep and snoring. He did not present an attractive appearance, but Miss Balfour pulled the coverings more closely round him without any feeling of revulsion. The arm she had covered was pyjama-clad, and a pile of clothes laid with moderate tidiness on a chair bore witness that Adam Ferrier had put him to bed.

"Like a—an elderly baby," said Miss Balfour to herself. "It was *very* good of him."

She went quietly up to bed, said her prayers with a special plea that guidance might be given her to deal with Montagu, and after a while fell asleep.

But she did not have a restful night, for her sleep was broken and full of annoying dreams. She came down to breakfast feeling old and tired and washed-out, and for all her sweetness of temper, could not help thinking that there was injustice somewhere, or else why should Montagu be rosy, beaming and brisk, with an enormous appetite for his favourite breakfast, grilled kidneys and bacon.

He showed concern when Miss Balfour refused them and nibbled a small piece of toast with her coffee.

"I am so sorry you have no appetite, my dear Dorothea," he said, anxiously. "I really think, you know, that perhaps you don't go out enough. Nothing like fresh air and exercise to give you an appetite. Look at me. Fit as a fiddle and hungry as a hunter."

"Well, Montagu," exclaimed Miss Balfour, stung into unmasking her hidden batteries and firing a shot before she had intended to. "It's the first time I have ever heard of *pub-crawling* as a means of getting fresh air and exercise!"

Mr. Milner was so startled that he jumped in his chair, a deeper tint crept into his pink cheeks, and he eyed his sister-in-law very uneasily indeed.

At last, as she said no more and continued quietly to eat her toast, he succeeded in producing a laugh.

"You—you were joking, of course," he said, hopefully.

Miss Balfour only smiled, but when she spoke next it appeared, to his great relief, that she had changed the subject.

"I was wondering," she said. "Whether we should have some of the Lenoxes to dinner one evening, and Mr. Ferrier and his mother. Food is quite easy to manage now, and—"

"A splendid idea!" cried Montagu, heartily. "I suppose it wouldn't be too much for Edna?"

"Edna loves a party, and, of course, we would get Mrs. Lyall in to help with washing-up," Miss Balfour answered. "Edna assures me that a bit of life about the place makes up for any extra work she may have to do. Then, Montagu, there is the question of what to drink. I think it is time you really looked properly at what is in the wine-cellar. I know Papa laid down some good wine, and it has never been touched since his death, apart from an odd bottle of sherry. Belle detested any form of wine or spirits, and I do not know enough about them to make it any use my looking."

Mr. Milner disclaimed interest in the contents of the wine-cellar rather too hastily.

"That may be," said Miss Balfour. "But I do think, Montagu, that if you feel you want to—to have an extra drink or two, now and then, it would be far better for you to drink your own good wine in your own house, than to ruin your stomach with the stuff you must get in a public-house."

Appalled, Mr. Milner stared at the sister-in-law who put these views so calmly before him in as matter-of-fact a manner as though she were telling him that coffee was bad for his liver.

"I—I—" he began, feebly, and could think of nothing whatever to say.

"I understand, though, that it is for the company that people visit bars, as much as for the actual drink," pursued Miss Balfour. "And I am beginning to think that you must be finding life here very dull. Perhaps it was a mistake, our setting up house together, and you would really be happier on your own."

"Stop, Dorothea! Stop!" shouted Mr. Milner, suddenly finding his tongue. "If you turn me out, I *will* take to drink out of boredom and unhappiness! If you would just come out with me now and again— I don't want you to sacrifice your peaceful life to me, of course, but if, now and then—"

Miss Balfour began to laugh. "My dear Montagu, I should only disgrace you in a public bar!" she said. "One glass of anything is enough to make my head spin. You would always be having to bring me home in a taxi—"

"Good God, Dorothea! You surely do not imagine that I propose taking you into a pub?" exclaimed Mr. Milner, profoundly shocked.

Miss Balfour gurgled with unsuppressed mirth. "Oh, dear, Montagu, I am sorry!" she gasped. "But you do look so dreadfully shocked!"

"I *am* shocked," he said, stiffly. "What I intended to suggest was that you might go to a play or a concert with me occasionally."

"Only occasionally? And why not the pictures, if there happens to be a good one?" asked Miss Balfour.

"Would you come?"

"Indeed I would. I should love to go to the theatre and out to dinner."

"Then why have we never done it?" he wondered.

"Well, Montagu, you have never asked me," said Miss Balfour. "And now, here is the key of the wine-cellar. I wish you would go and see what we have down there."

CHAPTER 21

"ROWAN, my dear child," said Mrs. Lenox, firmly. "If you are going out to dinner at Number Four with the rest of us, you really must have a new dress. Your green taffeta is hardly decent any longer, it is all splitting at the seams with sheer old age."

"Oh, it isn't as bad as all that, Mummy, and I wanted to wait until Christmas to get a new one," said Rowan.

But she coloured a little, avoiding her mother's eye, as she muttered that the green taffeta would do once more, and Mrs. Lenox was worried.

She had not a notion of the truth, which was that Rowan had no money. She had not been paid at all by Martin Tinker or his wife since the children had started lessons again in September, and almost all her savings had been drawn by this time to pay her share of the household expenses which she gave her mother each month. In her heart Rowan knew that it could not possibly go on. After Christmas she would have to find another job.

Arriving at the dingy house on the morning after Mrs. Lenox had spoken to her about her old dress, Rowan found the children huddled in a scared group in the dining-room. Viola, of course, was in floods of tears, Orlando looked as if he were going to be sick, even Rosalind was pale and subdued.

"Well, children," said Rowan, with determined cheerfulness. "Why haven't you got the lesson-books out? What's happened?"

Orlando stared at her out of wide, alarmed eyes, saying nothing. Viola sobbed.

Rosalind mumbled: "We've not had any breakfast, an' Father's gone an' Mother's crying in the studio. And we don't know what to do."

Rowan considered for a minute. Then she said decidedly: "The first thing is to get you all some breakfast. Rosalind, you could set the table, couldn't you? And Viola can stop crying and help. Orlando, you come to the kitchen with me and we'll make some toast."

The kitchen was in wild confusion, and there was not much to eat as far as Rowan could see, but she found a loaf and some butter, and Orlando obediently watched the slices she put in the toaster under the gas grill while she filled the kettle to make tea.

"I never saw such beautiful toast," she declared, as she piled it on a plate to keep hot after it was buttered.

"Is it good to make beautiful toast?" asked Orlando, very seriously. He looked less pinched and green, to Rowan's relief, but she knew he was still upset.

"Of course. It's good to do anything well," said Rowan. "Can you carry the toast into the dining-room very carefully, while I bring the tea?"

Orlando nodded and set off with the laden plate held firmly in both small square hands.

As soon as she had settled the children to their tea and toast, she poured out another cup and took it up to the studio.

Mrs. Tinker, her face almost unrecognizable, it was so blotched and swollen with crying, was crouched on the edge of the model's dais in a wretched heap, still shaken by racking sobs.

"Take it away, I don't want it!" she muttered, when Rowan came up to her.

"Nonsense. You must drink it while it's hot," said Rowan. "Could you tell me what has happened, or would you rather not?"

"Oh, you may as well know," said Mrs. Tinker, pushing back a lank wisp of hair and taking the cup which Rowan offered her. "Martin's deserted us, that's all. He's raised some money somehow and gone off."

"You mean—he's not coming back *ever*?"

"Not unless he finds himself without cash," replied Mrs. Tinker, with a long quivering sigh. "And if he's gone to the South Seas, as he says, he won't be able to get back in any case."

Rowan stood staring at her. At last:

"What will become of you—and the children?" she asked.

"Oh, I'll work, of course. I'll have to," replied Mrs. Tinker, with a sort of desperate calm. "My aunt will take the two girls, and they can go to the village school, and I'll send her as much money as I can."

"And—and—Orlando? Is he going to go to your aunt's too?"

Mrs. Tinker shook her head. "No. She won't hear of having Orlando," she said, reluctantly. "She—you see, she knows he isn't my child, and though I've told her many times that he is almost like my own to me, and begged her by telephone—I rang her up as soon as I'd read Martin's letter—*begged* her to take him with Rosalind and Viola, she won't do it."

"So—what's going to happen to him?" Rowan spoke through stiff, dry lips.

"My aunt wants me to get him into some sort of institution," sighed Mrs. Tinker. "I *can't* keep him with me."

"You might just as well kill him with a knife!" Rowan cried passionately, the anger and distress she had been restraining suddenly welling up and bubbling over. "It will be the end of Orlando!"

Mrs. Tinker stared at her miserably. "Well, what am I to do?"

"I'll take him home with me," said Rowan.

"My dear child, how can you? What would your mother say? And—I won't have much money to spare for him, poor child," said Mrs. Tinker. "I must think of the girls first, after all."

"I'll be able to pay for him," Rowan said, recklessly. "I'll get another job in the New Year, and he won't cost a lot to keep. Do please let me have him!"

"You must ask your mother first," said Mrs. Tinker; and she stuck to this, though Rowan wanted to pack Orlando's few clothes and take him away to Kirkaldy Crescent at once.

"I shall have him," was all Rowan said. Her head was high, the crusading light was burning in her eyes as she dashed out of the house and down the noisy dirty street to the nearest bus-stop.

A young man hanging about in a doorway on the opposite side saw her go, and after a momentary hesitation, followed her, scowling.

At the bus-stop he spoke to her abruptly.

"Hullo," he said. "Why are you going off in the morning?"

Rowan swung round. "Angus," she said, without any sign of pleasure or surprise. "I thought you'd be at a lecture." Angus's evil genius was in charge that morning. "I wanted to see that fellow Tinker that you're so keen on," he muttered.

"Well, you're too late, if you mean Martin Tinker. He's gone," said Rowan, coldly. "Nor am I keen on him, as you put it."

"Rot. Don't tell me. You'd never go on teaching the chap's brats for nothing if you weren't!" Angus retorted. "He's a handsome brute, I'll allow you, if you fancy brawn by the stone."

Rowan turned and gave him her full attention. "Are you telling me that you've been *spying* on me?" she demanded, incredulously.

"Call it that if you like," he said, already ashamed, but too late.

"There doesn't seem to be anything else I *can* call it," said Rowan. "Here's the bus. Good-bye."

She sprang lightly on to the bus and was borne away, and before the conductor had come for her fare had forgotten Angus completely in her anxiety over Orlando.

"But Rowan, *darling*, how can you do a thing like this? It's a very serious step to take, it requires endless consideration," said Mrs. Lenox, in reply to Rowan's statement that Martin Tinker had deserted his family and as Orlando had nowhere to go, she was going to bring him to live at Kirkaldy Crescent.

"There isn't time for talking it over, Mummy," said Rowan, with the steely calm which her mother recognized with dread. "I'd rather see Orlando dead than shoved into some institution, and Mrs. Tinker can't keep him if she's working, and her aunt won't have him. If you won't have him here, then I must go somewhere and take him with me."

"If Mrs. Tinker can't do that, how can you?" asked Mrs. Lenox, hopelessly.

"Because her job is stage work and B.B.C., and I'd answer one of those advertisements for a cook, child of school age welcome," replied Rowan, at once. "I've thought it all out, Mummy."

"Well—bring the child here for the Christmas holidays, then," said Mrs. Lenox. "It will give everyone time to think, if nothing else. But, of course, the whole thing is madness!"

Rowan, ignoring this last remark, flung her arms round her mother's neck. "Mummy, you're a darling!" she cried.

And so Orlando, puzzled but acquiescent, was brought to Number Six Kirkaldy Crescent. Rowan did not know whether he realized how final was the break with his old life, but she did know that he depended on her, and she vowed with all the ardent generosity that was her weakness and her strength not to fail him.

In the flurry of packing the girls' things and seeing them off at the station, helping Mrs. Tinker to collect her one or two personal household goods, and putting Orlando's clothes and toys into a suitcase and taking him home with her, Rowan did not have a moment to think about Angus until she went to bed that night.

Then she remembered, and was suddenly hot with anger again. That Angus should be such a fool as to imagine she was in love with Martin Tinker was bad enough, she thought, an insult both to her taste and her morals. But that he should actually cut a class to hang about outside the Tinkers' house, spying on her, was unforgivable.

"I've stood a lot from Angus because I am sorry for him," she said to herself. "But this is the finish. He must find another dancing partner, someone who will think he's wonderful all round. I shall write to him in the morning. It isn't fair to either of us to go on any longer. We don't seem able to be friends, and I certainly can never be anything else to him."

It is not easy for a girl deliberately to throw away her most constant escort and admirer, no matter how tiresome he may be, and Rowan did not enjoy writing her letter. But she was too straightforward to let things remain as they were between her and Angus, now that she had discovered to what lengths his jealous possessiveness could carry him. So the letter was written, and she posted it at the top of the Crescent when she took Orlando out with her to do the shopping for her mother.

A family conclave had been held the evening before, while Rowan was helping her charge with his bath, and though the Lenoxes all agreed that Rowan was mad, none of them was willing to say outright that Orlando must be banished to an institution of any kind.

Mrs. Lenox had a scribbled note from Mrs. Tinker, which she read out to Murray, Willow and Hazel—Holly, having fortunately elected to make Orlando's supper and take it upstairs, was also absent.

"I don't suppose there's anywhere the poor little brute could be dumped," said Murray. "He isn't an orphan, and I imagine that as Mrs. Tinker accepted him, he'd count legally as one of her children. But what's to become of him beats me."

Mrs. Lenox sighed. "He is a dear little boy," she said. "I don't know when I have seen a child I liked so much. And he really would be very little trouble here—"

"Can you afford to keep him, Mummy?" asked Willow, bluntly.

"Not really, unless Mrs. Tinker is able to send money from time to time," Mrs. Lenox admitted. "But you heard what she said in her letter—that she would do her very best, and she hoped her husband might—"

"From what Rowan says about *him*, you may as well give up that idea at once," said Murray.

"Couldn't we all give just a very little more towards the housekeeping?" suggested Hazel. "I know Rowan says she's going to do it all, but honestly I don't see how she can."

"Poor old Rowan!" said Murray. "She's on the rocks, thanks to sticking to these people. Doesn't Mrs. Tinker say she hasn't had a penny the whole of this term?"

"If only Rowan wouldn't embroil herself with such odd people!" mourned Mrs. Lenox. "There she is, poor child, her clothes in rags and her savings all gone, and Orlando on her hands into the bargain!"

"I'm going to give Rowan some of my things. In a month or two I won't be able to get into them, so she may as well have them now," said Willow.

"Well, that's good of you, Willow, but we're no nearer settling what is to be done with the child!" said Mrs. Lenox.

"Why don't you ask Miss Dorothea what she thinks?" said Hazel, suddenly. "She often has good ideas. You'll probably have a chance when we dine with her and Mr. Milner to-morrow."

Mrs. Lenox protested that it was ridiculous to bother Miss Dorothea with all their problems, but her family were pretty sure that she would consult their neighbour about Orlando, and left it at that.

Miss Balfour knew a little already about Orlando, for she met Rowan and him hand in hand, as she came round the corner of Linden Terrace into the Crescent, and stopped to speak to them.

"This is Orlando Tinker, Miss Dorothea. He has come to stay with us," said Rowan.

Orlando put out his hand with grave politeness and Miss Balfour shook it, equally courteously.

Orlando said to Rowan when they were walking on again: "That's a nice little lady. I'll make a picksher of her. Her face is like a sheep-dog."

"Is it? I hadn't noticed," said Rowan, surprised, but realizing that there was a faint resemblance between Miss Balfour and a wise elderly collie.

"I don't mean to be rude," Orlando said, anxiously.

"You aren't rude," Rowan assured him. "Now, you must help me to choose a nice big cabbage for dinner. And then, if we've time, we might buy some Christmas presents for you to send to the girls."

"I *do* like living with you," said Orlando, contentedly. "I hope I can stay for years *an*' years."

"So do I," answered Rowan, her hold on his woollen-gloved fingers tightening, as she wondered how her mother would agree with this sentiment.

Mrs. Lenox was pleased to have a boy in the house again, but it was quite absurd, she knew, to take Orlando into their household in this haphazard way, without his father's consent and with only a vague grateful letter from the woman he thought of as his mother.

She said this to Miss Balfour when, after an excellent dinner with wine from the cellar of Number Four, the whole party had gone upstairs to the drawing-room, and she had an opportunity of talking to her hostess aside.

"I really don't know quite what to do," she ended. "It would be simple if we could just adopt him outright, even though we can't afford it."

Miss Balfour said: "I don't suppose his father will trouble about him, poor little boy. And Mrs. Tinker would probably be thankful to leave him to you. I think you should make an arrangement with her, in writing, that she undertakes to send you what she can towards his keep, and you are given a free hand to look after him and his education until he is eighteen and can decide his future for himself. Of course, she should be allowed to see him if she wishes, and have him for visits, but you ought to insist that if you have the responsibility of his upbringing, you must not be interfered with. Would you like me to ask Mr. Ferrier about it?"

"I think I'll get Murray to speak to Charles Ferrier about drafting a suitable letter," said Mrs Lenox, thoughtfully. And added: "You didn't make any suggestions about what should be done if we didn't keep him, Miss Dorothea."

Miss Balfour smiled. "I knew you meant to keep him, my dear," she said.

"Rowan does, at any rate," said Mrs. Lenox, ruefully.

"Dear Rowan. There's something—something *splendid* about her," said Miss Balfour. "I can't describe it any other way, but, of course, you know, better than I do, what I mean."

"Yes, I know, and extremely awkward and uncomfortable it makes things at times," responded Rowan's mother, with feeling. "All the same, you wouldn't change her."

"No," agreed Mrs. Lenox. "I wouldn't change her."

They both looked across the room, so pleasant now with its new covers of warm ivory, its gay cushions and dark blue curtains, to a small sofa where Rowan and Charles Ferrier were sitting side by side. They did not seem to be talking much; they looked contented and at ease.

Rowan was wearing the old green taffeta, but Charles did not see that it was old. All he knew was that its rich dark sheen made her colouring clearer and more brilliant than ever, and that he had never met any girl before, and never would again, who was so absolutely in tune with him. No doubt they might disagree in small things, but essentially they were at one.

"Dine with me to-morrow and dance afterwards," he said.

Rowan frowned, then turned to him and said: "I've lost my job. Martin Tinker has gone off into the blue, Mrs. Tinker has left for London to find work, the little girls are with their great-aunt, and—I've brought Orlando next door to live with us. I'm going to look after him."

Charles looked soberly back at her face, now sparkling with defiance, and said: "I see. It's a big responsibility, isn't it?"

"Yes. An awfully big responsibility."

"Why did you tell me about it?" he asked.

"I don't know." The defiance gave place to a puzzled look. "Somehow I seemed to *have* to tell you, Charles."

("Her face changes like water in a hill-burn, it's all clear and sparkling, and yet deep," he thought, dazzled.)

"Come and dine and dance with me, just the same," he said, aloud. "Orlando will be in bed by then, won't he?"

"Yes, of course. But—but—"

"But nothing. Say yes, Rowan."

"All right. I'd love to come—just this once," said Rowan.

She was very quiet for the remainder of the evening, very quiet going home. A bigger problem even than that of Orlando had suddenly presented itself to her, and she did not know how to deal with it. She was fond of Charles, and she thought that he was fond of her. But she had pledged herself to look after Orlando, and could not fail him, and she had known that she must let Charles understand that she was not a free agent. One could hardly expect a man to fall in love with one seriously and have to include a small boy, who was no relation, in his affections. Charles ought to consider this before his feelings were too deeply involved, so that he could withdraw and look about for another girl, one not so encumbered.

"I've tried to let him know. I think he did know what I meant," Rowan said to herself. "It was the only fair thing to do, and the only sensible thing, too."

As if to provide further proof of how sensible she was, she let several tears fall on the ill-used old green taffeta before she stepped out of it, shook it, and hung it up in her cupboard.

CHAPTER 22

NOW THAT the stabbing pain in his side had eased up a bit, Angus was surprised and pleased to find that he was not uncomfortable, as long as he didn't try to take a deep breath. Even more surprising was the fact that he felt warm, though he was lying in snow. He had always supposed that snow was cold, yet here he was, cosy as if he were tucked up in bed, and sleepy too.

He wondered vaguely if he ought to shout and let the others know where he was, but decided against it. After all, when the rope broke and he went over, they could hardly help knowing that he had gone. And it seemed so unimportant that it didn't matter. Nothing mattered except the soft snow blanketing him. He tried to think of Rowan, whose letter had enraged him so much that he had rashly joined the climbing party to avoid spending the Christmas vacation in Edinburgh, but her face and figure, even her voice, eluded his tired memory. Funny, he thought drowsily, that he couldn't remember Rowan; but he had behaved so badly, he admitted it now to himself. . . . And all the time he had known in his heart that she would never have given a thought to Martin Tinker. He had fallen far from the heights where he had meant to content himself with her friendship, and it was no fault of hers. Rowan, the person who counted most in his life, he couldn't remember at all, and yet he could picture the pointed pale face, the soft straight hair like a field-mouse's coat, of little Morag Mac-Donald, the girl from Skye. He had only to shut his eyes to see her. From the moment when she and the other girl had joined them at Fort William, Morag and he had been friends. To hear her call him "Angus" in her soft lilting voice gave a new charm to his name. He must be Highland, she insisted. He looked and thought and felt like a Highlander, and—her big eyes kindling—he danced like one. Only a Highlander could dance like that! And when he told her his story, she was sure of it. He must take his degree and do his National Service, she said, and then come and farm on one of the islands; but before that, in the Easter vacation, he must come and stay with her people in Skye.

It was true. He felt a kinship with this land of wild high mountains quite apart from Morag; he had felt it as soon as he got out of the train after the long tiresome journey, and he felt it now, lying under the snow-covered, ice-bound crag that had cast him off.

Dreamily he began to think of the islands Morag loved, and back to his wayward memory came the sound of Hazel singing in an Edinburgh drawing-room.

"Land of Heart's desire,
    Isle of Youth
Dear Western Isle,
    Gleaming in sunlight. . . ."

And suddenly, instead of the twilight thickening on snowy wastes, he saw the Isle, the silver-white sands, the long blue and green seas breaking gently on them in creaming foam, the flowery meadows behind, the golden sky. He could hear the soft crash of the waves, and smell bog-myrtle and heather mingling with sea-salt . . . and there was some-one coming down the beach towards him.

"Rowan?" he muttered, questioningly, only to realize with a pang of unbearable anguish that it was not Rowan. He knew then that it would never be Rowan for him. For a moment the vision faded, and then the pain passed and the Isle was there again, and it was Morag whom he saw holding out her hands to him. Morag's soft voice sounded in his ears.

"Oh, Angus! Angus!"

He opened his dim eyes, the lovely Island vanished, but Morag was still there, bending over him.

Angus smiled at her in sudden complete content, and slid away into unconsciousness.

*   *   *

It was the twenty-second of January. The Lenoxes were having a small evening party, and Miss Balfour, as she dressed for it, remembered that it was her birthday.

There was nothing surprising in her having forgotten that she was sixty-nine to-day, for many years had passed since anyone had noticed her birthday. Belle had always ignored it and her own, as if, by refusing to acknowledge the inexorable march of the years, she could stay their passing.

Poor Belle, thought Miss Balfour, she had missed everything that made life sweet, from the small pleasure of exchanging gifts and greetings on an anniversary to the married happiness she could have found with Montagu!

Had Belle been other than she was, the old house would have been a cheerful happy home long ago, instead of only during the past half year. Happy, certainly, it was now, as was everyone living under its roof, from Willow, content as a nesting-bird on the top floor, to Edna, tunelessly chanting the latest songs from the films in the basement.

The new light paper and paint had helped, of course, as had the fresh coverings on chairs and sofas, and her own pretty clothes and softly waved hair; but besides these aids to cheerfulness there was something more.

The atmosphere of Number Four Kirkaldy Crescent had altered, its former heavy gloom was entirely dispersed, and Dorothea Balfour knew that this had only come about because Belle was no longer there to cast a blight over it.

Dorothea could not wish her sister back. She felt wicked about it, but unrepentant, for in the meantime several people were much happier than they could have been if Belle were still living.

As for the party given by Montagu and herself at Christmas for some of their neighbours and their children from Linden Terrace, Miss Balfour could not even begin to imagine what Belle would have said about that.

No, things were as they were, and better so, and Miss Balfour hoped that if she and Belle met when her own turn came to leave this world, and if they still bothered about its affairs, she would be able to talk on equal terms to her sister, and explain everything.

In the meantime, it was delightful to be going to a party on one's birthday, squired by an amiable brother-in-law, wearing a new and becoming gown, and with one's hair nicely arranged.

A knock at the door brought her round from the mirror in which she was admiring the reflection of her festive self.

"Come in!" she called, with a last glance at the soft fall of the long velvet skirt of rich dark brown—"Like the wallflowers in the garden at Kersland," she thought.

Edna came in, dressed in a thick coat over her black and white afternoon uniform, a lace cap perched on her head.

"If you please'm, I'm ready. Will I just go round?" she asked.

It was an understood thing by this time that Edna should help at any party given by the Lenoxes, and she enjoyed them all at least as much as any of their guests.

"Yes, of course, Edna. I expect Mrs. Lenox will be very pleased to have you there early, you are such a help," said Miss Balfour.

Instead of going, Edna took a step farther into the room, drew a long breath, and said very rapidly: "Miss Dorothea, you look just beautiful to-night! Sort of—sort of *regal*!"

Then she bolted like a rabbit.

"Regal!" murmured Miss Balfour. "How absurd! But it was nice of Edna to say so, for all that."

She picked up the fur coat which Montagu had insisted on giving her for Christmas, and made her way down to the drawing-room floor.

Her brother-in-law was hovering on the landing, waiting for her.

"Come into the drawing-room for a minute, Dorothea," he said. "We have plenty of time. Willow and Archie have only just gone next door."

He sounded embarrassed, and for an instant Miss Balfour wondered uneasily if he had some confession to make, then she felt embarrassed herself, and very much ashamed of her suspicions, for he had opened an old-fashioned jeweller's case of rubbed velvet, and was saying:

"For your birthday, my dear. A small offering with my love. It isn't anything much, but I saw it and thought it looked like you."

On its faded green bed lay a necklace of topazes set in elaborately worked pale gold, as delicate as flowers.

Miss Balfour touched the pretty thing with one finger, but made no attempt to take the case from Mr. Milner.

"Don't you like it?" he asked, disappointed.

"It's—beautiful, Montagu. I can't believe it's for me," said Miss Balfour. "How *good* of you! How very, very kind! I haven't had a birthday present since Mamma died—and how did you know it was my birthday?"

"There was an old birthday book away at the back of a pigeon-hole in the writing-desk," he said. "I found it when I tried to push some papers in. . . . Put on the necklace, Dorothea. It is exactly right for your dress."

But when she had lifted the necklace from its case and admired the winking golden eyes of the topazes in their paler gold setting, Miss Balfour handed it to Mr. Milner with a smile.

"Will you put it on for me, Montagu, please?" she said, some instinct telling her that this was what he would like.

He fastened it round her neck with his usual deftness, stood back to approve the effect, then helped her into her fur coat, and the two, arm in arm, went out of their house and up the steps of Number Six in great content.

"It is just going to be family and you and Mr. Milner, who count as family," Mrs. Lenox had said, when she invited them. "Willow doesn't care for the idea of a lot of people just now, and the others agreed. So please don't expect anything very grand or exciting."

"Just family" seemed to include not only Adam Ferrier, but his mother and his cousin Charles as well, so there was a sufficiently large number gathered in the Lenoxes' drawing-room to make it look quite well-filled. The Christmas decorations, the dozens of cards that had covered every flat-topped piece of furniture, were all gone, but the long room with its bowls of hyacinths scenting the air, and the big bowls of glossy-leaved rhododendrons dark against the pale walls still had a festive look, which the laughter and talk of its occupants enhanced.

Miss Balfour, accepting a glass of sherry from Murray, thought how nice everyone looked, the men in dinner-jackets, the girls in their pretty frocks, Mrs. Ferrier poised and elegant in midnight blue chiffon, Mrs. Lenox in her old black lace which showed up her still pretty neck and arms.

Willow was wearing black, too, and a little matronly air, absurd and rather touching. Holly in dark green, Hazel radiant in silver, and dear Rowan in red. It made her look rather pale, and she was not as gay as usual. Orlando trotted busily to and fro carrying a plate of savoury biscuits which he offered, nudging people with the plate if they did not notice him, and leaving a trail of biscuits behind him as he went. He discovered this in time, set the plate carefully on a low stool, and went back on his tracks picking up the fallen, and then carefully replacing them on the plate.

Mrs. Lenox, who had come to stand beside Miss Balfour's chair, laughed as she watched this.

"What does it matter?" she said. "He is the only person who is eating them, and he's happy and good. He is a *dear* little boy, Miss Dorothea. I shall miss him when he goes to school, even though it is only in the mornings."

"I knew you would keep him, and I am so glad for his sake," said Miss Balfour.

"Oh, yes! I couldn't send him away now," said Mrs. Lenox. "And Martin Tinker seems to have a germ of conscience after all. He wrote to his wife and sent her a little money, though he said he would never come back again. Mrs. Tinker came to see me and told me all this. She sent her husband a letter by air-mail—about Orlando's being here and everything—and then he wrote again and promised to let her have money when he could, some of it specially for Orlando. He said—Mrs. Tinker read that bit out to me—that if people had turned up who wanted to saddle themselves with the brat he wouldn't interfere, he was only too glad to be quit of family worries, and realized now he had got away how bad married life had been for his painting! I could hardly contain myself. I was boiling with fury when Mrs. Tinker read all this, but she took it quite as a matter of course. Glad to be quit of *him*, I expect, poor soul!"

"How strange people are!" murmured Miss Balfour.

Mrs. Ferrier crossed the room to join them. "Let me sit with you and watch the young people," she asked, and when she had taken a chair near Miss Balfour's, she added: "Mrs. Lenox, do sit down for a moment. They are all quite happy without us."

So the three sat together, looking on and thinking their own thoughts, all different, all alike.

Mrs. Ferrier thought of her son and rejoiced in his happiness. Unlike many mothers of only sons, she considered that Adam was extremely fortunate in the girl he had chosen. An early spring wedding, they had decided, while Willow would still be able to appear at it. Mrs. Ferrier hoped that dear Charles would be as lucky as Adam. Had he set his heart on Rowan Lenox? Would Rowan come to care for him in return? She was everything Maud Ferrier could wish for Charles, but that went for nothing, it all hung on whether the child would come to love him. There was that boy, the one she danced with so beautifully, who looked rather like Robert Burns in the sulks. . . . Mrs. Ferrier wished that she could arrange a marriage between Charles and Rowan, and just settle the affair out of hand. She was perfectly certain they would be a good match. Then her common-sense told her to stop being silly and think of something else.

Hazel was radiant this evening, her mother thought. Seeing her now for the first time, no one would believe that she was generally considered the least attractive of the Lenox girls. To-night she was as vivid as Rowan, prettier than Willow—though it was not fair to Willow to compare her with anyone just at present.

Willow was taking the discomfort of pregnancy and the thickening of her lissom shape very well. It was charming to see Archie's care of her, and her own reaction to the attentions which formerly she had been all too apt to respond to with pettishness.

Reviewing her family, Mrs. Lenox felt that she had reason to be satisfied with both Willow and Hazel and their prospects of happiness. Yes, and Holly was turning out so well. Her mother could hardly be thankful enough that the terrible lumpish stage, giggles and sulks and behaving like a plough-boy, which had made the holiday at Kersland less agreeable than usual, had passed. She had certainly improved greatly, and the credit for this was due to Madame Perrot, Mr. Milner, Mrs. Ferrier, so greatly admired by Holly—and Murray.

Murray had been very good about taking Holly out, he had even squired her to a dance or two and seen that she had plenty of partners. Perhaps it was because he seemed to have no young woman of his own at the moment, and was missing Hazel, who was absorbed in Adam.

As he had remarked casually just a few days before that he did not mean to marry until he was thirty at least, Mrs. Lenox considered it much better for him to devote his attention to Holly instead of rousing hopes doomed never to be fulfilled in other girls. Besides—to have her darling Murray at home for a few years longer, until he met the lucky, lucky girl who would be his wife! Surely it was natural for a mother to wish it? And Murray was perfectly happy. . . .

At the thought that Murray was happy, Mrs. Lenox realized with a guilty pang that she had forgotten Rowan, and Rowan was not happy at all. She might pretend she was nervous at the prospect of her new job in the little school to which Orlando was going, but her mother knew that she was worrying herself silly over that foolish boy Angus Todd's accident. It was typical of him, Mrs. Lenox thought angrily, to rush off on a climbing expedition out of sheer temper, and then to fall off some part of Ben Nevis and break an arm and several ribs and get pneumonia into the bargain! Of course, she would have been sorry, Mrs. Lenox told herself, if he had not recovered, but he was getting better—only Rowan seemed to feel it was her fault in some way, and had become pale and quiet in consequence.

At the other end of the room Murray, finding himself beside Rowan with no one else near them for the moment, nudged her gently.

"Look at those three," he murmured. "Mummy, Miss Dorothea and Mrs. Ferrier. The Fates, or the witches in *Macbeth*, or the Three Graces? All thinking of their young, by the look of them!"

"Miss Dorothea hasn't any young of her own," said Rowan, uneasily. "And I—I don't want to be thought about!"

"She's got old Monty, a handful if there ever was one! But I agree with you. I don't want to be thought about either," Murray answered, quite cheerfully. "Which is all the more reason for behaving as if we don't need thinking over, duckie."

"Oh, Murray! Are you unhappy—"

"Am I unhappy, too, you were going to say, weren't you? Well, I don't mind telling you that I'm not exactly uproariously happy, but I expect to recover."

"Well, so do I," Rowan retorted. "And I'm more worried than unhappy, really. Tell me, what's wrong with *you*?"

Murray pulled her back into the shadow of one of the long window curtains. "Just the usual," he said lightly. "I thought Susan Rattray would wait for me—we're both too young to marry—and she's decided she doesn't want to. In fact, she's met some fellow who's ready to marry her as soon as she likes. That's all."

"Susan is only a year younger than me," said Rowan. "She is old enough to marry—"

"And, of course, you think you are too?"

Rowan flushed. "I'm—it's different—" she began, rather incoherently. "Susan has some money of her own, and a mother she'd be happier away from, and—and—I'm not thinking about marriage," she ended, more firmly. "For one thing, there's Orlando."

"Orlando!" Murray repeated. "My dear good girl, surely you've realized by now that Mummy has taken over

Orlando? You won't have much say in his affairs and you may as well get used to the idea at once. It's far more sensible, anyhow."

Then, as she said nothing: "You don't mind, do you, Red Rowan? It is much the best thing that could happen," he said.

"No, I don't mind," she said, slowly. "It's just rather a surprise."

"Well, cheer up, then!" urged Murray. "I'll have to go and dish out more sherry and make bright conversation, and I don't like leaving you moping in a corner."

"I'll be all right. Only—if you could keep people away from me for a minute or two—"

"You're not pining for that Byronic dancer of yours, are you?" asked Murray, with a sharp glance at her downcast face.

"Oh, no!"

"Good. Then I'll try to head Charles Ferrier off. I suppose he's whom you mean by 'people'?"

Rowan caught him by the sleeve as he turned to leave her.

"Murray! You—you aren't *desperately* unhappy about Susan?"

"No, 'tis not so deep as a well," said Murray. "I told you. I'll get over it."

He nodded at her, smiled, and moved away.

Rowan knew that he was quite badly hurt, and she thought how different was his way of facing it from Angus Todd's.

Not that Angus had been badly hurt by her, or so she hoped, and he seemed to have got over it. But she had had a severe shock at the news of his accident, and had blamed herself for it. It had been a very great relief to have a letter in a round clear hand from someone called Morag MacDonald, who said that Angus couldn't write himself, but was "doing nicely". It was quite plain that the writer had been sitting beside Angus while she wrote and that they were friends, perhaps would soon be more than friends. There was no longer any need for Rowan to feel responsible for Angus, and though she was truly glad, she could not help feeling that she had lost something. It would be a long time before she forgot him; every time she danced she would remember him, and always there would be certain favourite tunes which would bring him back to her mind.

She knew that she had never been even half in love with Angus, but the fright of hearing about his fall was too recent for her to want to think of any other man. Rowan felt that she did not want to love anyone except her family for a long time. The sight of Willow's content and Hazel's shining happiness did not shake her, for there was Murray to weight the balance on the other side.

"I'd like just to be friends with someone," she thought, and unconsciously her glance went across the room to Charles Ferrier's fair head, bent towards Holly in the attitude of courteous attention which Rowan knew meant that his thoughts were wandering.

Miss Balfour saw Rowan's look, and smiled to herself. Dear child, she was upset and out of tune for love at the moment, but she would recover, and, of course, she would turn to Charles Ferrier and they would be happy. It might not be for a little time yet, but they were young. They could afford to wait.

With a little pang, Miss Balfour remembered that her own time was short, but she reproved herself for even this momentary repining She had had almost six months of such happiness and content as she had never dared to hope for. If she died at this very minute she could still count herself blessed. And she felt that she owed a great deal of it all to Rowan—under God.

Rowan's impulsive visit on the day of Belle's funeral had been the start. It had been a kind warm hand stretched out to draw her into the friendly family circle of her neighbours next door. She would have made the acquaintance of the Lenoxes, no doubt, in time, but with Rowan's help she had become their friend and they hers. Nor could she ever have come to terms with Montagu if it had not been for the new ease and confidence which knowing the Lenoxes had given her. Bless them all, she thought, and especially Rowan. . . .

She sat in a pleasant reverie until Mrs. Lenox roused her by saying: "I'm sure it is time we all went down to supper," and she saw that everyone was beginning to move towards the door.

Miss Balfour gave a last look round at all her friends as she rose and gathered her little bag and her lace scarf. She wanted to have a mind picture of them to carry away with her on her birthday, when they were looking even nicer than usual.

Willow's hand was tucked into the crook of Archie's arm confidingly and Archie appeared to have grown taller and broader in some mysterious way. Hazel and Adam had eyes only for one another, Murray was obviously drawing Holly's attention to them, while Mrs. Ferrier gazed at her son with dispassionate affection as if she found him silly but understandably so. Mrs. Lenox had been seized by Orlando, alarmed lest the extra hour granted to him might run out before supper was even begun, and Montagu was hurrying to give an arm to his sister-in-law, rosy and beaming, in his element because it was a party.

If only Rowan would be kind to Charles. . . . Miss Balfour held her breath as she watched the girl slowly push aside the curtain that had partly screened her. Charles was looking towards her. He seemed to know that Rowan's next move was of immense importance to both of them.

"Oh, Rowan, *do*—" implored Miss Balfour, inwardly. And as if Rowan had heard the words, she gave Miss Balfour one look.

She was pale still, but the light was coming back to her eyes. Turning, she smiled across the room at Charles.